J.S. ROEBUCK

The Bishop & The Pawn

For my family. Yes, all of you.

"Samyaza also has taught sorcery, to whom you have given authority over those who are associated with him."

-THE BOOK OF ENOCH

Contents

1

White Smoke

W hite smoke! The smoke billowed softly from the chimney of the Sistine Chapel high above the crowd in Saint Peter's Square. A new pope had been elected! The gathering known as the conclave had been in session for almost two weeks, deliberating. The previously sitting pope, Francis, passed away nearly a month before. The gathering of cardinals from around the world was long awaited as they slowly arrived. It took more than a few weeks for some of them to arrange travel plans. With the extended media attention and the time the conclave had taken to deliberate, the suspense in Vatican City was causing the crowd in Saint Peter's Square to have the tension of a water tank bursting at the seams. Members of the Roman Catholic Church, and of the faith in general, had come from all over the world to wait for the news in the grand square of the Vatican.

It was early March when the conference of cardinals began. There was nowhere for incoming tourists to stay in the surrounding area of Rome. Everything was booked. All of Italy was bustling after the funeral of Pope Francis, and after the burial and mourning, the people wanted to know who would be the next pope. Throughout each day during the papal conclave, St. Peter's Square was packed shoulder to shoulder with fans and mourners alike. At night, smaller groups sat out with lit candles in memory of their deceased holy father, waiting and praying for what might come next.

When the smoke flowed white from the chimney late that spring morning, enough people in the square were watching that a complete uproar of cheers could be heard for miles. Bishop Liam Shepherd Thompson listened to the shouts in the distance as he looked over the River Tiber. Bishop Liam had taken a tour of the Castel Sant'Angelo nearby the Vatican early that morning. His eyes doubled in size with excitement. *They have decided! Please, Lord, let whoever he is be a great pope,* he thought as he climbed down the staircase of one of the castle towers. Bishop Liam reached the bottom and stepped out to the streets of Rome. He was so excited to get back to the Vatican and participate in the celebration that Liam skipped out on almost the entire second half of the tour he'd already paid for and headed up the street.

The trip was Bishop Liam's first to Europe. Originally from New Zealand, he had immigrated to Australia while attending university. After taking up the cloth, he quickly rose to the honorable position of bishop in the Diocese of Parramatta in Sydney, Australia. Bishop Liam was finally seeing Vatican City at age fifty-two for the first time. He was spry for his age and quickly jogged up the street back toward the holy city. Liam was an average-height man; he had curly brown hair that rimmed the edges under his traditional saturno and flopped as he jogged the sidewalk.

Liam was brought along to the Vatican by special invitation

of his cardinal. The cardinal and Liam knew each other well, and he included Liam on his trip as a travel companion and assistant. Since the conclave kept the cardinals behind closed doors, once in session, Bishop Liam was free to take in the sights and make a vacation out of the visit. He spent several days assisting his cardinal and attending a few meetings after arrival. Liam spent time walking the Vatican gardens and museums, and sitting and discussing with other church leaders and random tourists who had traveled for the occasion their thoughts on who might be selected for the pope. He even spent hours in the evenings out amongst the mourners with candles lit, paying his respects to Pope Francis.

Bishop Liam had, by this time, spent almost thirty years working within the church in some capacity or another. He had unanimously been elected for the post of bishop after a great deal of outreach and aid work he completed with local groups in Australia that grasped public attention and grew the church significantly in his area. The fires in Australia that ripped across the continent had caused such devastation in recent years that there was tremendous need; not only from the impact it had on the ecosystem but also the local economy and the people's spirits. It would take a generation to recover for many of the towns caught in the middle of the disaster. Bishop Liam had stepped up, asking people in the country to, for once, think of themselves as one family, as children of humanity, all in need. It became his historic "when we help our fellow man, we help ourselves" speech that went viral online.

The Australian Cardinal, Bartholomew Johns, had quickly noticed Liam and his impact on the world and the church. Johns had even gone secretly once to hear Liam speak at an aid station when Liam was helping with supplies and medical assistance. Bishop Liam was delivering a load of rations purchased through an organization that reached out to the bishop after his viral speech. Johns had never before seen so many people of different backgrounds support one individual. Liam stayed at that aid station for three days, long after the supplies were unloaded and the TV cameras had left. Volunteers recorded and uploaded videos of Bishop Liam's morning masses, which he organized while visiting. His words rallied the members of the camp and bolstered his increasing following on social media. Some of his masses were recorded for the diocese's website, which started to get shared by church members and went viral online.

Being a guest of the cardinal, Bishop Liam didn't have to worry about accommodations for his stay. He was put up in one of the many dormitories within the walls of Vatican City. The journey had already been the trip of a lifetime for Liam, visiting Europe and being a special guest of his cardinal, staying within the Vatican. It was all more than he ever would have asked for. Liam was a simple man and he loved good food. The local cuisine was terrific compared to his usual diet choices back home of soda and something from the fridge thrown between two slices of white bread. After four days in the Vatican, waiting on the conclave, Liam finally decided to start venturing out further to sample local restaurants and see other nearby historical, artistic, and religious sites beyond the Vatican walls. Rome was an adventure he was looking forward to taking on and exploring for a few days. Liam hoped the conclave might take a little longer to give his vacation the extra time he selfishly wanted. As Bishop Liam jogged, he thought, *even if this adventure has to come to an end, it was still a grand experience.*

Having hurried out in front of the Castel Sant'Angelo and along the street in such excitement, Bishop Liam continued running for almost an entire block before realizing he could get a cab. He kept close to the Vatican so he wouldn't be far when the announcement came. He ran out into the street, waving his arms and wearing his bishop's hat and gown, an odd sight in a regular town but not near the Vatican. A cab stopped, and he hopped around to the side and slid into the back of the old car. Liam didn't need to tell the cab driver, who conveniently spoke English and Italian, where he was heading.

The driver turned around and gave one look in the back at Bishop Liam's collar and said, "Vatican?" After a nod from Liam, he hit the gas.

While taking the short cab ride, Liam had a minute to check his phone. He flipped through several notifications about routine updates and church business back home. One of his sisters had asked him if he'd heard anything yet and then had texted again that she saw the news and wanted details. Liam checked a news report showing images and video feeds of the white smoke and drone footage of the crowd cheering and celebrating in St. Peter's Square. His phone suddenly rang. It nearly jumped out of his hand when the vibration startled Liam. *Cardinal Johns* appeared on his caller ID; it was his traveling companion.

Must be out of conclave, already got his phone, and wants to see where I'm at and if I've heard. Liam hadn't been able to communicate with Cardinal Johns during the last week. Liam knew he should take any call from the cardinal ASAP. Johns had promised Liam he'd be the first call he made after the doors opened.

The cab quickly found itself stuck in bumper-to-bumper traffic out of nowhere. Tourists and locals alike were rushing back to the square. The mob all had the same agenda—to get back immediately and see who the new pope would be.

"Hello, Cardinal Johns!" Liam said excitedly as he put his phone to his ear under the brim of his hat. "Hold on one second. I need to pay my cab driver."

Liam didn't want to wait in traffic and miss something. He tossed some Euros into the front seat, more than enough to cover the fare, thanked the driver, and hopped out into the street. Liam began weaving between cars rather than pushing through the crowd on the sidewalk.

"Sorry about that, cardinal," Liam said as he put his phone back to his ear. "Good to hear you're finally—"

Liam couldn't finish his thought before the Cardinal interrupted. "Bishop Liam, where are you right now?"

The street was getting packed, and Liam was swept into a large group, moving towards the Vatican gates. He stopped in the crowd and looked around. "I'm—about two blocks out from Saint Peter's Square. I'm on my way back. I hope I don't miss too much!" He couldn't hide the childlike excitement in his voice. "I know you can't say, but is it someone you expected?" Liam was anxious to get a hint from Cardinal Johns about the decision before the announcement.

Johns couldn't help but explode into laughter on the line. Liam had to hold the phone away. It was so unexpectedly loud in his ear. "Hahaha! Bishop Liam, my good friend, I promise you won't miss a thing, mate. Work your way through the crowd to the gates as soon as you reach the square. Tell any member of the Swiss Guard your name and that you're lookin' fer me; they'll bring ya right to us."

The cardinal's behavior was a little strange. Liam was sure that Cardinal Johns had more important things to do at that moment rather than worry about getting him into the Vatican past the square. *Who's "us"?* He thought to himself. Liam initially assumed he would wait outside with the rest of the crowd, but he wasn't going to complain. He thought perhaps Johns was able to get him a backstage pass kind of access, but that didn't explain why every member of the Swiss Guard would be looking for him.

The Swiss Guard was the private police force of the Vatican City. With crowds flooding the square and all the attention, Liam couldn't help but think he would be the least of anyone's concerns. "Alright, Cardinal Johns. I'll get through, find a guard, and get to you as soon as possible. Is everything alright?" Liam started to wonder if something was wrong.

"Everything is as it should be," the Cardinal replied in an oddly cryptic way. "Just get here. We'll see you soon."

The call disconnected. Bishop Liam had made it to the far east side of St. Peter's Square. The crowd was growing by the minute. Liam found a stone ledge to climb onto to get a better view of the square and find a path of least resistance. The middle of the square was the most congested around the great obelisk at its center. He figured, rather than try and push through the thick of the crowd, it was best to work his way around the outskirts and walk the extended half circle skirting the inner square over to the main gates. Liam looked across the square and saw the obelisk towering high above the heads in the crowd. The low morning sun leaned far over the rooftops, almost reaching the obelisk's base.

People in the crowd were cheering, waving flags from all

different countries, and children were being hoisted up onto parents' shoulders to get a better look. Bishop Liam turned his gaze to the Sistine Chapel's roof and chimney. He could see the white smoke dancing in the wind for the first time. He got goosebumps, and a strong sense of joy was overwhelming him from within. He was excited to be on site for such a historic moment and allowed on the inside, behind the curtain, so to speak, for the worldwide event.

Maybe my vacation/adventure isn't quite over, he thought as he hopped down and followed the path he'd mapped around the crowd.

As Liam finished his long walk around the square and made it to the gate, he saw three Swiss Guardsmen, unmistakable in their blue, yellow, and red uniforms. Liam approached the closest guard. The other two had their hands full with a couple of tourists arguing to get in past the gate. Liam made sure not to run up onto the guard too aggressively so as not to alarm him needlessly.

"Excuse me, sir. Officer? Sorry, I'm not sure how to address you gentlemen. I'm Bishop Liam Thompson. I was told to come to one of you and ask for my cardinal. Cardinal Bartholomew Johns. He said you would know where he is?"

The guard's eyes popped. He stood up straight, and put his hand to his ear.

Liam noticed the curly cord coming from behind the guard's cap. I always *wondered if they had radios in those getups.*

The guardsman rambled something excitedly in Italian. Liam didn't know the dialect well enough but caught that "Bishop Thompson" was part of the statement. The other two guardsmen must have thought his words were important. As they heard the call come into their earpieces, the men looked in Liam's direction with just as much awe as the first guard standing before him, which made Liam feel somewhat self-conscious.

What's the big deal? We have a new pope, and these guys are looking at me like I'm covered in muck or something, Liam wondered.

The first guard looked behind himself through the long metal bars in the gate and then back to Liam. He said something, first in Italian, this time directed at Liam, not the radio. Liam had to ask, in the little bit of Italian he knew, for the Swiss Guardsman to repeat himself in English if he could.

"Oh, of course. Please, father, this way," the guard repeated, the second time in English.

The other two Swiss Guards watched awkwardly as Liam and the first guard went through the gate, completely ignoring the tourists still yelling at them.

The Swiss Guardsman's pace was swift. Liam made sure he kept up with the young man speedwalking along. The guard only looked back occasionally to ensure Liam was close behind. He was obviously in a hurry and was making a beeline for the conclave. They walked through several large halls and corridors. Some areas seemed off-limits to the general public, and Liam did not see them when he toured for the first few days. When they arrived at a large door, the guard stopped abruptly. Around the door handles was a rope and a seal that had recently been broken. They had arrived at the Sistine Chapel.

Bishop Liam felt as if he was somewhere he wasn't supposed to be. The conclave was for cardinals and necessary staff only. The day the new pope was elected was no day for a tourist to be in the way. Liam found himself thinking he should go back out to where the other guards had been arguing with those tourists. He stood outside the door; his heart raced as the guard entered.

I shouldn't go in, right? Liam couldn't recall all the rules, but he was almost sure you had to be a cardinal to go into that room. The guard pushed the door open and it swung with grace. He stepped back out of the doorway to the side as if beckoning Bishop Liam to enter—sort of an "after you, sir" gesture. Liam could hear inside the door. The room was roaring with dozens of discussions in dozens of languages.

Liam stepped inside and started to take in the room around and above before looking at the faces in front of him. The place was beautiful. The elaborate architecture and ornate paintings covering the room wall to ceiling took Liam's breath away. The Sistine Chapel had been off limits until the conclave was over, so the great chapel was the only part of the Vatican Liam had wanted to see on his visit that he was waiting for. After briefly gazing at the ceiling above, Liam heard someone clear his throat. He looked down and saw all eyes trained on him in the doorway. Cardinals crowded everywhere, huddled in small groups. They had been whispering, but now all looked patiently in Liam's direction. As Liam looked on from the doorway, easing in slowly, the room grew silent.

One cardinal he didn't recognize yelled in English back into the crowd, "Cardinal Johns! He is here!"

The crowd split, and Liam could see Johns rushing his way. Johns was an older native Australian man with a receding gray hairline and a bulbous nose. Liam couldn't help but wonder if he was in trouble or was being called on to do some errand. His mind was swimming but calming as Johns grinned ear to ear while he walked up to him.

"My dear Bishop Thompson," Cardinal Johns said as soon as he was face to face with Liam.

His words struck Liam as a bit formal since Johns had never referred to him as "dear" anything before, but they had become good friends and colleagues. Liam saw all eyes trained on him, and the crowd of cardinals was utterly silent. Liam was so out of sorts all he could get out as a reply was, "Yes?"

"Close that door!" Cardinal Johns yelled and motioned at the Swiss Guard with his back still holding the door open.

Bishop Liam looked over his shoulder at the door as it thudded shut and then back to Johns. "I came as soon as I could. What's going on? Wasn't a decision made?" Liam said, perplexed.

Once the guard closed the door, Johns continued, "My dear friend—"

Again, with the "dear" stuff? Liam thought. What is this about?

Cardinal Johns went on, "—it is the decision of this conclave—that the new Holy Father—is the man standing before me now!"

2

The New Pope

Liam didn't know what to expect when he walked in the doors of the Sistine Chapel, but being told he was the new pope was never an idea he'd entertained. Bishop Liam always pictured the pope as an ancient, holier-than-though-art, stuck-up, but humble, big-to-do cardinal like Johns or one of the other red caps. Cardinal Johns bounced along, ushering Liam this way and that amongst the crowd. Johns introduced him to some of the other cardinals as they walked further into the room.

"My goodness, I don't know what to say," Liam kept repeating in a daze.

"What's that accent? I can't quite place it?" a cardinal asked.

"I'm originally from New Zealand but immigrated to Australia as an adult, so my accent is a little mixed." Liam had already said this many times before in his life.

Another cardinal asked a similar question, "Thought you were from Australia, father. What region accent is that?"

Johns answered for Liam that time, "Born in New Zealand, immigrated to Australia, so a little o' both." The clarification on Liam's accent just—kept—happening.

"Originally from New Zealand, immigrated to Australia" became Liam's new catchphrase for most of the day as he tried to learn many new names and faces. The cardinals and papal staff moved with Liam across the room toward another exit. The new pope received blessings, prayers, and handshakes from everyone who could get close enough. Most of what happened from there was a complete blur for Liam until he reached the end of the day and found time to process everything.

The man was in shock. Liam had lived his whole life for the church but never wanted to be in charge. Leadership had been thrown on him before, in a much smaller sense, in his appointment as bishop back in Australia. Even that was difficult for him to agree to take on until he decided he could do more for people from the position. At no time in the last 500 years had an election of a pope from such a country, circumstance, age group, or position occurred. Liam was young compared to recently elected popes from the last century. Most popes were in their seventies at the time of their election. Liam had most of his fifties yet to live. He learned later from Johns that the decision to look for someone younger was made almost immediately in the conclave discussions. Everyone was eager to progress in a different direction than again put someone into a seat with only a tiny shred of life left in them. The church, for lack of a lighter way of putting it, was dying and losing members, money, and momentum all over the world. Modern society and technology seemed to be pushing religion and spirituality further from the people's minds and priorities.

"Johns, how is it that I can be elected pope? I'm not even a cardinal!" Liam said as he was being pushed to the back of the long room toward the exit.

"Accordin' to the 'oly church, any baptized catholic could become pope," Johns whispered as he maneuvered Liam by the shoulder.

"But it's always a cardinal! I'm not prepared for this. It would be better if you did it, Johns. You'd do great!" Liam said shakily.

"Nah mate, that life ain't for me. True, it's almost always a cardinal, but the world has seen you, Bishop Liam. We cannot refute what we have all seen and 'eard of you. I honestly didn't do much to convince the others. A few prestigious cardinals led the rally to vote for you. I was consult'n as your cardinal on the decision," the Australian replied as he ushered Liam towards an exit.

From the details and admiration Liam was getting from Father Johns and his fellow cardinals, Liam deduced he had been nominated in the first place by a cardinal other than Johns because of his recent philanthropy work and projects that were getting attention in the media. Once Liam was brought up by one of the cardinals, the conclave exploded into an array of stories and rumors heard, messages received, clips of Liam's masses, speeches, and videos shared online. The cardinals almost unanimously felt that the Creator was calling them to Bishop Liam Thompson before they even arrived at the conference.

Liam also learned that, according to Johns, there had been a lot more talk in the leadership lately about the "interesting New Zealander everyone was calling Shepherd" online. Shepherd was the trending nickname tagged on all the videos of Liam that had been going viral in the last year.

The cardinals took time to look further into Liam's background before arriving for conclave and emailed each other back and forth. Unknown to Liam, witnesses were questioned by church members all over New Zealand and Australia during the last week. The conclave decided about Liam early on, but they withheld the vote until they received word back from their agents whether the Shepherd was as holy as they had all hoped and heard. Apparently, the vetting had all come back approved, and with no concerns from the review team, they put out the white smoke.

Along with the confirmation and the perceived "divine providence as never before seen in conclave history," as one news outlet later reported hearing from a cardinal, which also exploded the story, the conclave had voted unanimously to elect Bishop Liam Shepherd Thompson, "The Shepherd," as the new pope in that early spring of 2023.

Liam was led down a hallway by a few members of the papal staff. They all introduced themselves to Liam, who barely caught their complicated Italian and Spanish names. He asked Cardinal Johns to stay by his side, and Johns was there helping move Liam along, who looked to be in a stupor. Johns sat Liam down at a desk chair in a small sitting room off the hallway outside the chapel. He was offered some water, which he took but held and did not drink. Liam grasped the glass of water like one would a worry-stone as a child about to go to his first dentist appointment. Impostor syndrome, as it's called, was filling him to his ears.

Liam had grown up in a small home in the Chain Hills outside Dunedin, New Zealand. His parents stayed together all his life. Both Liam's mother and father passed away in the last decade. They were the type of older couple that stuck together through everything, and when his mother eventually had been taken by cancer, his father's broken heart took him soon after. Liam grew up with three sisters, Emily, Clare, and Beth. There was a lot of female energy in that house. Liam and his father would stick together on fishing trips so that they had a chance to get some masculine energy out from time to time, away from the girls at home. Adventures outdoors were their way of bonding as father and son should. One older sister and two younger kept Liam's restless spirit in check, and he was there for them whenever they needed a strong brother.

From the Thompson family's back porch, the view stretched out over the Chain Hills and down to meet with other neighborhood properties before touching the sea's edge. Having ships out his back window, castles and cathedrals nearby, and living in a small island nation in the southernmost parts of the Pacific almost demanded a young man with any spine or curiosity to develop a sense of wonder and adventure about the world. Liam had decided in his youth that he wanted to either be a big part of the world or make a change in it for the better. Little did he know, back then, that becoming pope would be the fruition of that lifelong dream.

As Liam sat, holding his worry water, trying to return to the moment and get out of his head, another hand popped up under his nose, looking to be shaken. Someone else was trying to introduce themselves to him, but Liam was in such a fog he hardly noticed till the man was practically in his lap. The man was slowly inching forward and trying to catch Liam's gaze from the stupor he understandably was lingering in.

"Sorry, what was your name again?" Liam said as he mentally re-entered the moment.

"Marco. It's an honor to meet you and work with The Shepherd. I've heard much about you, father."

Camerlengo-Cardinal Marco Morelli, or just Marco, as everyone called him, was a Spanish cardinal who had been working in the Vatican very close with the former pope until his recent passing. In more common political terms, the camerlengo was an executive assistant or liaison to the pope, like a temporary sitting vice-president. Marco was a tall, slender man compared to Liam. He had furled, long dark hair that he bound in a ponytail falling behind his back.

Liam finally started to bring his attention more into the present. Talking with Marco helped anchor him back to reality. Also, the occasional tap on the shoulder from Cardinal Johns kept him grounded in the present.

There were several documents for Liam to sign. Marco, Johns, a papal staff attorney, and a tall, lanky man who looked like the Secret Service sat with Liam while he reviewed the paperwork. There were many contracts, confidentiality agreements, non-disclosures, Swiss Guard and Entity Protocol Agreements—the list just went on. Some lunch was brought in, and the day continued with Liam signing page after page after page.

Next, Liam was taken to a room where he had outfits tailored, sewn, and fitted on the spot. Since he was already being measured, he was fitted for new clothes for his general wardrobe while being prepared for the rest of the day.

Liam whispered to Johns as a tailor wrapped a tape measure around his left ankle, "Has anyone even thought to ask me if I want to be pope?"

"Jeez, Liam! Blimey, why not?" was Johns' hushed Aussie reaction. "You're always up in my office talkin' 'ow you want to do more fer the world. And we all know you don't wanna do it. I told the whole damn conclave you'd never want the job in a million years!"

"So then, why am I doing this? Why was I elected?"

"Liam, my boy, we picked the man best for the job, not the man who wanted it the most," Johns explained.

Along with deciding on a few clothing options, Bishop Liam was free to choose his new name as pope. Liam quickly decided to be Pope Leo XIV, after Pope Leo the Great, who had met Attila the Hun outside Rome himself in 452 A.D. to save the city from being sacked. Leo was an old religious hero in some ways to Liam. After that came the fitting for the Ring of the Fisherman, the ceremonial ring of the pope. Liam was given a temporary ring and told another one would be presented later that evening. Liam thought that was awfully fast, given that the ring was personalized, and insisted waiting was fine. But it was insisted back by the tall, lanky secret service man, *Yanis, or maybe Janis was his name?* Liam couldn't remember his name for sure. In any case, the Entity Agent was adamant that the ring must be on the pope's finger before the end of his first day.

Liam followed the same trend as the last pope and set aside the pageantry and ornate outfit of the traditional papal wardrobe and instead wore a simple white gown and cap. After his speech, Liam was ushered to a dinner where he gave a blessing and could eat some of what was passed around. Liam got small bites in between explaining where New Zealand was and why he didn't exactly sound as Australian as Johns. The dinner ended abruptly, and the new pope found himself being escorted to his chambers for the evening. As the papal staff suspected, Liam said he would want to reside in the dormitories amongst the other staff members permanently. Scaling down from the stately single suite to a humble dormitory fitted more with the message he wanted to make sure the new Holy Father conveyed to the world.

Formerly Bishop Liam Shepherd Thompson, now Pope Leo XIV, the Leader of the Roman Catholic Church, found himself alone for the first moment all day. Other than using the lavatory once or twice, these were his first moments of privacy behind a closed door. He let his face, back, and neck all relax as he slumped into the first chair he saw. With his eyes closed for a moment, Liam prayed and asked the Creator, *is this really happening? Is this because of what I've wanted to do since I was a boy? To help the world. Is this fate? Was my whole life leading to this, and I didn't know it?*

As Liam contemplated predestination and fate, he popped his eyes back open. The ceiling and the room were less ornate than the rest of the building they were in. The way the walls reached for the high ceiling up from the small floor space below made the room feel tight. There was old antique furniture in every corner. Looking around, Liam saw a roll-top desk, a long, thin table near the entrance with a few chairs, a bathroom, a bed, a nightstand, dresser, and a wardrobe. Electrical and plumbing updates had been made to the room over time more than the others, and it was apparent the bed had yet to be slept in recently. Liam thought the room had even been a part of some tours. The bed looked recently remade and prepped for the new Holy Father's first night. The bed was a large four-poster, the strangest feature of the room.

Even though the ceiling was extremely high, the bedposts stretched all the way from floor to ceiling, where they even recessed slightly in. The headboard was a very ornate, wood-carved back panel with a tall middle section that arched and waved in swooping patterns down on each side towards the floor around the head of the bed. The room was spotted with small pieces of artwork hung on the wall, mostly antique oil paintings of different places in the Vatican and historical sites around Rome. Long tapestries were tucked into the corners and around the single large window. Most of the modern updates were to the electrical sockets, lighting fixtures, and lavatory off his suite. It was a full bath that appeared to have been updated at least in the last twenty years. The modern look was quite a jump compared to the other parts of the Vatican hundreds of years old.

Liam was surprised to notice there were pajamas laid out for him. He laughed into the empty high ceiling of the room when he pulled the long flowing robe up to his neck, looking down at it lying in front of him. The garment was a sleeping gown that he wouldn't be caught dead in, public or not. Liam looked around the empty room and tossed the gown over his shoulder. He went to the side of the bed and found his travel bag, which he'd requested an assistant of some cardinal earlier in the day to grab for him when Liam was asked about his personal effects. Liam pulled out his favorite pajama pants, flip flops, and hooded sweatshirt he brought from home in his luggage. After slipping into his favorite pj's, he felt like himself again for a minute. As his body relaxed, Liam realized the adrenaline was holding up his posture and demeanor throughout the day. He felt his body grow stiff and sore. There was a TV in the corner across from him. Liam walked over, sat on the bed's edge, and found a remote on the nightstand. He pointed it at the TV, clicked it on, and found a local news station. His speech from earlier was playing on different stations throughout the evening ever since it was broadcast live. Liam only had about one hour to assemble the speech with Johns and Marco earlier that afternoon.

Liam saw himself on the screen, standing at the microphone on the balcony above Saint Peter's Square earlier that day. He turned the volume up to hear what part of his speech it was on.

"It's not myself that has been elected, but all of you. The world needs us all to step up and do the hard things we'd rather not. The church is here to save you, not the other way around. Do not send the church money. Instead, give it to your fellow man in need. Do not try to save the church; instead, try to save your neighbor. Save each other first, and together, we'll save the world. The church comes after. It is time for all communities of believers and faiths on Earth to lift each other up and take hold of the future that our Creator designed for us. Too many wars have been fought over whose God is more peaceful. Too many a people have been crushed by others who believe their God is most loving. This is not my papacy, but all of ours. This is your church, and you do not belong to it. It belongs to you. I will use every resource and revenue at my disposal to make this world better than how we found it. My life's mission has been to make a permanent impact in this world for the betterment of all humanity. I thank you all for giving this bishop from New Zealand a chance to complete that mission to its fullest."

The speech replay coverage cut from there and returned to a local news anchor. Liam wondered how the church leadership worldwide would receive his new "don't give the church money" approach. He could envision them already plotting to remove him from the papal office the moment his speech ended. Sitting on the bed in his favorite pajamas humbled Liam and reminded him of his home. Liam reflected and took the time to pray more. He spoke more deep and honest words than he had in a long time. He was thanking the Creator for the opportunity. He humbled himself and asked for wisdom and guidance. Liam had never actually heard the Creator whisper to him in any way before. Nothing other than what he thought were certain feelings, signs, or paths he was being called to over the years. He wondered, *in these prayers, in this place, with this responsibility on my shoulders now, are my prayers somehow... different?*

As Liam was about to say his *amen*, there was a quick wrap on the door. Liam felt his heart jump past his lungs and into his throat. He hadn't realized just how quiet the room was until the knock at the door echoed into the stately chamber. Liam stepped up to get to the door. It was Marco. Liam had gotten so caught up in the day's activities he'd forgotten Marco was coming that evening. It was time for the new pope to receive his official Ring of the Fisherman.

3

The Chest and the Fisherman's Key

L iam pulled the door back and slid aside for Marco to enter the room. Marco was closely followed by two men in suits who looked like Secret Service agents, similar to the Entity representative Liam had met earlier that day. The two men entered behind Marco, lugging an enormous chest of some kind between them. The chest was old and heavy. The men set it down with a thud on the end of the long table that stood behind the door across from the end of his Holiness' bed.

"Your Holiness—" Marco said. He was a young cardinal, as Liam was a young pope. The Camerlengo was in his mid-forties, and his long, black, wavy Italian hair no longer had a cap pinned atop it as he had for the ceremonies earlier in the day.

Liam interjected, "Please. I would ask those of you that I'll be working with more closely to call me something different. I know it's tradition, but I fear I'll develop a complex if I get called 'your Holiness' at every turn. Can I ask to please be called something else?"

Marco smiled and replied, "It may take some time to get others to follow suit, but what other names did you have in mind?"

"My name, Bishop Thompson, Liam, father, bishop, or padre. Honestly, I'm good with anything that doesn't have 'holy' in the title."

Marco said, "How about I call you, as everyone seems to know you, Shepherd?"

"I guess—it's at least one of my names," said Liam reluctantly.

"I like it!" Marco smiled with delight. "The people like it. It's a beautiful coincidence, I think, that the next man to shepherd the people of God already be a Shepherd, not only in name but in works." His smile hung on his face a little longer than you'd typically expect, almost like he held it intentionally to show his enthusiasm a bit further.

Liam smiled and nodded, accepting his new name, which Marco was sure to spread among the rest of the Vatican staff.

"Shepherd it is," Marco confirmed one more time.

Liam, or Shepherd now, stepped behind the table across from Marco. The two agents had been standing quietly at the end of the room, farthest from the chest, since they sat the large box down.

Shepherd asked, "I'm sure you're about to tell me, but what is this? I thought your visit this evening was just for the ring."

Marco replied, "The two go together, actually. The ring is not just jewelry; before we get to that, these are agents Rossi and Bruno. They are members of the Entity, entrusted with, among other things, holding this chest till the new pope's election."

Shepherd's eyes widened with boyhood excitement. The Entity was the Secret Service of the pope—the agents of the

Vatican Nation. Shepherd signed documents earlier giving him authorization and access to the Vatican Archives, and behind the mysterious curtain of the Entity. Shepherd saw a few agents here and there while he did tours his first week in Italy. Anything behind the Entity's curtain was kept top secret, never to be revealed to the public. The Vatican had exemption upon exemption with Italian and international authorities to protect itself and conceal its secrets. There were plenty of conspiracy theories about the Entity, and the organization's real purpose was shrouded in mysterious origins.

Marco continued, "Rossi and Bruno are two of our best men. As such, they alone have been entrusted with this chest for several weeks since the late Pope Francis' passing. This chest has been handed down for over 500 years and has never left the walls of Vatican City."

"It's good to meet you, gentlemen," Shepherd said, nodding to Rossi and Bruno, who each gave a minor nod in reply. "What's it called?" he asked of the chest.

"Ha! Everything seems to have a special name around here, right? But this chest doesn't," he chuckled. "Hmm. Some of us call it 'the pope chest' from time to time." Marco held in a silent laugh. Rossi and Bruno didn't break character from their secret agent stance at the opposite end of the table. Shepherd saw the younger agent, Bruno, at least crack a smile. Marco regained his serious demeanor, "We simply call it 'the chest' in the protocols."

"Protocols?"

"Yes. Some of the documents you signed today. One was to agree to this presentation now of the chest and the Entity Protocols designated to it." Marco lightly bowed to the agents, waiting stoically to the side, "Thank you, gentlemen. I'm glad his Holi—Shepherd met you both this evening. You are dismissed to return to your previous posts."

Rossi and Bruno nodded and let themselves out, closing the door firmly behind them.

"Alright, now what is in this chest, Marco?" Shepherd said as he slapped a hand on top of the old elaborate box.

The pope chest was made of a combination of wood and metal. The edging and rivets were iron, while the main faces and classic treasure chest arched top were made of yellow-stained chestnut. It had artistic indents and grooves cut in beautiful patterns and mechanical bearings all around it with complex, interlinking cogs. The chest looked more like something from a steampunk pirate ship than a Vatican Museum.

"No one, Shepherd, that is, no one alive now, knows what's in this chest," Marco replied, with a straight face this time. "The chest has been handed down from Holy Father to Holy Father since the early sixteenth century. It has survived under the care of each pope and the Entity. According to the protocols, the chest has always resided in the pope's quarters, these solitary chambers. Only the pope can open it or have access alone at any time. When the pope passes on, or in the rare case, retires, the chest will be removed by the Entity, monitored, and protected as it has been these last few weeks, under multiple guards. We also watch the guards on camera now, and the key to the chest is unknown to the guards."

Marco sat down and continued, "Only three people in the Vatican know the key to this chest. Myself, as the Camerlengo, the locksmith we keep on staff, and now you, our new pope." He pulled from inside his pocket a small antique-looking jewelry box. The box was tiny but appeared even smaller by the ring inside when Marco opened it to show Shepherd the contents. It was the Ring of the Fisherman. Shepherd knew about this ring only from what he had read online once or twice years ago. He was still wearing the temporary one given to him earlier that day.

The ring usually served as a papal seal and was even kissed by visitors and guests of the pope. In modern times, it was more of a symbolic item of the papal office. Shepherd peered down at the ring as Marco displayed it on the table. The ring was golden and rounded on top, with engraved artwork of Saint Peter fishing from a boat with a net. Arched around the top of the image of Saint Peter, letters were etched saying, "Leo XIV."

Marco commented on the ring as he pushed the box out, presenting it in front of Shepherd. "The ring itself is the key. Each pope has worn the Ring of the Fisherman since the early thirteenth century. There have been many versions of the ring. No one knows for sure the design of its original brother, but there has been a new ring for each pope since the chest and the ring were paired together. Each ring has a different size, shape, and face engraved into it, and our locksmith reconfigures the locking mechanism on the chest to coincide with the new key. Please, try it on Shepherd."

Shepherd took the ring from the box and slowly placed it on his right-hand ring finger. The fit was cold and unfamiliar but snug. "How do you know the locksmith doesn't look at what's inside the chest when setting up the locking mechanism?" he asked.

Marco answered, "As part of the protocols, we always take special care that the chest is placed under the watchful, trustworthy eyes of the Entity, even when it is in the locksmith's shop. When the locksmith triggers a reset from the closed position, the chest has a sliding, iron secondary lid that rolls up and goes over the contents, snapping it closed from outside access, but he can still work on the outer locking mechanism. When the lid is opened and the locksmith goes to reset the keyhole, the secondary door flips into place and is kept shut till his work is done. After the key is reset, the lid can be re-shut, and the sliding inner door snaps back out of the way so the chest can be opened correctly. All of this is also done under close supervision by two members of the Entity. Entity recruits are pulled from the most devout dioceses across the world. They are the most trustworthy agents of the church."

Shepherd's eyes gleamed with astonishment as he peered over the intricate cogs and ornate carvings in the structure of the chest. "This thing is quite the contraption then. I wonder who designed such a device."

Marco cracked a smile and said, "None other than Leonardo Da Vinci himself was the designer of the chest."

Shepherd's heart skipped a beat, and he fell back into a chair facing Marco when he heard that. *He couldn't be serious! Da Vinci?*

Marco read Shepherd's look. "Oh yes. It wouldn't be a Vatican secret without somehow involving Da Vinci." He couldn't help but laugh a little bit at that statement.

Shepherd found himself itching with excitement, sitting in his pajamas as he looked at the chest with eager anticipation. He looked down at the ring on his finger as he held his right hand up, palm down in front of the chest. He flexed his fingers out and twiddled the ring with his thumb from the underside of his hand. Shepherd made a fist, pointed the ring towards the chest, and glanced at Marco. "How does the ring, or the key, work? Do I place it on the plate here?"

"The entire ring is the key. So, you'll have to remove it from your finger. Take it off and hold it in your fingers, then push the face of the ring back through that round hole in front. When the ring touches the back, you'll feel it stop. Then, with some forward pressure, give it a twist to the right. The opposite motion will lock the chest. The ring stays in the lock whenever the chest is open. The ring will not come out unless the chest is closed. You will need to ensure it is closed and put your ring back on once you are done each time."

"Part of the protocols?"

"Exactly," Marco said.

Shepherd inquired, "Should I open it now?" as he pulled off the ring and leaned in to push it to the keyhole.

"No, no, Shepherd! Remember, no one can see its contents except the pope. That's you and only you. I'll get an earful from Janis, the Commander of the Entity Order if he hears I was in the room when you opened that thing. I don't want to have to take another one of his lie detector tests and sign more non-disclosures any more than you probably do." Marco looked more serious now. "The chest is one of the parts of being Holy Father that is strictly handed down immediately upon the new pope's election. It has been put forth since its inception into the inheritance of the position as one of the most important, yet secretive, ceremonies of the—passing of the cloak, as it were. You are the new spiritual leader of the entire Roman Catholic Church. From here on out, your entire life is under the public eye." Marco smiled again. "And if you think the Creator was guiding your life before, don't be surprised if you feel him nudge you a little harder than usual now from time to time." Marco looked back down at the chest from Shepherd's gaze. "This is kept private, just for you, as it was for your predecessors. Take refuge in this one part of being the new Holy Father that is kept secret for your eyes only. I hope you will use whatever is inside wisely and carefully."

The wisdom Marco shared struck Shepherd as profound. He had already seen a lot of solid qualities in Marco that he liked. This was another checkmark in Shepherd's mind that Marco had great insights and could likely be relied on for council in the future. Shepherd nodded and casually glanced around the room. He was anxious to see what the prominent treasure chest in front of him held. His interest and anxiousness to proceed must have shown because Marco picked up on them.

Marco moved to the door. "Well, this has undoubtedly been quite an unexpectedly exhausting day for you, Shepherd. I'm sure you would like to have some time to yourself to relax this evening," he said.

Shepherd slipped the ring back on and walked Marco out. After everything they'd gone through together for the first day, Marco could not have been more right about how worn out and mentally and physically drained Shepherd already started to feel the moment he came into the room and slipped on his pajamas. Shepherd began to feel the fatigue seep into the front of his forehead, pushing down on his eyes, but looking at the mysterious chest on the table gave his spirit more energy from his curiosity reserves. Noticing the out Marco was giving him moving toward the door, Shepherd nodded his head again and instinctively gave a half-yawn. After a thank you and quick embrace, Shepherd excused Camerlengo Marco and closed the door behind him.

Shepherd found himself, once again, alone in the bedchamber in the Vatican. He looked back from the door and leaned against it. He stared up at the ceiling, then let his gaze fall in line with the chest sitting on the table. Shepherd looked back down at his new Fisherman's Ring and lifted his eyes to the chest.

*Well, I gotta at least open it tonight, h*e thought to himself, as his eyes were already starting to feel heavy, and the need for sleep was battling his curiosity. Shepherd walked back across the room to the table and circled until he was on the opposite side, standing over the chest where Marco had stood while giving him the rundown on the chest's origins and design.

"Leonardo Da Vinci," Shepherd whispered into the room, feeling the history and ominousness of the moment. He ran his hands over the top of the chest, inspecting its intricacies with his fingertips. When he reached the ring keyhole, Shepherd felt around its edges and tapped it with his pointer finger. Shepherd's excitement took on a level of nervousness as he slid the ring off again and placed it in his palm.

After a brief moment of contemplation and a deep breath, Shepherd pushed the Fisherman's Ring into the hole at the front of the chest. The head of the ring passed through the opening. He wiggled it a little and felt the face align itself perfectly at the back. *Must be something magnetic in the ring.* Once the ring felt snug, Shepherd kept the pressure forward and turned the key to the right. There was a harsh jolt after a little struggle, and once it rotated about ninety degrees, Shepherd heard a loud *kerchunk!*

The sound reminded him of the noise an iron bar jail cell key would make in old westerns he watched with his father as a kid back in Dunedin. His father was an outdoorsman at heart who loved nature, especially the sea and fishing. Part of Shepherd's love for the outdoors had expanded into a passion for wild west adventures. His father would read Louis L'Amour novels about cowboys and watch John Wayne on the television with young Shepherd right next to him on the couch. Shepherd grew up watching "The Duke," as John Wayne was called. Seeing the stories unfold on screen where the good guy takes out the bad guy, the hero gets the girl, and the desperate townsfolk are saved repeatedly with cowboy heroism and frontier justice gave Shepherd an adventurous, yet moral, compass in his youth. That compass was part of what led him to the church through his family. He didn't want to be just a part of the story; he wanted to be *The Duke*, but it seemed he was going to be *The Shepherd* instead.

Shepherd returned from his thoughts on his childhood to the adventure at hand. The chest was unlocked. He placed a hand on each front corner of the lid and gave it a jerk upward. The lid lifted with unexpected ease due to a spring mechanism in the back of the hinge that was revealed as it opened. Shepherd expected the lid to be rusted and stuck on such an ancient-looking box but then felt silly remembering the last pope had access, and the locksmith had just worked on it maybe a few hours before. Shepherd hoped for some dramatic whoosh of mist or dust when the seal broke on the chest, but there was no such dramatization. The lid swung up with a creaking sound that made a practical man like Shepherd wish he knew where to find WD-40 in a place like the Vatican.

He peered over the lid into the chest. Deep inside, the lower half was filled with stacks of old papers, some leather booklets, and a few larger old books bound with leather straps. He grabbed one of the more oversized books and looked it over closer. The binding and cover were plain. Shepherd flipped from the front to the first actual page and found writing inside the book.

Pius XII, 1939-1958 A.D.

Shepherd flipped through the first few pages and quickly realized what he was holding. It was a journal. He scanned a few more pages from the other booklets in the chest and saw similar journals with different popes' names and years on them. These were the secret journals of all the popes in recent history.

What did Marco say? About how far back this chest has been handed down? Shepherd thought to himself in the quiet of his bedchambers as he shuffled through the papers into the bottom of the chest and found a very tattered small booklet down in the bottom. It had pages made of cloth rather than parchment.

The cover and binding were made from a much more degraded material, which looked to have been handled quite a bit. The first pages of the journal read:

Alexander VI, 1492-1503 A.D.

Atop the pile in the chest was a newer-looking hardcover notebook with an elastic band wrapped around it. Shepherd peeled back the strap and opened the journal.

Francis, 2013-

Shepherd flattened the journal on the table and gave the name and date a somewhat somber look. After a few seconds, he pursed his lips, grabbed a pen from a nearby desk, and filled in the year *"2023 A.D."* at the end. He noticed in the previous two journals that the end year was filled with different ink and penmanship, just as he had done. The next pope always filled in the end dates.

I guess it's up to whoever comes next to fill in that part, Shepherd confirmed in his mind as he carried Pope Francis', his predecessor's, journal over to the bed. After turning on a small lamp on the nearest nightstand, he set the journal down for a moment on his comforter. Shepherd crossed the room length to turn off the main lights above. On his return to the bed, he slumped into the covers and rolled to his back. He let out a long groaning sigh that only older men with a tight back, or anyone who's been a father for a day, makes. He stared at the ceiling for a few seconds, pondering his current reality and if it might all go away in the morning. Shepherd reached back over, grabbed the journal, and pulled it open under the light from his lamp.

I suppose I'll start with where Francis left off, he thought.

Shepherd opened the journal and began to read the most recent entry. He did not get very far before Pope Francis' cursive blurred together under his heavy eyelids, and he found himself out cold, his hands grasping the pages beneath his sagged chin.

4

Holy Eyes Only

The first month as Pope Leo XIV went by in a blur for Shepherd. The name Leo XIV was ceremonial, but everyone in the Vatican, and thanks to the media the rest of the world, had taken to the simple name of "Shepherd" or "The Shepherd" in all his greetings and news stories. The daily schedule for a pope was very regimented and organized. It may have been Shepherd's first rodeo, but the staff of the Vatican quickly ushered him along day by day as he fell into the routine. Shepherd usually took breakfast with Camerlengo Marco and an occasional cardinal with a private concern or one who'd asked for a brief audience, all so the Holy Father could multi-task with what little time he had before a morning mass and prayers. The afternoons were filled with meetings and occasional public appearances or speeches.

Once evening came, usually more quickly than Shepherd liked, he would take dinner with anyone in the Vatican able to attend. Shepherd never wanted a private meal. He knew that all the men and women who had dedicated their lives to the church needed to see who their new spiritual leader was. Shepherd required himself to get to know every face that worked within the walls; he was adamant about that. At dinner, he would ask for someone new to sit next to him each night when he entered the dining hall. He wanted to get a chance to sit down and meet each person one-on-one at some point but to take a less formal approach. From the Swiss Guard at the front gate to the sisters who ran the daycare for the few staff with children, Shepherd showed interest in every one of them. The dinners were a favorite time of Shepherd's. The man was clearly a foodie, and Italy had already sparked his interest quickly when he had arrived on his initial trip with Johns and sampled some of the local cuisine. Pasta was Shepherd's weakness, and there's nothing quite like authentic Italian pasta. His mother's spaghetti had been a family staple growing up in a lower-income home. Spaghetti was cheap, and it filled the plates of him and his three sisters, a reminder of the feeling of a full belly whenever he twisted it in his fork. The experience was an excellent comfort for Shepherd during a fast-paced and stressful time in his life. He had the growing waistline already to prove it in just a short while.

One evening, Shepherd asked a priest who worked in the library's curation department to join him. The librarian's name was Samuel. He shared with Shepherd all manner of stories of how excited everyone he spoke with in the libraries and galleries were to see someone younger, like Shepherd, as pontiff. Samuel shared that he, too, hoped to see a leader such as Shepherd take the position.

"With all the turmoil going on in our time, it's so inspiring to see a leader of our church with a passion for changing the world for the better. Most want to avoid ruffling feathers and increase membership." Samuel blushed after making that bold statement early in the evening.

The encouragement and hope from others continued to put into perspective for Shepherd what was expected and needed from him. He always dreamed of a chance to be in a position of influence where the Creator could use him to make a lasting impact during his time on Earth. Becoming pope was clearly his moment, and he wasn't wasting any time. Shepherd had appointed his replacement to the diocese back home in Australia he had to leave behind. Taking care of business back home first, Shepherd quickly worked with cardinals in the church to release funds and some aid for a few groups he had worked with in Australia during the fire disasters that he knew were in great need when he departed. That was one of his first acts, ensuring the home he was leaving was in capable hands and cared for. The second task Shepherd put before himself was to learn everything he could about the position, authority, duties, and resources within the pope's purview. Shepherd wanted to know what he potentially could or couldn't do from his papal seat. Shepherd wanted to understand every option and resource at his disposal to find the best outlets for change and impact. He learned since the Vatican is not just a church but is also a city-state, the position of pope wasn't as simple as just head of the church. The pope was also technically the "King" of the Vatican and had a ruling authority over its internal government. Although many of the rules were old and antiquated, they were still in the fine print. When it came to concerns of funds and projects, there was a council that weighed in on everything. Shepherd wanted to know where all the money went. He wondered what happened with all the Peter's Pence money sent each year to support the Roman Catholic Church Capital.

Shepherd was to be given a wage, as each pope is offered, but like many before, he refused. He only asked that the funds be given to specific charities and aid organizations of his choosing. Shepherd made it clear he didn't want the church to have any money behind its walls other than what was needed to keep the lights on. He wanted every penny that flowed into the church to flow right back out to help its people and the world they were a part of. The policies and changes he was enacting already had a massive reverse psychological impact on the masses. Hearing his message and seeing the decisions being made for the church on the public stage was causing ripples. The success was also thanks to assistance from Marco and a new website he set up, *theshepherdsflock.va.* Instead of the church asking for any funds for themselves, *theshepherdsflock.va* showed anyone willing to donate precisely where the funds would go, and every program was vetted and verified. Organizations around the world could submit their own applications for needs in their communities to be posted on the site. The website allowed funding to go right where it would be most helpful. Shepherd and Marco included recommendations, along with insights from other advisors and the cardinal council. The website posted options for organizations that could be funded where they felt an urgent need, or donors could pick and choose where they saw a specific need they wanted to assist. Within a week of the site's launch, it had already tallied 400 million subscribers, a staggering new record for anything of its kind. The site also facilitated the changing hands of over $50 million in funds from organizations with plenty to give to those with plenty of need. The site's initiative was already being applauded in the media as one of the most impactful crowdfunding programs to the date.

Shepherd felt his vision was coming alive already. *Save each other first, and together, we'll save the world; the church comes later.* For a moment at dinner, he thought back to his first speech, remembering those crucial words. He wanted to inspire people to change and to look out for each other. The revival was happening, and the momentum was already filling Shepherd's spirit. The part of his speech indicating "the church comes later" was very intentional on his part. The new agenda rooted out several greedier parties amongst leadership in the church, who were quickly replaced with those the council decided had their hearts and intentions in the right place. With the worst of those wanting to line their pockets removed, there were rumblings of concerns about the longevity of Shepherd's plan and whether the church was to really "come later." The issue of keeping the lights on was resolved with an ingenious idea from one of Marco's interns on the staff, who had a little bit of marketing knowledge. When the website was launched, a simple checkbox option was added on the last page of each donation transaction screen. Next to the checkbox, a brief description was included asking if the donor would increase their giving by just one percent to give for the church to continue supporting and maintaining the website. The option to give more was also available, but one percent was the default. Most donors were happy to click the checkbox, but a surprising percentage opted for more than the minimum. In fact, along with the first week's $50 million in donations to organizations and communities, an additional $1.5 million was donated through the site to the church.

When Shepherd's lessons in the business of the church and meetings were done for the day, and dinner was through, he would retire to his bed chambers. Apparently, the fact that most of the other popes had been elderly and had earlier—bedtimes got the staff into a bit of a routine that had settled long before Shepherd's time. Dinner was at 5 pm sharp, and the hallways of the Vatican were dimly lit by the time the sun set most evenings. The early lights-out schedule gave Shepherd ample time to rest, occasionally call family and friends back home, and read up on his *pope files* as he had started to call the journals in the chest. Shepherd flipped further into the journals each night. Every evening, after he had showered the day off and slipped into his favorite pajamas, Shepherd looked through the chest and cracked open a journal.

Shepherd now had a few extra pairs of pj's since his previous office staff back in Australia mailed his clothes from the diocese's barracks. When the package arrived, inside were some baked congratulatory cookies in the cutout shape of sheep, for The Shepherd, by some enthusiastic church members. The joke had completely floored Shepherd one morning while sitting with Marco at breakfast when he first opened the package. A sense of hope and joy was growing inside the Vatican walls. The people said the spirit of optimism flowed from the Vatican City gates to the world once Shepherd entered the picture. The world seemed to have its eyes on the Vatican more so than at any time in recent history. There were expectations of influence and grandeur, and Shepherd was gearing up to deliver.

Shepherd was excited to be getting into a new journal that night. He finished Pope Francis' small body of work the night before. Francis hadn't been much for journaling. Most of his entries were months apart and seemed forced in their wording as if he were writing in the journal because he felt it was an obligation or an unwanted chore. In any case, Shepherd gave it the respect it deserved and read the whole thing cover-to-cover in the late hours over his first few weeks. Shepherd decided he'd alternate new and old journals, looking for an older one in the chest to skip back to that night.

The chest was placed sitting in a corner next to the roll-top desk across from his bed. Shepherd decided to stay in the pope's traditional suite a bit longer before moving to a more spartan quarters. It had been easier to go to and from the room for all his meetings and meals. He figured if the room would sit empty otherwise, no one would think it odd to "suffer" a little luxury of living conditions for convenience's sake and to save the treasury some coin. A few visitors had already used the extra dormitory space he wasn't occupying. Shepherd tied his pajama pants off after brushing his teeth and set his phone on its wireless charger on his nightstand. The screen lit up with the battery indicator, time, and a wallpaper of the view from his parents' old back porch in New Zealand. Distant waves and a familiar sunset hid behind the digital clock on Shepherd's phone screen. Every time his phone lit up and he saw that view, he was reminded of the peace and comfort he dreamt of for all people. Shepherd slipped off his Fisherman's Ring and slid it into the keyhole at the front of the Da Vinci-designed chest. *So cool*, he always thought to himself when he would slip the ring in and turn it as a key to the open position.

The pope chest clicked through its complex opening routine, and Shepherd flipped back the lid. He reached right for Pope Julius II's journal, which rested upright in the bottom right corner.

Julius II, 1503-1513 A.D.

The cover had coating of dust on it. Shepherd remembered lifting and brushing it when rifling through the chest his first evening as pope and could see his finger marks. He reflected on how his appointment to pope already felt like a lifetime ago or as if it was a different lifetime altogether. He felt fortunate to have become pope at an age where he could continue to make an impact for decades. *Lord willing, if my health lets me,* he thought with a pat on his already growing belly.

After Shepherd wiped the dust on the journal away with a rag from his bathroom sink, he flopped down on his bed and flicked on the nightstand lamp to get more than just the ambient vanity light from the bathroom doorway behind him. Pope Julius II wrote in Spanish. Some pages had inserts where an English-speaking pope somewhere between that time and the far past had translated a page here and there. At Shepherd's high school, way back in his teen years, they required Spanish each year as a language course in New Zealand. It was either that or Māori, which was only a local New Zealand dialect he had no use for if he was anywhere but New Zealand. So, when Shepherd was a student wanting to get out in the world, he opted for the broader world language option.

Feeling fluent enough to take a stab at it, Shepherd attempted to muddle through some of the untranslated pages. He quickly realized that the Spanish writings of the past did not so easily translate to the language spoken and written anymore. Translating the Old Spanish, which looked more like Latin in part, was a task he unfortunately wasn't equipped to adequately tackle after all. Julius II had put more on paper than most other popes since his time. His journal wasn't the most oversized in the chest, but it was filled, each and every page. Shepherd wasn't about to try and get through the entire thing. He was curious, at least, after spending most of his time over the last two weeks just looking into the mind of Pope Francis and where he had left off.

According to his own entries, Francis spent little time reading the older journals. He, *"Read the full journal of his predecessor and a few interesting historical anecdotes from the past, but the future is where my interests lie,"* was how he put it.

Shepherd flipped deep into the journal of Julius II looking for something good. As he scanned and skimmed, he started to notice some sections and pages had a unique marker on them. It was simple and small, so he didn't take notice at first. It was a circle with a crosshair-*x* in the center. The mark didn't look like a chapter, header, or break marker and was randomly displaced throughout the text. Shepherd mostly took notice since it was clearly in a different ink than the rest of the journal. He picked one and investigated the writing in that section since it was a translated page.

Pope Julius II, November 4, 1510 A.D.

I am about to leave for the next campaign, leading our military to another victory for our papacy. I am not sure when I shall return. I visited the prisoner one last time before our caravan leaves in the morning. He no longer tries to plead for his release. He only sits and stares like a stone when I visit now.

The prisoner has refrained from speaking on my last few visits. It seems he no longer wishes to provide anything of use. I told him if I never came back there could be others, but that he may be forgotten down in that place. Good riddance. Let him be lost. Let his secrets stay buried with him down in that dark hole under the square.

Shepherd didn't know what to make of the entry. *Prisoner?*

He puzzled to himself. *The Vatican had prisoners?* Shepherd flipped to another section ahead of the one he'd just read. It was a year or so earlier in Pope Julius II's writings. There it was again, another segment marked by the x-circle symbol along with a paragraph about a "prisoner."

Who was this prisoner? What had he done? Why did the church have him? So many questions. It seemed like an interesting Vatican secret to check out. The kind of thing Shepherd's mystery-thriller-prone personality was unable to resist. Shepherd had a thought. He popped out of bed and ran to the Da Vinci chest in the corner. Shepherd slid on the smooth marble floor tiles and swung the pope chest open. He grabbed the first journal he saw and flipped through. It had four or five of the same x-circle hash marks. *Someone had gone through the journals and marked these sections later. A more recent pope did this to the older ones' journals.*

Shepherd flipped through one journal after the other, *prisoner—prisoner—prisoner.* He kept seeing the word.

Each section that was marked in every journal made the same reference to the same "prisoner." As Shepherd sat looking at the different entries, seeing which might be best to pick and read in-depth first, he realized the date range he was looking across. The journals he'd just searched through with the markings spanned at least a couple hundred years.

It can't be the same prisoner, can it?

He quickly grabbed a journal from Pope John Paul II and flipped through it. Ten to fifteen pages in, the x-circle mark was in the same red ink. John Paul II wrote in English, and as Shepherd read the entry, it only became more intriguing.

Pope John Paul II December 22, 1988 A.D.

I found it! I finally figured it out! I took a trip down to see the prisoner today. Using Pope Julius II's journal, I found the key inside the chest and used it to open the entrance that was installed in the main papal chambers. The prisoner was incredible. I should hope to visit again. One can imagine there is a lot to learn from someone who has been around since the days of Creation.

Shepherd found another entry with the prisoner marking and read again:

Pope John Paul II, January 3, 2001 A.D.
Well, Y2K didn't happen after all. I made a bet with the prisoner. I owed him a few books for that one. I took three new novels down on my visit just yesterday, as I do for each new year since I discovered him.

Shepherd dropped the journal to the floor with a *clack* of the hardback binding to the tile below. The sound slightly popped him back to reality. He only just then realized he'd stood up from kneeling in front of the pope chest at some point. Shepherd stepped back and sat down on his bed.

"Since Creation? That can't—that can't mean what it sounds like! Why would such a being be a prisoner? Why does the Vatican—have a prisoner? None of this makes any sense!" He found himself dumbfounded, staring blankly into the room's dark corners.

Shepherd began to pull some of the other journals with the prisoner section markings out and lined them up chronologically atop the long table in the center space of his bedchamber. He quickly realized that most of the pages translated to English were the pages in journals with the prisoner mark. Shepherd worked late into the night, unable to even think about sleep after what he'd discovered. He got sticky notes from the roll-top desk drawer and started marking journal covers and pages to find and reference where the different prisoner sections were. Shepherd spent hours on his makeshift filing system till he had at least 300 years sifted through and labeled, and there was around 200 years to go. Some journals had no entry of the prisoner, such as Francis'. A handful had just one or two entries, but some of the oldest included many long entries referencing the mysterious Vatican prisoner. Shepherd grabbed a pad and a pen and began to take notes. He soon learned that the journals with more entries had more insights, and he stuck with them for what he was able to stay awake and read. That night, Shepherd passed out asleep at the end of the long table, with his face resting on stacks of paper.

5

Secrets Hiding More Secrets

S hepherd woke the next morning to his cheek stuck with drool against the cover of an open journal's pages. He learned the night before from the journals that there was indeed a prisoner in the Vatican somewhere. He was always just referred to as "the prisoner" in all the journals. Shepherd pieced together a few facts and was developing his own theories. Based on what was mentioned in little bits of the journals he was able to dive into so far—only the pope and the Entity had access to the prisoner, but somehow, no one else knew of his existence. There were also references to some other "key" in the chest and a "shortcut" to the prison that was installed in the late 1990s. Shepherd had wanted to investigate these new findings as early as possible, but the sun was already peaking its way over the highest rooftops that hindered the dawn from breaking through his window each morning. The pope's full morning routine was about to commence. Shepherd had to shrug off his curiosities, and instead of going further down a rabbit hole, adorned his daily responsibilities.

Shepherd got dressed in his more casual Holy Father attire. He usually changed clothes again after breakfast before he led prayer and mass. It was a routine he'd grown accustomed to after several wardrobe changes so that *The Shepherd* wouldn't have coffee stains when being broadcast to the rest of the world. Shepherd locked his pope chest after placing the last journal back inside and slipped out of his bedchamber into the hallway, closing the door quietly behind. Slowly, over the previous few weeks, Shepherd convinced the Swiss Guard, Thomas, posted outside his door, that it might be alright for him to stand watch a little further down the hallway. Shepherd disliked the feeling of someone hovering a few feet outside the door from where he was sleeping, and a little more space put him at ease. When Shepherd stepped out of his room, Thomas was at the opposite end of the hall, not looking toward Shepherd's door. Shepherd started to make it a sort of game to be out the door and halfway down the hallway before Thomas noticed. To his boyish glee, Shepherd had nearly given Thomas the slip that day and was almost around the corner before he was caught.

"The Shepherd is on his way to breakfast," Thomas said, giving his other Swiss Guard and staff members the heads-up on his earpiece.

Shepherd heard him just as he was leaving earshot. "New record," he said out loud in delight to himself as he entered the dining room.

Marco, Shepherd's new trusted companion in his papal life, was already seated at the table. He was sipping a tiny espresso, his usual choice unless an upset stomach called for tea. Marco was leafing through a morning paper for something worth reading. He sat down his cup as he stood to greet Shepherd.

"Please! Don't get up, Marco. The later in the day I see the first ceremonious or courteous gesture, the longer I feel relaxed and myself," said Shepherd as he approached the table. "The more laid back we keep these breakfasts that are out of the public eye, the more I'll appreciate you for it." Shepherd had already given Marco and most of the staff a similar speech a few times.

The idea that Shepherd was the pope but didn't want to be treated as such, unless ceremony demanded, was becoming more expected and socially accepted. Shepherd was fighting what traditions he could to maintain those parts of his personality he thought were essential and self-defining. Shepherd discussed the topic one evening with Cardinal Johns before Johns returned to Australia the week before. Johns stayed for Shepherd's first week as pope, but having been gone from his dioceses for several weeks during the conclave, he was pushing his time away. Plus, Shepherd wanted him to get back and check how things were going for his home church since he left. Johns had helped steer Shepherd in the right direction in the past, and Shepherd leaned on Johns for wisdom when doubts crept into his mind.

"How do I not forget who I am, Cardinal Johns?" Shepherd questioned one night. "How do I keep this—" He motioned to his papal attire and the beautiful city around him. "—all of this from changing me? I want to use my influence to help people as much as possible. I'm nervous, though, that this place and the weight of the world will change who I am. I'm not sure if I'll be the same person after I've been in the Vatican for years."

Johns told Shepherd, "You're scrappy, Liam." Johns hadn't adopted calling him "Shepherd" like everyone else yet. "If you let too much of who ya are change, then you're no longer the same man our Creator guided us cardinals to elect. Try to recognize what is necessary, and what is jus' tradition. What is necessary may need a strict, intentional thinkin' pope, but I believe the traditions of this church could use more of that scrappy bishop from down under that can't help but shake things up a bit, eh?"

Shepherd already wanted to take a similar approach to what Cardinal Johns advised, and the conversation encouraged him all that much more, having his mentor's endorsement.

As Shepherd dwelled on Johns' thoughts and pulled up his chair, the smell of coffee took hold of his senses. He sat down and quickly added some cream and sugar from a nearby tray to take a sip as fast as possible. The Vatican staff knew how to make an excellent cup of coffee. Italy was already known for great coffee; the Vatican took it to the next level.

Marco, noticing Shepherd's haste and reactions, couldn't help but comment. "You know, Shepherd, if the early evenings retirement to your chambers and getting into your *secret pope chest* keep you up so late, I'm sure there are other things we could schedule in your night—like sleep."

Shepherd wasn't alert enough yet to hold in an abrupt chuckle, which made him slightly nose-gargle his coffee. He smiled it away and wiped his nose as he looked over at Marco. "Good Lord! I can feel that in my sinuses," Shepherd said, wiping a trickle of coffee from under his nose with a napkin. Marco, you can't do that to me before we've even eaten. Whew! That's one way to let the caffeine hit you hard and quick."

Marco bounced with a little laugh, "Sorry, Shepherd. You look so obviously like you've been at something all night again." He was aware Shepherd was up late reviewing whatever mysteries were in the pope chest. Shepherd was sure at that point Marco had deduced some journal or secret documents were in the chest, and he, of course, wasn't very far off.

"I can't help myself. I want to learn as much as I can, as fast as I can, about all the facets of this position that can be used for the greater good. I think I'm onto something exciting that I just got new insight about." Shepherd had to be vague with Marco due to the Entity Protocols, but he was curious how much he could say to see if Marco knew any inside information about the prisoner.

"Is that—ink on your face?" Marco leaned over the table and looked closer at Shepherd's left cheek as he raised a hand to it. "Yes, it is! And it looks like some writing stamped on there with it!" Marco laughed again as Shepherd quickly grabbed a napkin to wipe it away. "You've obviously been reading something you can't say much about, so what CAN you say?" Marco inquired.

Shepherd grabbed a slice of toast from a center platter and began spreading thick butter across its rough, charred surface. "Well, I've seen a few—old reports and writings of some form or another, records if you will. And they keep referring to a prisoner, here in the Vatican, over and over. And these—documents are separated by many years, yet they refer to the same prisoner."

"How many years are we talking about Shepherd?" Marco asked, taking a sip of his espresso.

"Many. Too many. An inhuman amount of time," Shepherd replied vaguely again.

Marco contemplated for a minute, "Just 'prisoner'? No name or other identifying information? Maybe details on where this prisoner is held?"

Shepherd looked disappointed and shook his head. "It sounds like you have no idea what I'm talking about," he lamented.

Marco seemed to be searching his memory for a moment. Then he spoke, "I do recall one time hearing an Entity guard mention to another that he had moved to the prisoner detail as I passed them in the hallway. This was years ago. I didn't understand the comment at the time. I still don't. The words have always stuck with me, though. The guard detail sounded important the way he spoke, and I recall thinking at the time that it was odd to hear anyone in Vatican City speaking about a prisoner. There's never been any prison or prisoner here that I can recall. The closest thing to a prison is a few small rooms with cots and toilets used for holding cells by the Swiss Guard and the Entity. And those are most often used to detain drunks that wander onto the property at night and harass the guards, or the occasional rowdy tourist. Sometimes vandals try to get into areas restricted from the public."

"I see, that's something—the Entity guard comment. Ever hear about it again or follow up?" Shepherd asked.

"There is an area restricted to only Entity members that supposedly has a back door that doesn't leave the office building it's in but goes somewhere undisclosed."

"Maybe I can inquire to some of the Entity about it later this evening?" Shepherd said optimistically.

"Well, it's Entity only. And that applies to even The Shepherd. No one is allowed into that area, not even the pope. They won't budge on it. Pope Francis asked to pass the guard post down that corridor once or twice, if I recall correctly, during his time. They told him he would have to use the Holy Father's shortcut entrance," Marco said.

"I read about a shortcut! Where is this other entrance? Do you know?" asked Shepherd.

"I wasn't sure what they were talking about, and Francis never commented on it after the incident."

"I haven't yet reviewed all the documents on the subject. Maybe I'll spend some more time looking into it another evening in the next week," Shepherd said as he sat back in his chair, chewing some toast. He changed the subject to the morning's schedule. Marco shifted gears and reviewed a few notes he took to go over during breakfast—a few cancellations, and some additions to the afternoon meetings. The evening was looking clear again. As excited as Shepherd was to get back into researching the prisoner, he compartmentalized, set aside his passion project, and dove into the day.

The evening came fast, as always. After another insightful dinner, chatting with sister Agatha, who had been at the Vatican since she took her vows over forty-five years ago, Shepherd found himself back in his own quiet space behind closed doors. He took a little time to process his day, shower, brush his teeth, and throw on his usual pj's. His pajamas were never washed and pressed so neatly before becoming pope. Every night when he returned to his tiny apartment space, they were laid out crisp and clean by the staff. It was a small luxury that he appreciated every time. Special treatment, to that extent, was so out of place for someone of his character that it forced him into a daily moment of humility and self-reflection.

Shepherd tied his plaid pajama pants off into a bow and slumped down into the chair next to the pope chest. As he slouched down into the chair further and further, he tilted his head left and reached his hand out to tap the lid. "I've got to figure this out tonight! I'm too distracted by this to let the mystery bleed into another day," he said adamantly.

Shepherd was naturally curious as a cat, and the *Hardy Boy* in him needed to solve the case. If he was going to give his daily activities the attention they warranted, then the mystery of the prisoner needed to be put to bed first. A stirring question in the back of his mind would always keep Shepherd distracted from the goings on of the day. The prisoner, if he still existed, or wherever he was, Shepherd needed an answer. He slid the pope chest in front of him on the tile floor, facing the chair. After popping his Fisherman's Ring into the keyhole and clicking the chest open, he grabbed the journal with the most prisoner x-marks, Julius II, and began scanning the text. Shepherd occasionally updated notes and took pauses at times to pace, think through ideas, and search about the room.

There was a key to be found and some secret door in the very room where he was sleeping. That much was certain from how the journals of previous popes described coming and going from their visits to the prisoner. There were references to a secret door in the room and another key in the chest, which he had already looked over from top to bottom twenty times. After pacing and pacing, Shepherd slumped again back into his new favorite chair. The back of the chair was tall and made him feel small due to its towering stature behind him. The further he slumped down, the closer he felt to a former childlike state of mind, trying to clear his thoughts. The pope chest was on the floor facing him. As he slumped to where his neck was at the crease of the back and the seat cushion, he stared at the open lid of the chest now meeting his lowered eyeline. His bed headboard was just out of focus behind the chest lid. On the underside of the lid, which Shepherd now had a straight look at, something was carved. Shepherd's eyes had just started to get droopy as the night got away from him, but they widened immediately at the realization of what symbol he was staring at. It was the same symbol used in the journals to mark the passages about the prisoner. The underside of the pope chest lid had a small circle in the center, with an *x*.

The other key was staring Shepherd in the face for quite a while before he realized it. He leaned forward and reached out to touch the lid of the chest. The inside lid surface was smooth except for the prisoner symbol. As Shepherd ran his fingers over it, he could feel it give some, like it was a separate detached piece. He pushed in, and the lid made a *click*. Shepherd released the pressure backward, and the symbol popped out like a round peg. Underneath the round wooden end with the emblem was a short cylindrical key about an inch deep. The wood was attached to metal and ended in a short stubby key with complex facets and grooves.

Shepherd smiled and clenched the key in his hand. *I've got to find this keyhole!* Now that he knew the size and shape of the keyhole, he scanned the room from the corner. Shepherd stood up to get a better view around the entire space. He was looking for a small round hole about an inch in diameter.

"It probably wouldn't be in plain sigh—" Shepherd was starting to voice his thoughts but was quickly silenced by another epiphany. Halfway through scanning the room in a circle, he stopped on his headboard. He noticed the wooden ornate piece of furniture came to a peak at the center. The peak had the prisoner's symbol on it with a small one-inch round hole at the center of the *x*. Shepherd leaped onto his bed like a cat and pulled himself up next to the headboard. He stood there momentarily, looking at the newfound key in his hand and the possible secret lock before him. "Johns said to stay scrappy," he said as he slid the key in and turned it just like the chest lock, and there was a loud *click*.

The headboard stayed on the wall, but the bed Shepherd was standing on began to lift. He quickly jumped off the side and slid back, landing on his backside on the cold floor. Loud mechanical gears could be heard shifting behind the wall. Shepherd watched, seated from the floor, while his bedposts disappeared into the ceiling above, and the base of the poles kept rising out of the floor below. His bed stopped eight feet in the air on four tall stilts. Shepherd looked back down at the headboard. He could now see that the center section of the headboard looked like a door when it was visible, extending all the way to the floor with no bed in front. Shepherd walked toward the door. He stood barefoot in front of it for a moment, admiring the woodwork and craftsmanship. He pushed the middle of the frame since it had no knob. It clicked and swung open into the room just like a magnetic lock cabinet. Shepherd peered into the dark opening and felt a little bit of fear tingling on the back of his neck. After a pause, he looked up at his bed hanging suspended. He chuckled, "Ha! Who knew the pope had monsters under his bed!"

6

The Monster Under the Pope's Bed

Shepherd tried to let his eyes adjust to see if he could find any shapes in the darkness that filled the passage behind his headboard. There was nothing in the black space ahead. He stepped over to the nightstand, grabbed his mobile phone off the charger, and swiped it open to access the flashlight feature. He slid on his flip-flops and went back to the secret door. The bright, tiny LED wasn't enough to fill the space, but as Shepherd peered around the left side, he found an old industrial light switch. The switch was a large lever that could be flipped one way to close a circuit of electricity and flopped down the opposite way to break the circuit and shut something off. Shepherd threw the switch. Several lights flickered inside, and the hallway became dimly lit. The fluorescent lights faded in and out quite a bit before giving a robust, solid glow. When they fully illuminated the space, Shepherd stepped inside.

The hallway was cold, and the air was stale. Cobwebs filled the corners, and some of the light bulbs above never flickered all the way on. The space looked run down and derelict compared to the rest of the surrounding pristine Vatican interiors. The hallway was probably the only space anywhere in the city that didn't look upkept as Shepherd dwelled on it. To his right was a wall about five feet away; to his left was a dark, foreboding hallway. Shepherd stepped to the left and kept his phone light forward. The hallway had a slight curve to its direction as it went on. Shepherd was wearing sandals, and the only sound you could hear in the corridor was the dirt particles grinding under his feet against the harsh concrete floors between *flip-flops*. The walls along the entire hallway were covered in a thick foam with sound-canceling qualities. Shepherd put his ear up next to it and could tell the foam drowned out ambient noise.

The hallway must be between the surrounding walls throughout the building, and the foam keeps anyone coming and going from being heard.

Shepherd shuffled a few yards down the hallway and came to a corner. As he rounded it, the hallway continued in a curved, angled downhill direction. Shepherd followed the hallway for what felt like several hundred meters. Most of the lights along the hallway were out, and Shepherd relied heavily on his tiny cellphone light as he went deeper and further in, but luckily, his eyes continued to adjust.

Around the last bend, the tunnel cut short abruptly, and Shepherd found himself standing at another door. The door was more evident than the previous and had a good old-fashioned turn knob on it, which Shepherd gave a stiff crank, and pulled toward him. The creaking sound was enough to make anyone wince, and the door cracked like it was brittle as chalk when it swung from the frame. As the door opened, a brighter light filled in from the doorway. Shepherd let his eyes adjust back again to the brightness and stepped into the newfound room.

The first thing Shepherd noticed was a desk with a man sitting behind it in the center of a room. The desk lit up the man's face from a small bank of security monitor screens. Shepherd recognized the man sitting behind the counter as Agent Rossi, one of the Entity agents that brought the pope chest into his room that first night. Shepherd hadn't seen the man since, and his initial reaction was to step forward and say "hi" despite the confusing circumstances, but Shepherd held his tongue for the moment. He quickly took more stock of the situation, looking about the room as he felt the front of his pajamas with his hands. For a second, Shepherd had an instinct to turn back to the door and close himself back into the passage, but as he let that thought fade, Agent Rossi looked up.

Rossi bolted out of his seat, "Your Holiness!" he said.

"Please, I've been going by Shepherd with everyone, if you don't mind. It's Rossi, isn't it?" Shepherd replied.

"Yes, your Holi—yes, Shepherd," Rossi replied nervously.

Shepherd took a look around the rest of the room as he stepped forward in his flip-flops to meet Rossi. The room was plain, empty, and open. It only had one desk station in the center, surrounded by vast, gray concrete floor space. Shepherd approached the desk and noticed it was circular, with a rotating chair in the middle so that its occupant could have a whole 360-degree spin of the monitors, desk surface, and view of the room over the counter edge around the desk. It was centered in a roughly thirty by thirty-foot room with a low wood rafter ceiling. The door Shepherd had entered by was directly across from another one on the far side of

Rossi's security post. The right wall that stretched the distance between encased a steel elevator door, an ancient iron door to the far side of that, and the opposite wall from the elevator was a blank stone surface.

"Rossi, I just came here from my bed chamber," Shepherd said in dismay.

"Yes, you found the entrance very quickly compared to others. I've heard previous popes didn't come down for years. Others never found the entrance at all," Rossi stated.

"Down?" Shepherd glanced toward the elevator.

"Yes, down. To visit with the prisoner," Rossi said.

Jackpot! Shepherd thought as his eyes lit up.

Shepherd tried to play it cool and hide his eagerness from Rossi. "Well, I would like to see him if that's alright. What's the procedure?"

"Of course, Shepherd. Yes, there are some strict rules and guidelines that I need to advise you of before sending you down the elevator. I'm not sure how much you already know from what you have seen in the chest, but the prisoner has stringent protocols." Rossi shuffled through a drawer in the desk area.

"Do you know who he is or why he is here?" Shepherd asked.

"Oh no, Shepherd, that information is for the Holy Father only. Our agenda is strictly secrecy and security." Rossi pulled out a small green jacket booklet from a drawer. "With that in mind—here are the rules we must enforce on you, Shepherd." Rossi read aloud and paraphrased for Shepherd. "The pope is the only person ever allowed into the elevator or out for standard visits, and only the Entity may accompany him if requested or if necessary for maintenance and repairs. The pope may only enter through his domicile entrance, and the

Entity guards may only enter from their adjacent entrance," he said, motioning to the opposing doors. He continued, "No form of communication device may ever pass the security post; that's where we are now."

"How far does the elevator go?" Shepherd interjected.

"120 meters down."

"Why so far?" Shepherd asked, placing his mobile phone on the desk.

"You'll find that we Entity guards aren't much for answers. We won't say anything about any matters we're in charge of for the church, especially the prisoner, Shepherd. The prisoner protocol is to be followed and passed down; that is all the Entity knows and needs to know. That is part of our oath. The project is under the authority of the King of the Vatican, which is the Bishop of Rome, the pope, you." Rossi handed the notebook to Shepherd. "Please, take this with you. You may have more questions on the protocols."

"So, I'm in charge of what goes on down here more or less, but you guys ensure nothing, and no one else, gets in or out. Is that about everything? Everything else is a mystery to me so far, honestly." Shepherd fessed up a little to his lack of understanding.

Rossi smirked, "We are trained to like things that way and to keep quiet, father. Our prisoner guard rotation team goes under regular lie detector tests, confessions, psychological screenings, and background checks. This position is for life, and that's what we give to it, our lives."

"I see." Shepherd stopped viewing Rossi as an intimidating Entity Agent, but he was definitely a boy scout when it came to the rules. "Anything else I should know?"

"Yeah, don't ever touch him. That's the last on our orientation list."

"Shortest orientation I've ever attended," Shepherd joked. Rossi didn't react.

Rossi stepped through the gap in the round desktop station and made his way to the elevator door. Shepherd walked to meet him at the entryway.

"Rossi, where are we right now exactly? In the Vatican, I mean? I feel like that hallway curved around and went on for maybe more than a football pitch long," Shepherd inquired.

"We're under Saint Peter's Square. There are two tunnels to this spot directly beneath the obelisk at the center of the square. There's the winding tunnel you came down that was installed after the original prison, and the larger service tunnel that those double doors lead to take you directly to the Entity guard main building."

"So, we're directly under the obelisk in the square?"

Rossi nodded, "Yes. We're shallow enough I could hear the crowd cheer through the dirt when the announcement of your election was made. I was down here on duty that day. It's quite tranquil normally."

Rossi reached down and grabbed a keycard on a retractable lanyard attached to his belt. He touched it to a sensor panel beneath the elevator button. A loud beep rang out, and the indicator light on the elevator button above his card changed from yellow to bright green. The large doors opened and revealed a pretty spacious elevator inside. Shepherd assessed the area as large enough to fit a small car inside.

"Is this the only way up or down?" Shepherd asked nervously, realizing he was about to voluntarily be lowered in a box held by old cables into a 120-meter-deep hole in the Earth.

"There was once a spiral staircase before the elevator got installed in the '90s, but that has long since been walled up."

"You mean there's no emergency exit? Where's the *in case of fire, use stairs* option in this scenario?" Shepherd was having second thoughts about going down.

"If you have any trouble down there, Shepherd, use the phone just outside the doors. You pick it up, and the other end rings here at the security desk, which is manned 24/7," Rossi assured him as he stepped back from the elevator doors.

"Right, it would just be nice if there was a backup system or something."

"Well, that's certainly something we can look into if you'd like, father. Have to take it up with the commander later."

"Yes. Well, I'll see about that. And see you in a bit," Shepherd said with a faux authoritative tone as he passed in front of Rossi.

Shepherd stepped cautiously into the elevator. As he turned around to face back at Rossi, he saw that the doors were already beginning to close. Rossi didn't even wait for the doors before returning to his station and plopping back into his chair. Through the hairline crack, as the doors collided, Shepherd saw Rossi grab a travel mug and take a sip.

The elevator seemed bright compared to the security room. The walls were stainless-steel all around, reflecting Shepherd's image in different scrunched and stretched perspectives depending on the bow of the flat metal surfaces like a house of mirrors. Shepherd looked to the panel beside the doorway on his right, where a small display screen lit up. Directly below it were two simple buttons—an up arrow and a down arrow. Shepherd tilted his head in acknowledgment of the simplicity of the design and tapped the down arrow. *Only one place to stop on each end, I guess.*

There was no music in the elevator, for some reason that bothered Shepherd, and he made a mental note of mentioning it to Rossi when he got back up. He would typically have thought something like that to be trivial, but about thirty seconds into the lengthy elevator ride, Shepherd hummed show tunes and wished for something to fill the dead air. He needed a distraction from the fact that he was plunging deep down a dark hole, a thought that made Shepherd more anxious as the ride went further. Finally, there was an abrupt lunge, and Shepherd felt his inertia halt and then pop back up from the bottom.

The elevator doors made their classic *ding* and rolled open to reveal a stone wall across from the entrance. In the middle of the wall was a small bland yellow phone hanging by a tiny spike nail. It was a classic curly cord landline from the '80s. Shepherd walked over to the phone and picked it up, holding the receiver to his ear.

There was one long beep tone in the earpiece, and then Rossi came on. "Rossi here. Everything alright, Shepherd?"

"Yeah, just wanted to make sure this thing was working. I got down just fine. Thanks." Shepherd hung the receiver back on its wall mount and stepped over the long curly cord flopped loose on the ground by his feet.

Shepherd shuffled forward and found himself in a dimly lit, short hallway. The walls on each side and ceiling were all carved into heavy granite stone. As the elevator door closed, Shepherd peered around the short hallway. A brighter, more ambient light came from the end of the hallway five or six meters away from the elevator entryway. As he walked in that direction, Shepherd saw some furniture and other items on the floor in the long viewing room he was entering. A small chair was in front of him, next to a plate glass wall, and a chess set out on a table. The glass wall was massive, and the light was all spreading from behind it. The place was some type of observation room Shepherd was in, and then the entire left wall's lowest few meters from the floor was a thick plexiglass transparent panel. When Shepherd entered the space in front of the glass, he looked up and could see the rock wall rose further in the room space he was in up into a high cathedral-type ceiling, revealing a massive natural rock wall that stretched far above the glass area and rounded down to meet the floor at the back of the room on his side. The diggers must have started cutting into the rock from above, bored out of the side he stood in down to the floor depth, and then cut back into the rock to create the glass cell surrounded by solid granite. The room's floor was stone, just like the walls, and other than the chair and table with a chess board and its game pieces, there was nothing else to be found on Shepherd's side of the glass.

Shepherd turned to look behind the viewing glass. To the left of the chess set, there was what looked like a slider drawer, also made of plexiglass. The drawer had a handle and seemed designed for passing large items between the room and whoever was behind the glass. It was probably big enough to slide a large pizza box back in or maybe a few shoeboxes; that was about all it could fit.

Then Shepherd saw him—the prisoner. He was behind the glass, sitting in a tall back, green armchair, turned away from the glass at an angle and holding a book. The prisoner looked like a man. His beard was the first feature that stood out to Shepherd. His beard was long and dark matted brown. The man was tall and dressed nicely enough; he was in what might be described as prison pajamas. Similar to Shepherd's attire that evening, but no hood and all one color, gray. The man was wearing a black round-brim saturno, and his hair color matched his beard. The man's face and hair were unkempt but he seemed put together otherwise. He was lounging back with his feet on a small, padded ottoman in front of the armchair where he sat reading. The prisoner didn't indicate that he'd noticed Shepherd entering the space outside his glass-enclosed cell.

The man must have noticed Shepherd, for without lifting his head from his book, he called out, "I had a feeling I would be seeing a new face soon." Shepherd could deduce that the tone was steady, refined, and sarcastic.

Shepherd stepped closer to the glass. He could see small marble-sized holes that passed through, just enough for some ventilation and sound to travel. "My name is Shepherd. May I ask yours?" Shepherd thought it best to give the prisoner the benefit of the doubt and to start with introductions.

The words from Shepherd made the man finally move his eyes from the page he'd been scanning. He turned to the side, keeping his brim down, and gazed at Shepherd around the side of his chair. The prisoner had deep, almost black eyes. His hair was chocolate brown. The man grabbed a slip of paper from the side table next to his chair and slid it between the pages, marking his place. He closed the book and laid it on the stand next to him. He lifted himself from the chair and strode casually to the glass. The prisoner's face was shrouded mainly by the shadow of his hat. Shepherd naturally adjusted his body language as he approached and stepped back as if the tall, muscular build prisoner was getting into his personal bubble. Then, remembering the glass, Shepherd settled his posture and stood his ground.

"You are the new pontiff, are you not?" the prisoner inquired, ignoring Shepherd's introduction.

"Yes, I was elected about a month ago," Shepherd answered.

"You seem quite a bit younger than most others."

"I'm fifty-two. Yes, a little younger than your average pope, I suppose." Shepherd couldn't help but try to keep the conversation light with humor, which was his anxious defense mechanism.

"You said to call you Shepherd? Is that your surname? The papal name you have selected, perhaps? Although, I recall no others by such name." The prisoner turned, walked back towards his chair, and ran his hand along the top of its torn, upholstered back.

"Middle name and nickname of sorts. It's what I've asked everyone to call me instead of 'Holy Father.' My name is Bishop Liam Shepherd Thompson. Well, I'm Pope Leo XIV."

"Ah, another Leo. There has not been one of them down here since the turn of the last century. Leo XIII found the way down. Pius IX before him could barely fit down the stairs. He was such a large chap. Formerly a bishop—so a priest then," the prisoner said.

Shepherd's adrenaline was pumping into him with excitement, hearing the mysterious figure talk about old popes and knowing Leo XIII. "I'm sorry, what should I call you? Prisoner?"

The man sighed, "I have been known by many names, but you may call me Samyaza."

"You don't go by Sam or anything shorter, do you?"

Samyaza rolled his eyes and stepped back further from the

glass, turning his attention to a desk against the back wall of his cell. Stacks of books and papers were littered around the desk surface, along with pencils, paperweights, and a few rulers.

Shepherd wasn't sure how to proceed. "May—may I call you Sam?"

Samyaza turned back and snapped, "No, Priest!" His gaze was filled with disdain.

Things already seemed tense to Shepherd in their first interaction. He tried to read the room and backed off from the glass. He'd been so anxious to meet the prisoner that he didn't think about how Samyaza might have no interest in meeting him. Shepherd had a lot of questions, but deciding which to ask first was proving more difficult than he anticipated. He didn't think about what would happen once he found the prisoner, but he already knew a few things from the events of the evening. The prisoner was real; his name was Samyaza, not Sam. He was still under the Vatican, way under, and Shepherd was able to find a secret entrance from under his bed and take a nerve-clenching elevator ride to a hidden dungeon. It was already a big night, to say the least.

While Samyaza turned his back again to shuffle a few papers and books around, Shepherd took in the rest of the view. Behind the glass was a cell about the size of a shipping container longways. The room had clearly been designed to provide a reasonable length of space while keeping every inch of it in close view from the glass wall.

The cell's back wall was the same stone as everywhere else, only that wall was covered in pinned-up drawings. Beautiful chalk and black soot artwork filled the space on many parchments of different sizes. The sketches were of

68

landscapes and maps and contained lettering that Shepherd had never seen before. The artwork was incredibly realistic. The talent rivaled most of the work Shepherd had seen in the museums while touring when he first came to Italy. Strange plants and animals that looked like they had deformities or evolved wrong filled the pages covering the wall. Shepherd recognized what could be forms of dragons, dinosaurs, giants, and all kinds of other creatures that lined the space that backdropped Samyaza's living quarters.

One strange thing Shepherd noticed was that there was no toilet, or sink for that matter, in Samyaza's cell. The desk had a few drawers and a small lamp on it with a green shade. The chair at the desk was old and had been repeatedly repaired with layers of duct tape. The wall closest to the elevator area was lined to the ceiling with books, hundreds and hundreds of books. Samyaza's high-back green chair was nearest to that wall, and the pillar sticking out a little into his space by the glass looked like it had a TV stand next to it, but it was hard to see next to all the books and the two-way drawer. The opposite far end of the holding cell had a walled-up entrance that looked to be reinforced with concrete and steel bars. In front of the wall were boxes filled with supplies and loose clothes.

Shepherd wasn't about to turn around and walk away to ride back up the elevator without making a few more attempts at communicating. "I'm sorry to seem so ignorant, but why are you down here, Samyaza?" Shepherd asked, breaking the silence.

"I know you have many questions, but this is not the first encounter for me, Priest. Having been acquainted with new pope after new pope, you must understand, I grow tired of

69

answering the same trivial questions and telling all the same stories. I think you need to spend more time with those journals for which Monsieur Da Vinci made a chest." Samyaza roughed his hair with his hands in frustration as he walked over to a smaller stack of books to the side of his desk. He grabbed one of the books from the stack, placed it into the glass drawer, and slid it to Shepherd's side. "Here, Priest, take this and read it."

Shepherd walked over to the drawer and lifted the lid on his side to access the contents. The book was more of a journal, Shepherd could tell as he picked it up. Written on the cover, he could make out in English cursive, *Account of Samyaza, the Watcher, Chronicling 2350 B.C. – 1500 A.D.* in black ink. "Is this one of your journals?" Shepherd asked, holding the booklet.

"Think of it as my resolution for frequently asked questions, Priest. I do not mean to be impersonal on our first meeting, but I have grown tired of explaining certain stories and details over and over, and this is my system, so please respect it. If you read that cover-to-cover and return, I will attempt to answer what questions you have, but not before. I have no interest in storytelling for church boys." With that burn, Samyaza turned and plopped back down in his chair, crossed his legs onto the ottoman, reopened the book to his place, and set the bookmark aside as he continued reading.

Shepherd was somewhat speechless as he stood there holding the prisoner's journal. The vibe Shepherd was getting was similar to that of a mic drop. Finally, he spoke again, "Glad I at least got to introduce myself, and thank you for the journal." He did a half-hearted side wave goodbye, even though Samyaza wasn't looking, and headed toward the elevator. He was about to go out of sight of Samyaza when he heard him call out.

"Priest," Samyaza said without turning from his book.

"Yeah?"

"Please, do bring that back when you are finished. That one is my only copy, and I will not rewrite it again for the next pope."

"Of course. I'll return it to you as soon as I've finished. Thank you," Shepherd replied. He nodded and continued to walk back toward the exit.

"One last thing if you could, Priest?" Samyaza called louder one last time. "Ask the guard to bring down a wash basin and razor."

Shepherd grabbed at his protocols booklet copy in his sweatshirt front pocket. "Is that allow—"

"If the guard gives you grief about the protocols, just tell him to check page four, item one, amendment three. If I am to have new visitors, I will not be looking like a troll. Goodnight!" Samyaza belted.

Shepherd saw no need to confirm the last request and kept moving. The elevator doors immediately separated as he pressed the single up-arrow button. When Shepherd stepped inside, he looked over the journal that the prisoner Samyaza had passed to him. It was tattered and dingy, and the pages were soft on the edges as if it had been thumbed over and handled many times. Shepherd pressed the up arrow inside the elevator, and the doors proceeded to close.

On Shepherd's even longer journey back up the elevator shaft to where Rossi waited in the security room, he let the experience of meeting Samyaza sink in. Samyaza gave him almost nothing but his name, and barely that, but immediately handed over his journal that shared personal information of some kind? It seemed odd to Shepherd for any person to do such a thing so quickly without being requested or demanded, especially with the attitude Samyaza portrayed.

Shepherd initially started to see the journal as a sign of a trusting character but then reminded himself that the journal may be doctored with an agenda of sorts. Certainly, anyone who was kept a prisoner would have a singular end game, escape, but Shepherd still didn't even know the reason for Samyaza's imprisonment in the first place. With no answers from Samyaza yet, Rossi, Marco, or even the pope files, Shepherd had to look to the details in the pages he carried to get what he wanted, or at that point, he felt he needed.

7

The Watcher's Journal

Excerpts taken from the Journals of the Watcher, Samyaza, chronicling 2350 B.C. to 1500 A.D.

These entries are to chronicle the events experienced by myself, Samyaza, Head Chief of the Watchers, General of the Tribe of the First Father Adam, ender of the Bekori Wars, father of giants, and once wielder of the Cherubim Sword.

I have existed on one plane or another since before the dawn of what humans perceive as time. My fellow Watchers and I descended to Earth in the time that you now call Antediluvian, before the time of Noah's Ark and the Great Deluge that covered this entire world. These chronicles begin with my time immediately following the flood. Great upheaval and loss have fallen on me over the millennia, and I have traveled vast distances; hence, these writings are from many years after the actual events described. My kind, Watchers, have a near photographic memory, and the account should be more accurate than that of any mortal man's immediate memory.

I shall begin by chronicling the origins of my first imprisonment by the Creator. The Creator had finally sent his deluge to wipe out all on the Earth except for Noah and his family within the

Ark that the Creator tasked him with building. I and my other Watchers were being punished by the Creator for the mark we left on this world without his approval. We were swept up by the flood and cast out of this world. The Creator took up my Watchers, and their physical bodies were destroyed, leaving only their spirits and consciousness scattered to roam in the phantom realm. The Creator had other designs for my punishment. I was swept deep under the waters covering the Earth as the entire surface of the planet was engulfed in the Great Deluge. Without air for my lungs, my physical body went limp and unconscious while my spirit drifted into the phantom realm and followed as my body was swept further and further north. Eventually, my body stopped drifting and settled to the bottom. I watched as the Creator's prison formed all around my physical form. I lay deep in the water for many days until the water level began to get lower and lower. As the sea became shallow, the temperature began to drop, and ice crystals started growing exponentially. Soon, my body was frozen solid under nearly twenty meters of ice. This was the punishment the Creator had designed for me—to be locked in ice, unable to be revived, my spirit trapped in the phantom realm with no way to move further than 100 meters from that frozen spot. There were no humans within what must have been thousands of kilometers. Also, by then, I was sure Noah and his family were the only humans currently left on the planet. They could have been on the complete opposite side of the world at that point, starting a new civilization on whatever rock their Ark wrecked onto as the waters eventually settled.

I was trapped in that state for thousands of years. From what on most recent calendars was roughly 2350 B.C., as best I can see has been figured. I was never conscious in my physical body during the entirety of my frozen imprisonment. From what I have best been able to deduce with more recent scientific information and

74

what is known about polar ice cap migrations, I was caught in a glacier moving south from what is now called Newfoundland in Upper Canada. The glacier carried my body little by little further south into what I have now learned is the continent called the "New World."

While my body stayed trapped and lifeless, my spirit drifted in that space between physical and spirit, the phantom realm. That is the name we angelics gave upon its first existence. It is the space where we Watchers go when outside our bodies. Death is not something that has a simple answer to beings like Watchers. Unable to travel far from my body, I watched as the ice and snow moved and shifted in minute increments over centuries. I floated around my body, stuck in a realm outside human contact, watching the physical world age around me. The climate shifted slowly, and the glacier became shallower. Close to the end of my imprisonment, I could tell that I had slowly shifted and drifted under the ice to be near the eastern coast of the continent. My phantom form could sit atop the snow, look over a hillside, and see the ocean stretching into the distance. No sign of humans existed for many years, but the coast drew closer. Life began to show up more and more around my icy prison. Birds flew overhead, small creatures began to cross the frozen tundra occasionally, and I could see trees growing along the coastal areas where a stream exited the mainland and spilled into a bay. Trapped in what felt like a never-ending time capsule, there was nothing to do except sit in one's thoughts and observe the slowly changing landscape.

Then, one day, there were humans again. I saw a wooden ship; the front had the head of a dragon, and round shields lined the rails along the sides. It had two large square sails, and oars were coming out the sides as I watched it enter the little bay down the hill from my prison. I have since learned these people were called Danes and later Vikings and were some of the very first settlers from Europe that came to this continent. I was lucky to have been so close to an early settlement. I learned later that most indigenous people of the continent were south and west of where my body had migrated to over all that time and that most other colonies started much further south, down the coast of the continent. I may have spent hundreds more years trapped if I had not been in such a spot.

I have calculated that time to be around 1030 A.D. when the settlement first reached the shores of Newfoundland from Greenland. I sat on that hill and watched the small settlement slowly grow into a little village. The Viking people landed and established their homes and boundaries. The first thing they did was build housing structures near the base of the hill from my prison. No person came remotely close to my spot for the first several months. The settlement was roughly three kilometers away; the closest anyone ever ventured was still hundreds and hundreds of meters too far. Based on the shelters they built and the tools I could make out they were using, there had been few mechanical advances since my previous time free on Earth before the Great Deluge. If anything, it seemed that mankind's technology had taken many steps backward. The Vikings appeared to be primarily simple carpenters, hunters, gatherers, and ironsmiths of a sort. The fact that they had made such large ships indicated they had traveled across a large body of water, but I had no idea the scope of how much the Earth's surface had changed to know where they had traveled from with any certainty yet.

The colonists cut down many trees and constructed a small fort of spiked walls, creating a decent defensive perimeter. There were about twenty-four people in total. I had counted over the first few days after their arrival. They made the journey with the intention of staying. One of their first projects after the ship had been unloaded was dismantling the mast and flipping the ship upside down to turn it into a large wooden lodge. The idea was ingenious, and it made me hopeful for how intelligent mankind may have become in the time I was confined to the ice alone. The colony consisted of some small family groups with children. I made up names for all of them over the many months, observing out of sheer boredom and curiosity. With nothing else to entertain me, I gave them all nicknames and tried to construct narratives for all of them. I could observe the children playing games together in groups and chasing each other sometimes during the day. At night, the fires below were a new regular comfort, warming the loneliness of my darkest years away for the first time in thousands.

The colony seemed to be faring well over the first year, and then, finally, one evening, I saw a man walking in my direction. It was one of the Vikings from the colony I called Ben. Ben was carrying a weapon, a bow and arrow. The bow was an interesting sign. I had been in the ice for so long that I was sure that mankind would have advanced further in weapon technology over thousands of years. Yet, here was a man with a simple wood bow, a primitive weapon technology during my own time long before the flood. It made me wonder if this man was from a more primitive tribe than what others might exist on the planet or if perhaps mankind had not recovered well. I also considered that other cataclysmic events hindered societal growth and advances, possibly even wars.

Ben was moving along slowly, scanning the trees ahead. He was hunting. He looked strange, different to me up close; at first, it was hard to place what it was. Then it occurred to me that I had never seen a man aged past normal full adulthood; this man had wrinkled skin and grayed hair. Signs of aging past prime adulthood did not exist before the Great Deluge. No man or woman, even hundreds of years old, looked much older past thirty years. He was also much shorter than I expected up close. I thought perhaps his growth was stunted, but I later learned the average height of humans had gone down by three to four feet.

As I observed Ben walking in my direction, I moved to the closest point in the phantom realm that the position of my body would let me reach. He was crouching and moving along some trees, growing closer and closer, swiveling his head slowly as he watched for prey. I was trapped in an invisible space, looking right at Ben as he crept through the woods. I began focusing and remembering what it was like before I was trapped when I had moved back into my physical body from my phantom form. I had done it many times before, but always back to my own body. I focused hard on this feeling and decided to try something since this may be my only chance to get free.

The hunter was oblivious to my presence, and as he moved into the same space as me in the physical world, I was able to take possession of him. Possession is how Watchers move in and out of control of physical beings from the phantom realm. It was a new experience, something I was not sure I could do. I only knew of one Watcher before who was without physicality and had achieved this. It was strange. I could see some of the hunter's memories, see the faces and names of his family and friends. He had been hiking, looking for game on a trail, and going further than expected in my direction. I could tell that his consciousness was moving aside while I took over. I was able to take in and absorb the hunter's language and common knowledge. The journey he and his people had taken across a vast cold sea was an incredible experience from which to take on memories. I learned later that this was the experience all my Watchers were doomed to live out for the rest of their existence, but that is another story.

I took a moment to acclimate to being in a physical form for the *first time in over 3000 years. I took deep breaths and tasted the cold, ice-crystal-laced arctic air. I gazed up into the evening sky, bursting with stars in the northern twilight. I could feel the cold wind bite my cheeks and smell the pine on the air from nearby trees. The bitter wind of that place was icy and whistling as it whipped around the hunter's thick hair. I peered down to the village and then to the place where I knew my body was buried in the snow. The hunter had a bow and an axe on his back, which was enough to do some digging. I went to work on excavating my own remains from the ice. Luckily, enough time had gone by that my body was only three feet from the surface at that point, and after one evening of hacking and chiseling, part of my body was exposed to the air. I used what I found in a pack the hunter carried to strike flint and start a fire. My Watcher body would not burn in flames, so I piled logs and brush to burn all around and even over the top of my body to melt the ice and snow to thaw myself out. A few hours after sunset, the fire had done its work, and my body was free enough to drag from the ice and set it comfortably near the fire.*

The flames had gotten relatively high, drawing the attention of some of the other Viking settlers down below. I had inadvertently set up a signal fire that made them send out a search party, no doubt looking for the Viking whose body I had possessed. I could see three men coming in my direction from the colony when my body was finally ready. I planned to transfer back into my body, let the poor hunter I had taken over go free, and then I would work out the rest from there. I needed to get back into my body before they arrived. As the men approached, I released the possession I had taken over the hunter, but as I left him for the phantom realm, his body started to convulse. There was nothing I could do. He fell over, lifeless and dead. I did not know that leaving his body would kill the man! I quickly jumped into my body. All my limbs popped back to life with a jolt. Every part of me was stiff but movable. What would have been impossible in a human body took only a few seconds to regain strength for in my Watcher body. My form immediately began to shrink. I was ten feet tall as a Watcher before, and the adaptations of my body to look similar to humans nearby took over autonomously and brought me down closer to six feet.

The three men came into the warm light of the fire just as I was able to stand up. My clothes had been burned off while the fire was thawing me, so I stood there naked and dripping wet in the cold snow near the flames, standing over the lifeless body of their companion. The scene had to have been terrifying because the men wasted no time in shouting threats in my direction and waving their swords and axes. I was still taking in everything that had just happened and the knowledge I had learned from possessing the Viking and did not have much time to think. One of the men began to draw a bow, so I turned and used my only just loosened-up legs to run in the other direction. I had nothing to fear from their weapons, but I did not want there to be stories of a naked killer in the woods that arrows bounced off of, so I ran. It felt good to run again for the first time and be back in my body. I kept going for a while, enjoying the feeling of—feeling anything again for the first time in forever. While running, I determined there was no other option but to escape from the other men. Their dead companion would have been enough for them to accuse me of killing the hunter, rightfully so, and then I would have to fight my way out of the colony, possibly harming others. I ran all through the rest of that first night south along the coast, away from the Viking colony. I never saw it or its people again. I am sure the Vikings hunted me for a while, but it is not hard to stay ahead of humans when you need nothing to survive and only minimal rest.

Back in my Watcher body, I could brave the elements with little discomfort. I felt the cold and harshness of being back in the physical world but welcomed even the discomfort as a change from the nothingness of the phantom realm. It was thrilling just to feel alive again. I continued traveling south along the coastline into what later became the original American colonies. At the time, they were only populated by indigenous. Over time, I had fashioned clothes, weapons, knives, tools, and other essentials to make life easier as I traveled. Food and water were unnecessary luxuries, but luxuries were welcome. I decided that even if I encountered other humans, I would conceal my identity as a Watcher and keep my distance as much as I could manage. I wanted my return to the human world to pass unnoticed.

I did not yet have any idea of the Creator's presence or influence with mankind anymore on Earth. I was not sure if any human or angelic beings in the world would notice my existence. I was an escaped prisoner, and I was on the lamb. It made sense that I might keep my identity hidden until there was any necessary or relevant reason for it to be known. I wished to draw no attention to myself that could hasten my return to the ice prison or the Creator. I traveled and stayed hidden. The first few human tribes I encountered were possibly Cheyenne or Chippewa. I did not make any contact whatsoever, so I do not know for sure. Also, I had been so devastated by causing the Viking's death with my possession. I had taken a life by accident to escape. Yes, it was a means to an end, but it was an act I swore as I ran through the woods that first night I would never commit again. I wanted to ensure I avoided getting into a situation where I may be tempted to harness such a power. Similar to that, I have always had the ability to feel someone's emotions when I touch their skin. It is my gift as a Watcher. Initially, I was much more powerful before I descended to Earth, but I developed the skill well again over time. I always used *that ability to help others; this power of possession seemed much more dangerous. It was a muscle I planned never to flex again and let atrophy if possible.*

I traveled alone this way for around 100 years in the New World. I made my way as a nomad slowly down the eastern coast of what is now called the Americas. Eventually, I made my way closer to the equator of the planet. I enjoyed that the planet's climate grew warmer as I traveled further south. Before the flood, the Earth's axis had no tilt. It became tilted when the continents shifted with the events of the Great Deluge and the turmoil of the tectonic plates. Seasons did not exist before the flood. The closer I got to the equator, the closer I felt back to home in the time before there was any winter. The climate drew me further and further south.

I eventually came across the Mexica people. After all my travels, I found what I thought to be the most prominent, most sophisticated culture on the planet, or at least on that continent at the time, from what I had seen traveling. I decided that if I were going to reconnect with humankind, this would be the place I would make an attempt. I had wandered long enough, and purpose is part of what drives a Watcher; we need to be doing something that matters to help mankind; it is all we are created to be.

My hope was to slowly and secretly fit into Mexica society. I failed. I had observed them in secret for a while, working on learning their language and culture, but I was easily discovered by a group of farmers one day. The men threw spears at me, and when they saw them bounce off my skin, they approached me as if I were a god. When I offered to share knowledge with them, they claimed I was Quetzalcoatl returned and took me to one of their leaders, who took me to another leader, who eventually escorted me to the city of Tollan. I quickly informed the king, Ehecatl was his name, that I was not this Quetzalcoatl, and that I was an ancient immortal traveling the world, wanting to aid his people.

The king made me one of his advisors. I was given the name Huitzilopochtli and lived out my earliest time in Tollan at the palace, advising the king and helping the Mexica people advance as best they could. I helped them make small steps at a time. The city of Tollan became a marvel to the rest of the Mexica civilization. As they progressed, the rest of the civilization caught up around it. There were new mathematics, aqueducts, agriculture, games, and written language. I gave them the bow and arrow but stopped there. I explained mining to them once, but they had no interest in precious metals or iron. I saw no need to give an entire civilization the desire to make more powerful weapons from tzohar, orichalcum, or steel when they were more content without these advances. It had never occurred to me that some of the advances we Watchers gave to mankind before would not only be lost but possibly were not even necessary.

Upon the king's death, I decided not to advise his successor but to live amongst the people and have a regular life. I took the time to build a modest home outside the city with my own hands, and no one disturbed the immortal living outside the walls. I had nothing to fear. I opened a shop and collected my own herbs and remedies to help those I saw in need. The people would get confused, bring me offerings from time to time, and treat me as a god.

Eventually, after a few centuries, I concluded that my cultural involvement would be minimal going forward. Understanding more of the universe and the stars was one area where I continued to provide people with a wealth of knowledge to help broaden their perspective of life and understanding without giving them massive religious, philosophical, or technological advances or ideas. Astronomy was something I had wanted to spend time on with a more advanced culture. I still had no real idea exactly how many years had passed, but with my knowledge of the stars, I began to make specific calculations of how much time had elapsed and my approximate location on the Earth.

During this time, I discovered the changes in the Earth's axis, rotation, the cause of the seasons, and the calendar of the Mexica people was fine-tuned and made to be highly accurate thanks to the work I had done with their educators and leaders. I quickly learned that my choice to avoid spiritual involvement with these people was a wise path. Omens were of great importance to their culture, and finding that eclipses and star patterns were predictable brought them new perspectives and understandings that enriched their minds and beliefs on their own.

By this point, I had established myself within the cultures as a sort of shaman. I was not a god to them anymore, thank goodness, I did not want that, but I was more of a guide of sorts. They looked to me for guidance when they had questions about the stars and weather patterns. If a crop was not doing well, they came to consult with me. I occasionally also assisted with advising on medicinal herbs and healing procedures. I helped them stave off plague and infection here and there. I was able to maintain this life for hundreds of years. I was content and felt I could stay this way indefinitely, but the world was forcing a change again. Near the end of the 15th century, a child who had come down with a strange illness was brought to my home.

The child had been brought to Tollan from a tiny coastal tribe. These tribes fished in the ocean, while the more inland cities relied on agriculture and the domestication of animals. The child was the daughter of a fisherman. I had been with the people long enough to learn all their dialects and spoke with the girl's father. He explained that a new people had come on massive wood ships from the sea, that they wore great shining garments like gods, and that these gods had weapons that shot fire from the ends of sticks. The man was describing a culture that was clearly more advanced. I was intrigued by the story and needed to investigate further for my curiosity, but there was still the matter of the sick girl. The child was deathly ill, clearly with some type of plague. From my understanding of disease, it seemed that these new travelers had brought a foreign sickness to the Mexica people, probably new to their entire continent. What I later learned was the bubonic plague from Europe, measles, and smallpox would decimate the Mexica people I had lived with for so long. I watched the beginning of the end of an entire culture in those final few years in the New World. The girl died quickly, and almost the entire city around me soon after.

The earliest visitors from Europe that contacted the Mexica people almost completely wiped them out with disease. Their culture was in shambles within one generation. The city of Tollan slowly became a ruin, and the rainforest overgrowth devoured everything. I felt tied to a dying horse and decided there was no longer any purpose for me in that place. The stories continued about travelers from across the sea coming and going every few years from different villages on the coast. I deduced that if I wanted to see these foreign disease-bringing gods for myself, I would have to find the villages that had the most contact and wait for their arrival.

It was not hard to pick a tribe. I selected the one that had the most warnings of disease being spread. The village with the highest death toll had over three visits already in the last eight years from two different expedition groups. I was well known amongst the people still as Huitzilopochtli of Tollan, easily recognizable, looking very different from the tribesmen of the New World in skin color, size, and hair. It was odd when I first learned that these physical attributes mattered to humans. Not only among these Mexica tribes, how they looked at each other, and myself, but in Europe especially. Very quickly, I learned that the concept of different races among humans was what held them back for the entire last 3,500 years. The plague of segregation and slavery rampant in Europe was one of the first visible signs I came across that my Watchers were out there somewhere influencing the world. Such a manipulated perception of nature could only come from the darkest minds of Watchers. Humans twist many ideas, but this one came from an otherworldly evil place.

While I waited at the village, I stayed in the empty hut of a deceased family of the tribe. Since that tribe had been impacted the most, an atmosphere of grief, death, and sickness lingered over them. The people would watch for the ships to return over the water in fear. At first, the travelers seemed friendly, but they brought only death. The diseases that the tribespeople could not fight off killed millions across the continent, and when the villagers resisted the shiny gods in any way, they "blew their fire sticks and swung their spears of shiny stone" at the villagers, killing them with ease till any resistance was thwarted. Many of the people were taken by the shiny gods against their will back onto the ships and were never seen again.

I waited for close to a year with the people of that village until one day, some fishermen spotted the ships returning into the bay. Most of the villagers ran when they saw the ships coming. Some of the stronger men in the village banded together to try and form a defense they had been preparing, but when the men from the boats landed on shore and shot three villagers within seconds, the rest quickly ran for the trees and gave up.

I spotted the men as they were reloading their fire sticks, guns, and their longboat was being pulled onto the beach by ship hands. I wanted to have an audience with these travelers, so I was not being *inconspicuous, and I sat out on the beach watching all this when they arrived. I wanted my presence not to seem threatening. With a complexion that is dissimilar to that of the natives, along with my taller stature, I would stick out regardless in that part of the world. I knew nothing of the language the visitors spoke, but a few of the local leaders had learned multiple words during the travelers' previous visits.*

One man attending the longboat saw me on the shore and could not take his eyes off me. He looked at me as if I was a long-lost ghost or relative. He was in a stupor and toppled to the side into the surf as the boat was being pulled out of the last few feet of water. He did not wait to pull the boat; he ran up to me and stared me right in the face. The man was speechless for a while and stepped back once the leader of the expedition got out of the boat and came forward.

That day was when I found a way to Europe with Christopher Columbus.

8

Getting to Know the Monster Under the Bed

Shepherd spent most of that first night after visiting the prisoner reading through the journal that Samyaza asked him to finish. The journal shed a lot of light on where the Watcher came from, but it also led to many new questions Shepherd was dying to get the answers to. The read took him three nights, but the entire journal was reviewed as promised. Shepherd made sure to read it cover to cover just in case Samyaza was the type to leave something specific to quiz Shepherd and check if he skipped anything.

The journals told of a being, Samyaza, imprisoned by the Creator during the great flood, or Great Deluge as he called it. The story of Noah's Ark and the flood was known to Shepherd since childhood. It was one of the first stories from the Bible most kids learned in many Sunday school children's bible classes. Shepherd assumed that Samyaza was imprisoned in the Vatican because that was where the Creator led him somehow to be captured again. It made sense; the Creator wanted him captive, and he escaped. Undoubtedly, the church rounded him up, put him down there, and threw away the key. It was a logical enough theory so far, but how did he get to the Vatican in the first place?

Was Samyaza also some type of angelic but demonic-possessing physical being? Not an angel, but not a human, really, either? Shepherd wasn't sure yet what to make of it all.

He went down several online archive rabbit holes and did a little searching as he read through Samyaza's accounts of his time imprisoned and right after his escape. Shepherd found a few historical and religious works about Watchers and even on Samyaza. Many myths and legends were tied to the Watchers with similar origin stories throughout history. As Shepherd researched and read late into the nights, he began writing questions he wanted to ask Samyaza. Some had already been answered in the journal, and he could see why this was Samyaza's way of first sharing parts of the story. All of it was completely unbelievable, though. The idea that there was a being living below the Vatican, an immortal from the dawn of humanity, all the way back at the beginning, was the type of mystery Shepherd dreamt of.

Shepherd had to know more. He had a drive growing in him to understand better who Samyaza was, why he was there, and maybe even what Samyaza might want. Shepherd had been keeping everything to himself. Not being able to share his discovery with anyone, even Johns or Marco, was very frustrating to someone of his character. The protocols demanded his silence, which was one part Rossi forgot to read, but it was right at the beginning of the booklet. One evening, Shepherd went to the guard post and questioned Rossi a bit harder as he ran his shift at the security post. He did not mind Shepherd or his questions so long as they didn't pertain to the prisoner. He seemed glad to have someone to help him pass the time at his post in that quiet room. All Shepherd had been able to get out of him that wasn't in the journals was that the prisoner's story was kept secret from all Entity members. The protocols had been the standing order of the Holy Father and King of the Vatican for over five centuries; only the pope could visit the prisoner, and Samyaza was never to leave his cell.

It was finally the first night after Shepherd finished Samyaza's journal. It was a Tuesday, and Shepherd changed his schedule during his morning breakfast with Marco to ensure nothing was planned after dinner to interfere with his evening agenda. The weekend and last few days had flown by in the wake of Shepherd's new secret adventure. He already felt it distracting from his priorities, but the mystery was something no man of any curious nature could help but be drawn towards. After speeding through dinner, a little more hastily than usual, Shepherd retreated to his fortress of solitude. He completed his usual evening routine, including pajama pants, he also wore a sweatshirt, and this time left his regular shoes on. Shepherd felt quite unprepared during his first encounter with Samyaza. He didn't want to ruin his second opportunity to make an impression. He grabbed his notes and pen, tucked Samyaza's journal under his arm, and popped the headboard entrance key from the pope chest.

Shepherd stepped onto his bed and slid the key into the round hole on his headboard, activating the lift to reveal the door in the backing behind his bed. He proceeded down the hallway and through the final door. Rossi was on duty again that evening at the security desk.

"Evening Shepherd. Going down to the prisoner this time?"

Rossi called out when he saw Shepherd coming through.

Shepherd strolled over to the elevator as Rossi came around the desk with his keycard. "Yes, I have a few questions for him this evening. I think he—"

"Oh, please, father, we have to take a lie detector test going over every part of any details we hear or learn while on duty for complete security. The less you tell me about the prisoner or your time with him, the less I must remember to disclose or worry about. I hope you understand. It will be a lot easier for us Entity security personnel if you don't share anything about the prisoner," Rossi pleaded.

Shepherd handed his journal to Rossi to inspect as they talked. "Well, I wouldn't want to get you guys into any deep water or cause extra paperwork. Fair enough, send me down then, I guess." Shepherd agreed, keeping the small talk to a minimum.

Rossi handed the journal back to Shepherd, passed his badge over the sensor, and opened the elevator doors. Shepherd completed the long elevator ride down for the second time. It felt like a quicker ride this go-round with less adrenaline. He arrived at the bottom, and the doors slid open, revealing the stone wall and yellow retro curly-cord phone. He rounded the corner to peer into Samyaza's living space. The furniture inside Samyaza's cell was slightly re-arranged, and it appeared at first glance that Samyaza had even tidied up some of his papers and books since Shepherd's last visit. Samyaza was sitting in his high-back green armchair again, just like when Shepherd last arrived. However, the chair was turned facing more towards the elevator this time rather than towards the opposite end of the cell where the desk and boxes were.

After taking note of the tidied-up cell, Shepherd next

noticed Samyaza had also cleaned himself up. His beard was trimmed short and neat, his lower neck was razor-shaved, and his hair was cut from shoulder length to a more modern man's short trim.

"Hello again, Samyaza. I see you shaved?" Shepherd tried to start the conversation lightly.

"Yes, it has been some time since I have had a new visitor. It seemed proper for me to shave. Amendments were added to the protocol to give me certain toiletries for such—occasions. I see you have brought my journal back. Have you read the entire account, Priest?" Samyaza inquired with his hands folded, still seated.

"Yes! Yes, I read it as requested, and you can call me Shepherd or Liam if you want, like everyone else does." Shepherd walked to the left side of the glass and placed the journal back in the two-way slide tray. He closed the lid and pressed the drawer back inside for Samyaza.

"What do you want now, Priest?" said Samyaza, ignoring Shepherd's request.

"I first wanted to thank you, Samyaza. Your journal was fascinating. I've never read anything like it before. Tell me, I must ask, is it all true? Your account of what took place all those years ago?" Shepherd replied, trying to mix pleasantries and interview questions.

"We Watchers have excellent memories. Similar to what you would call a photographic memory. This journal was written in the late 1800s—much later than the events. Still, it is as accurate as can be portrayed in words."

Shepherd went on, "The journal gave me a lot of information, but I was wondering if I could ask you more questions?"

Samyaza gave a long sigh. "There are always many questions,

even with the ones my journals answer. I suppose I can stomach a few. Let us get this over with." He moved over to his book pile and began to scan them as if looking for a new read.

Shepherd figured he'd fire away. "So Samyaza, you're a Watcher, and you're immortal, but why are you here? And why did the Creator imprison you before?"

Samyaza continued scanning his pile up and down before abruptly responding. "The Creator imprisoned me because we—disagreed on what was best for mankind. The reason I am here now, in this place, is because a man who once held your position decided imprisoning me was the Creator's 'next divine purpose.' At least, that is how Julius II justified his decision to trap me down here."

"I don't understand. What did you disagree with the Creator on? That humans should be saved in the Ark?"

"The Creator wanted the flood, and my Watchers and I, along with many humans, did not. We tried to stop the Great Deluge, and the account you read is the start of my punishment and the beginning of my journey that brought me to the Vatican."

"What exactly is a Watcher? There are only a few stories in history and literature, and it's hard to know what's true. I'm hoping you can set that straight."

"Watchers have been called by many names throughout human history and in different cultures. Demons would be the closest comparison or descriptor in this time with any accuracy. Yes, my Watchers are out there in the world, but only in the physical world through possession. And unlike my experience with the Viking, their hosts can survive after they leave their bodies."

"And the Creator destroyed their bodies, the other Watchers, but not yours, and put you in a physical prison?"

"Yes."

Shepherd tried to keep a casual composure, but his heart rate had spiked at hearing Samyaza refer to himself and his Watchers as demons so nonchalantly. "Why is that different for you? The possession? I remember in your journal, the Viking hunter, he died when you released him."

"You see, Priest, the experience disturbed me greatly. When I possessed the Viking, I had taken his memories, and when he died, it was like watching a part of myself die as well. I shall never use that power again. I do not understand why he died the moment I left his form, but the same is not the case for my Watchers. It may be because I still have my original physical body, and they do not, but from what I have learned, they do not kill the host if removed back to the phantom, or spiritual, realm."

"How did the Creator destroy their bodies? The other Watchers?"

"He cast them into the depths of the center of the Earth. One of the few in the solar system with enough heat and pressure to destroy a Watcher's body, other than the sun or the Cherubim Sword."

"The Cherubim Sword?" Shepherd interrupted.

"Please, do not create new questions with my answers, Priest. I am losing my patience for this line of questioning as it is." Samyaza expressed his discomfort and moved to another section of his book pile.

Shepherd looked to his notebook and continued, "This cell was designed just for you then?"

"Is that not obvious?" Samyaza pointed out. "No toiletry

facilities, why bother for a being that needs no food or water, has no reason to perspire, and without food intake has no— other bodily functions. There is no way in or out; the doorway was cemented up years ago. The cell is 120 meters down directly below the surface. Perfect depth to ensure that I may never possess any passerby in all directions in case I decide to go back on my oath."

"The design did seem like overkill for a normal human prisoner-type cell," Shepherd said embarrassingly. "And the possessions, I read a segment where you mentioned it only works on 'nonbelievers,' but I was curious what someone like you means by that?"

"Yes, essentially anyone in the Vatican is already safe, to begin with, especially my guards above, so I am told. I have not left this place in over 500 years; I expect I never will. Anyway, something about the humans that believe in and honor your Christ keeps Watchers from taking over. Salvation is like a protective shield."

"Or force field!" Shepherd said, slightly geeking out. He then retracted his excitement, seeing Samyaza was not amused. Shepherd decided to switch directions. "Are you— comfortable here, Samyaza?"

"Comfortable? The Priest asks me if I am comfortable on his second visit while going through his first questions?" Samyaza exclaimed, gazing up at the ceiling. He finally looked directly at Shepherd. "You are different from the rest, Priest. I am comfortable enough these days, I suppose. I do not exert enough energy to require much in the way of sleep. I enjoy my chair, though I have heard new designs called recliners are quite comfortable. I have plenty to read. I can even stay somewhat abreast of current culture and events for entertainment, and whatever I can get brought down helps me understand the outside world. I write and journal. After spending thousands of years outside my body, trapped in isolation, having a chair and these books to read was a luxurious change. I was fortunate to have time between my two imprisonments to at least see some of the New World before being locked up again," he said, lowering his gaze to the floor.

"You said you stay up with current events? Do you have the internet or something down here?" Shepherd asked.

"Ha! You really should read all the protocols in that booklet the guard gave you, Priest. No, but I convinced the last pope that made it down here to set me up with the TV." Samyaza motioned to the TV set in the far-left corner, right behind a concrete pillar on his side of the glass. It was mainly obscured from the outer viewing area, keeping Shepherd from seeing it before. The screen was paused on a show that he was streaming.

Samyaza continued, "I prefer reading, but this new venue of television and cinema has allowed me to view moving images of what is happening outside my prison. Some real, some fiction, but better than concrete walls and just—ink." He looked down at the floor again. "I do miss food. I know I shall never get any. The Entity would prefer not to have to set up a toilet down here for me, but since you're asking, I've wanted to try fast food ever since I learned of its popularity among humans. Their commercials have been teasing me for the last few decades."

Shepherd couldn't help but laugh. His reaction made Samyaza look back at him and give a curious grin.

"I feel as though you have had a sufficient turn. May I ask a few questions of you, Priest?" Samyaza posed.

"Go ahead, how rude of me. Yes. Ask away!" Shepherd heartily replied.

"I do not mean to keep pointing out your age. I know it can be rude, but you must understand my curiosity. It does make you an outlier from the age of popes who find their way down here. What made the cardinals choose you? I would like to know." Samyaza was somehow familiar with the election process.

Shepherd answered, "I ask myself the same question. I believe it was a combination of divine intervention, name association, and dumb luck. The cardinals claim it was providence, but it seemed like I was just the most popular name on social media at the time, for one reason or another."

Samyaza gave a skeptical look but accepted the answer. He continued his turn at questioning, "What do you hope to do with your station? As pope, you have a lot of influence and power." Samyaza crossed his arms and leaned back, resting his weight on his desk.

"Indeed. At first, I wanted to turn it down. But then a voice inside me nudged me on further. I knew I had to press on so I could change the world for the better. That has been my life's calling. I think that is what led me here."

Samyaza turned back to do more book pile scanning. "The way you humans talk. 'Led me here.' Huh!" he muttered, barely loud enough for Shepherd to hear.

Samyaza flipped silently through his books, his subtle queue for Shepherd to take a turn.

Shepherd once more focused back on his list of questions from his notebook. "Samyaza, what would you do if you were released?"

Samyaza stopped shuffling in front of his books. He stood for a minute, unflinching, looking down at the middle of the pile. With a blinding spin, he turned to look directly at Shepherd. He then popped over next to the glass between the two of them, and with such smooth steps, it appeared he was gliding. Shepherd pulled back and looked up to meet Samyaza's eyes as he drew up before the glass.

Samyaza looked stern, wincing at Shepherd with his bottomless black eyes. He raised his arms to rest his hands high, leaning on the glass. "If I were allowed to leave, I would finish the task I started when I came to Europe all those years ago. I would find the Sword of the Cherubim."

Shepherd had to shake his awe before asking, "I looked that up after reading about the sword in the beginning of your journal. What I've learned is it was the sword that stood guard with an angel at the entrance to the Garden of Eden. But that doesn't exist on Earth anymore, does it?"

"It does, and the writings and records that could lead me to the sword's location are in the Vatican Archives above us. I was close to discovering where it had moved to when I was locked away down here," Samyaza said, lowering his hands and giving a shrug.

"If the answer is in the archive library, could anyone else have found it by now?" Shepherd said.

"Not unless they let another Watcher into the Vatican. Three texts came off the Ark with Noah and his family—the earliest transcription of what you call Genesis, some other works of his grandfather, my friend Methuselah and his father Enoch, and Noah's own journals. The writings of Genesis were translated and carried on through history in different forms and interpretations, but the other two writings were never translated or copied. Written in the language of the Watchers, which it seems has since been forgotten by mankind. The only beings in existence that can now read those ancient scrolls are the Watchers themselves," Samyaza explained.

Shepherd tried to focus and not get hung up on Samyaza's casual mention of Methuselah, the oldest man to ever live, as a "friend," and he continued on topic. "You said moved to? The sword was moved?"

"Not quite. The Earth's surface moved. The Garden of Eden still exists, and the sword remains guarding its entrance but is no longer on the Earth's surface. When the Great Deluge occurred, the waters and tectonic plates were in such upheaval that the entire surface of the Earth collapsed in, sort of like a cracked chocolate shell on a melting ice cream cone, but now it has been re-frozen. The entire Earth's surface was re-arranged. The continents were made new as cards in a deck shuffled into an overlapping order. Noah's journals are star charts and maps referencing the earliest explorations from where Noah's family landed with the Ark. Those journals are the only known details of where the Garden of Eden was relocated."

"How do you know the garden survived the flood?" Shepherd asked.

"The sword. The Sword of the Cherubim at its gates would stave off the flood's destruction and preserve the garden in an encapsulated bubble of energy. I am certain the garden is deep beneath the Earth's surface, slowly eroding back to the top."

"What would you do with this sword if you got it? It's a weapon. Are you intending to fight someone?"

"I plan, as I have always planned, to use the sword on myself.

To destroy my own physical body," Samyaza stated plainly.

Shepherd was taken back a little by how casual that response was from Samyaza. "What will that accomplish? Why is death better than being immortal?"

Samyaza walked to his chair. "My physical life holds all the Watchers in place, like an anchor, to the physical realm. My fellow Watchers are trapped out there, bouncing from physical form back to the phantom realm, possessing one random host after another in glimpses. They create chaos and terror in the physical world. They grow confused and bored. They make people do terrible things just for their own psychotic entertainment. My Watchers have been trapped without their physical form between worlds for too long and have possessed so many people that they have lost touch with their conscience and character. Only their most vile characteristics can now make it to the surface and spread. In such a state, the Watchers have strayed from helping mankind and are now a blight on their spirits." Samyaza turned back to Shepherd and grimaced. "I wish to bring an end to this. My Watchers have left their marks on this world long enough; our time in this realm should be over. To whatever end."

Shepherd could see how it pained Samyaza to speak about his Watchers. "If that's the case, why has no one helped you find the sword? Ending all evil—that sounds like something worth at least looking into!" he stated enthusiastically.

Now, it was Samyaza's turn to laugh. "You may have read all of my first journal, but you clearly have not gotten through all the other pope's journals in that chest." Samyaza walked back to his desk and slipped another leather-bound journal from a large stack. He walked over to the transfer drawer and passed the booklet to Shepherd's side. "Here Priest. Take this and read it next."

Shepherd stepped over and grabbed the new journal from the drawer. *Journals of the Watcher, Samyaza, chronicling 1500-1523 A.D.*, was written on the cover. It was in the same handwriting as the previous one Samyaza gave him.

More homework, Shepherd thought to himself. He asked, "This one explains what happened after you came from the Americas?"

"My journey here across the Atlantic, and then what led me to this prison, Priest, yes. I had already journaled the voyage at the end of one of my medical books I brought from my time with the Mexica people, but it was somehow lost after arriving in Europe with my luggage. I transcribed it from memory into these new copies."

"Interesting. Thank you. I am curious—how do you know about the pope chest and journals?" Samyaza asked as he looked over the booklet.

"That chest is the only way for anyone other than the Entity to find a way down here. There used to be more of a procedure and more people in the know in the first twenty years or so, but that all changed after Clement VII." Samyaza showed agony in his face at the mention of that name. "Anyway, this saves me from having to play storyteller to a priest every night for the next month," he said quite bluntly.

"I see. Well, here, take mine for yourself in the meantime." Shepherd passed his journal, which he brought with his page of questions, into the drawer and slid it back through.

Samyaza walked to the drawer with a curious expression, shock, and a little intrigue. He picked the journal up, looked it over, and then back at Shepherd. "You would share this with me, Priest? Your personal journal?"

"Yes. You've let me get a look into your past, and your thoughts, seems only fair," Shepherd said.

Samyaza didn't know what to say for a moment. "I look forward to reading it. I have not had a new book in many years," he eventually said.

"That's awful! Any requests?" Shepherd asked.

Samyaza's eyes widened. "There are a few I wish to add to my library." He stepped back to his desk and opened a small drawer. He took out a loose piece of paper and passed it to Shepherd through the glass transfer drawer. It was a long list of books Samyaza had been keeping.

"I'll see what I can do." Shepherd felt that he needed to draw the visit to a close soon. He motioned to the chess table sitting to his right. "Would you be interested in a game next time I'm down?"

"You play, Priest? Why do all you popes play chess?"

Shepherd shook his head and scratched his neck as he replied, "I don't much anymore, really. Not since university, but I'm sure I can pick it back up again. My father was the first to teach me."

"As far as opponents go, I believe the expression *beggars cannot be choosers* applies. I will be seeing more of you then? Most others grew bored of these visits quickly. When I was of no use," Samyaza stated.

"What did they want to use you for?"

Samyaza turned his head, almost as if avoiding a blow. "Does not matter now, Priest. I have worn out my usefulness long ago. Nothing I can do for my Watchers or humans now from here."

Shepherd had to ask, "Has no one considered releasing you all this time?"

"Ha! Would not want to hurt their *job security*." Samyaza started chuckling while sitting back down in his chair.

"I'm not sure I understand."

"You read that journal, and you will, I'm sure, Priest."

"I see. I look forward to speaking with you more, Samyaza."

"I have little else to look forward to, but it does get old repeating one's story, and reliving the past is not something I relish," Samyaza stated as he unpaused his program on the TV. "Till next time, Priest."

"Next time," Shepherd confirmed. At that, Shepherd entered the elevator and headed back up to his room for the night with a new adventure to read.

9

Columbus Day

E xcerpts taken from the Journals of the Watcher, Samyaza, chronicling 1500-1523 A.D.

I later learned this year was 1503 AD. I had been staying with one of the coastal tribes in Central America, where there were multiple visits from the strange "shiny gods" and their enormous ships. A ship finally arrived after many months of waiting, and two long boats brought twenty of these visitors to shore. I sat waiting to greet them on the beach with a man from the village who had learned a bit of Portuguese and taught some local dialect to the sailors. The party made it ashore and flopped out of the boat onto the sand. One gentleman, with a grandiose feather in his helmet, came ashore with the assistance of two crew members who had already gotten out ahead of him. He was later introduced as Christopher Columbus.

Columbus had red hair, but silver highlights were beginning to take over and fill the edges of his beard. His mustache was almost entirely gray. He wore a shiny brass breastplate and helmet. His conquistador armor was adorned with red ropes, and the helmet bore a large ornate feather that must have been dyed red. He seemed to be putting on a show for the locals with his stature, but the man looked to be sickly. It was only a few years before his death; what exactly he suffered from was never diagnosed for sure, but he died at the age of fifty-five, three years after our meeting.

One of the crew members who helped Columbus out of the boat had been looking at me strangely ever since they came to shore. He lingered behind awkwardly when I approached. He would not take his eyes off me. His behavior vexed me, and I kept a close watch on the man in return. A meal was prepared for the visitors. I did not understand why the villagers were catering to these men who had brought so much death and suffering to them. Columbus and his men had taken whatever they wanted in the past, even making slaves of the villagers. The translator explained that this was the lesser of two evils for their people. If they fed the visitors more than they could eat and showered them with gifts, they would usually have their fill and leave with what was offered. Other times, when the visitors were met with resistance and turned away, the village was attacked by the "shiny gods," and they would kill many people with their "fire stick" weapons.

Sitting at the meal together, I was a guest of honor. Columbus and his people had caught on to this and noticed how I was getting more attention. He moved closer and tried to speak with me. I had only learned a few words of the Portuguese language. I figured I communicated well enough my interest in traveling with him to—to wherever he came from. Columbus reached out to shake my hand in agreement after we discussed my joining him on his return, and my gift of sensing emotions and thoughts pulled his feelings and twisted mind to me so I could see his intentions. I had honed my skill over many years and knew straight away that Columbus was not someone to be trifled with. The evil, selfish, exploiting nature of that man wreaked in the air of his consciousness as I took a *whiff, so to speak. He was foul, and from that moment on, I saw Columbus only as a means to an end to get to more civilized and populated parts of the world.*

During the evening dinner, among the tribal locals, I noticed the same crew member from before staring often in my direction. His glare became unnerving to me as the night lingered on. Columbus and his crew taught the locals on their previous visits how to brew different meads and ales that were ready for their return on this visit. The entire crew and half the village were wholly passed out, inebriated in the low firelight. The moon had risen full, high overhead. I sat up, sober, of course, unaffected by the alcohol as a Watcher. I stared at the moon for a while, letting my eyes adjust slightly to its crystal brightness against the black, matte, star-studded sky behind. I was excited about my future for the first time in thousands of years. I was going to see more of what the world had become since mankind rebuilt their civilization and looked forward to observing what other new technologies and ideas had come into the world. I had never seen human-made black powder guns before, just as the local Mexica people had not. I did not know that it was a very new weapon at the time on a world scale, but it was a massive step up in sophistication from anything on the New World continent I had observed thus far. I was startled by the sound of sand sliding and looked for what was moving. It was my stalker, the crewman who kept eyeing me, sitting up and moving in my direction. He looked around suspiciously, checking if anyone else was awake. He then tiptoed, hunched over around the fire next to me, and slumped down, leaning on the log holding my back up while I had been stargazing and daydreaming.

"Samyaza?" The crewman whispered my name out of nowhere. I realized quickly that these visitors did not know me by that name. I jumped back.

The crewman leaned closer to me. "Samyaza, it's me, Yekun, one of your Watchers," he said.

It was true. The man was one of my Watchers from the time before the Great Deluge, but he had possessed some sailor's body. Yekun had been one of my closest lieutenants in the earliest times known to man; when we Watchers did our task we were named for, Watch. After we descended to Earth, Yekun stayed with me and my tribe during my years with the First Father, Adam's house, through the Bekori Wars, and was stripped of his physical form along with the other Watchers when the Creator cast them to the depths of the Earth during his flood to wipe out everything on the surface we cared for and loved. I embraced my old friend once I realized it was really him in a stranger's body. Yekun explained how he and the other Watchers were trapped and lost, drifting in the phantom or spiritual realm, as whoever is reading this may call it. They wandered the Earth outside of physical space, formless and unable to even communicate with each other. Having lost their physical bodies, they had no form to be echoed in spirit, so they had no way to speak with or see each other in the phantom realm. Then, one of the Watchers moved to a place where in the physical space overlapping, a human was passing through, and he stepped into his form, possessing that man, just as I had possessed the Viking hunter when I first escaped my prison in the ice. Once this happened to any Watcher, they could shift back and forth from the physical and spiritual realms. More and more Watchers found the ability over time as the Earth's population grew and spread. More Watchers, coincidentally, passed into a person's space and could take over their body. This is how my Watchers still exist today.

Yekun told me stories late that night of the other Watchers, and how they had been fairing in Europe, as they called the new continent he came from. Some of the Watchers found each other after possessing humans in the physical world, and they banded together to survive in solitude, away from the world, which is comparable to how I had first lived after my escape from the ice. Most of the Watchers were scattered and alone as far as Yekun knew up to that point in time. Many of them had essentially snapped, mentally, after the flood, drifting in limbo for what felt like an endless dream. Then, at some point, they began shifting back to consciousness in a physical reality inhabiting a human's body.

Along with those circumstances, the Watchers took on the memories of any human they possessed, which confused them and broke their minds even further. A possessed human does not live forever, and they were forced to change hosts, causing the Watchers to have more and more overlapping memories, lives, and identities. The main difference from when I possessed the Vikings was that they did not kill their hosts upon leaving. They prolonged the host's life expectancy dramatically, but the host did not die when other Watchers exited them, just me, just my Viking many years ago. Eventually, some Watchers broke and forgot who they were. Some even chose to hide and forget, but the majority of those who had lost their way were bringing chaos into the world of man.

After that first night, Yekun and I kept our conversations to a minimum while onshore in the New World. Columbus and his crew were there with an agenda to take on new supplies, treasures, and slaves to bring back to Europe. The village had been so desperate to avoid having their own people taken that they captured twenty other natives from a neighboring tribe months ago and kept them as prisoners while waiting for the ships from Europe to arrive. Another way they bent their morals to appease the dreadful Europeans, a true sign of the desperation and terror Europeans had inflicted wherever they landed, tainting these more primitive people with their ideas of property.

Yekun was able to act as an even better translator for myself, and he solidified my plans to join the crew on their return. At first, Columbus needed help understanding my offering for passage, which was mere trinkets and jewelry. I had no need for possessions before, so I had nothing to offer in the means of currency to barter. Luckily, I also had no need for food and water, and Yekun was clever enough to realize this and offered to split his rations with me for the entire voyage, sweetening the deal. Columbus laughed and agreed, but most likely under the assumption we would both starve before arriving in Europe. With my travel secured and the ship loaded, I left the New World and we set sail out across the Atlantic.

The voyage with Columbus and his crew was one of profound enlightenment for me in more ways than one. My lieutenant, Yekun's possessed host, had already been a member of the crew when Yekun took control of his body. Yekun had last left the possession of a woman of some higher standing in the court of Spain; he explained to me one night as we swayed in our hammocks below deck. Yekun had seen that this ship was traveling to the Americas and wanted an adventure. He heard of the wonders in the New World, as everyone was calling it, and he had already seen enough of the civilized world.

Yekun and I made sure that we bunked next to each other in the crew quarters. He did an excellent job catching me up on languages such as Portuguese, Spanish, and some English, which I learned more of later. As Watchers, we knew a dialect no man could understand. Late at night, we would talk for hours alone in our own Watcher language. We knew that if anyone stirred or asked what we were talking about, we could explain it away, as I was teaching Yekun's host in some Mexica tongue, and no one would be the wiser. His host was a young man named Gabe, who had grown up in southern Spain. Gabe's body had lived a tough life on the streets and knew only a hungry stomach. This voyage, on which Yekun took his body just before setting sail, was to be his first. I was shocked when I felt my Watcher, Yekun's, emotions with my gift in our interactions. He did not feel any remorse or shame for possessing a young soul. It made me start to fear that my Watchers were losing their true selves and had completely lost sight of our original purpose.

Our vessel made its way across the Atlantic. Columbus called my presence a good omen from time to time, as he saw me working on deck whenever the sun came out. It was a coincidence, of course, but I was learning more and more about how superstitious humans had become, and I welcomed favor with Columbus even if it was happenstance. As we sailed on, I learned everything I could from Yekun. Along with getting acquainted with certain languages, Yekun updated me on many cultural and societal changes mankind had experienced since the days of the Great Deluge. There was a lot of time to cover, and information was limited during that age, with the printing press having only recently been invented. Yekun had been able to learn much from the memories of his hosts, along with his own research and experiences. He explained to me the significant changes in Earth and humans, as he could recall. Most of the stories were second or third-hand accounts or readings, and I could see he was unable to remember everything as a Watcher would in his own body. His memory was clouded by all the transitions between hosts over many centuries.

I learned from him on that voyage about how the Earth had shifted so much that there were entirely new continents yet to be explored and mapped. The Mexica, or Aztec people, and many other tribes I had left were lost to death and disease when Europeans came during that time. Little is known in history about the extensive cities and cultures that vastly populated the New World before I

110

left for Europe. Their history would not live on as strong as that of the people of the east Yekun was describing. It was strange to think that a small ship and a tiny germ had greatly devastated an entire culture of millions. Man had learned to build great ships and weapons again. The cannons on board the vessel were a powerful weapon to behold. These accomplishments were nothing when compared to the technology and magic we Watchers had helped man develop before the flood. Columbus let me fire a shot while the crew was going through battery drills one afternoon. It was fun, but I dare say it was almost laughable how this was the peak humanity had progressed back to. Noah had obviously left much of the Watcher's influence behind when he started his new world.

I asked Yekun what he understood about the Creator's involvement in the world since the flood. His answers in this regard were vexing. What was once just known as phantom and physical was now packaged for mankind, by themselves, into this new perspective called religion, reality, and spirituality. Yekun explained that there was a division of mankind many years ago after Noah's family started over new. Their languages were confused, and now there were many of these religions, worshiping different gods, similar gods, some worshiping "the God." As far as I could connect the dots, the Creator had been boxed into something different with over-explanation and misinterpretation over millennia. A nation called Hebrews followed the Creator's way as best they could, and then an event changed everything. I learned about Christ and the development of Christianity. I knew the Creator. I was always aware he planned to send his son one day, but the people had done something unexpected with his wisdom—they sold it to each other for money and power.

The histories of humankind vexed me deeply, as Yekun described all he had learned from his collected memories. Christianity had *blossomed into a massive church with political and social influences. Wars were being fought and carried out, even genocide over beliefs that all came from the same place. The more time passed, the more confused the religious philosophies that Yekun walked me through became. The Roman Empire's shift to a church-state had done a number on the teachings of the past. The Christ was fully a part of the Creator, that much Yekun knew to be true. Yekun did some experimenting years back and determined that anyone who was a true believer in Christ, or any child, could walk right through a Watcher trying to enter them from the phantom realm and not be possessed. Yekun discovered, and I concurred, that only a power from the Creator could explain such a phenomenon. The connection to the Creator kept the followers impervious to possession.*

Yekun told me stories of the splendid architecture and accomplishments of mankind he had witnessed. Humanity had certainly reclaimed the Earth, and they were starting to push back against nature again. Another realization I came to was that spirituality and physicality were drawing so far apart that mankind was truly lost once more in this time. The flood had allowed the world to start over, but it seemed man had squandered it. The religions, greed, Watcher influence, and governments had all gotten in the way, and now mankind seemed to be muddling in the dark once more, much as they were before us Watchers descended. But that old Watcher-guided world was long gone, and this new one was some strange foul beast.

I decided, even as confused as these structures of human society might be, that I needed to understand them if I was going to find purpose. Yekun had lost his purpose as a Watcher and now found fulfillment in adventure. Occasionally, I would see him slip and lose himself in his host's mind. Yekun would be gone, and Gabe would return confused and missing time, then he would be Yekun again. If I had been punished the same way as my Watchers, I could have been just as confounded as Yekun. I learned in our talks about an influential leader of the new church, called the pope. Columbus had even met this religious leader. He spoke of Pope Alexander VI one day on deck after some men had done morning prayers. From what I overheard, this man was in a position with a lot of power and influence. Columbus offered to grant me an audience with him once we arrived. It would be a short trip by land afterward, but he assured me we would make the journey together. Many crew members confirmed that Columbus retained an audience with the pope and other world leaders.

Columbus made the promise to take me to the pope because of what happened on the fifth week of our voyage. The ship found itself caught in an unpassable storm. All the crew was on deck, attempting to keep us perpendicular to the waves to get us clear of the worst of the storm as soon as possible. We were making excellent time but were risking everyone's lives in the process. I was on deck, tied to a lifeline, working on a topsail line when Columbus exited his cabin to get some air and see what all the commotion was about. Even a seasoned sailor such as him was feeling the heavy crash of the waves in his gut. He also had the most food and wine in him, to boot. As he spewed good wine overboard, we hit a breaker and the ship lunged with a thud. Columbus toppled over the railing, and I was the only one even remotely close enough to see him fall.

For a fraction of a second, I recalled reading his emotions and thought good riddance to such a foul creature, but then I remembered he was my connection to the leadership in Europe. I could not let the man disappear and drown. With a flash, I checked my lifeline and dove overboard. Columbus had fallen close enough to the side to catch the ship's rudder on his way past the stern. I grabbed him as I passed, just as he lost his grip on the rudder. The slack on my lifeline ran out with a jerk. I gripped Columbus' overcoat tight and waited. One of the crew saw our line in the water and rallied some others to come and pull us up along the port side. I hated hauling that human filth back on board, but at least my connection to the high seats in Europe was intact. Columbus declared that I would get the finest stores and rations and receive gifts on our arrival to Europe for saving his life.

Upon making landfall in Europe, I was shocked at the congestion of life at the ports in Spain. Piles of muck overran European cities. The Aztecs had better aquifer and sewer systems than the cities and villages of the more "advanced" Europeans. Their modes of travel, weaponry, and academia had progressed. However, they still seemed to expend more energy on luxury than logic when it came to the structure of their society, which they designed to appeal only to the wealthiest. Columbus took me to the Spanish Court, where we learned that the pope we expected to visit was not even the pope anymore! He had been replaced twice over! Once, by a Pius III, who died in less than a month! And then by the current pontiff, Julius II.

I thought my plan was about to hit another setback, but luckily, Columbus was as devious as he was devil. He told a bunch of cardinals at a party that he was so disappointed the pope would not get the gift he brought from the New World. Word got around to the Vatican, and a meeting was set within the month. I had not yet revealed my true identity, abilities, or immortality to anyone in Europe. Yekun had left for another voyage north in the New World by this time, drawn through the consciousness of his host. I was on my own. Pope Julius II welcomed me into the Vatican in 1504 with open arms. I decided that now was the time to reveal my nature as an immortal Watcher and see where that led. It had been nearly 300 years since I revealed myself to the Mexica people, and my Watchers were being labeled as these demon creatures. I had waited long enough. I was hiding, hoping the Creator would not notice my presence in the world. The hiding needed to end.

I revealed myself as a Watcher to Julius II. I explained to him my desire to set right what was wrong, to remove myself and my Watchers from the physical realm entirely. I explained my desire to research and find the Cherubim Sword. I was given access to the Vatican Archives. Among the archives, I found the original journals of Noah and Methuselah. I, of course, was the only one who knew what they really were. When I saw that the oldest text in the archive was written in Watcher, I kept the information to myself. I still wanted to be the only one who could read the texts, just as a precaution. Ironically, being cautious in some areas can cause one to be lax in others. I was so careful to protect the secrets of the texts, thinking that the pope would want to find the Garden of Eden for himself, I did not even consider another plot he had been developing since my arrival.

A little over a year after my first visit to the Vatican, Pope Julius II came to find me as I was working away in the archives. He told me that a new section of the archive had been discovered, opened by some excavators working on expanding the facilities underground. We both grabbed torches, and I followed with blind excitement as we traveled through a long, dark tunnel and down a deep, winding staircase. At the bottom were a dozen men who forced me behind a row of thick iron bars. I grabbed one around the neck with my arm as I struggled to get free. I cracked his neck before the others got out and shut the door.

Pope Julius II had tricked me into my new prison. He said he wanted the church's power to stay strong, and in his and his advisor's opinion, that could not happen if I completed my mission to remove evil from the world. For the light to gain members of its *army, it needed reminders of the fight against the dark to continue. Julius II explained that the idea was to lock me down here and throw away the key. Ensuring that the world would continue to know evil and, therefore, would always need the church's influence. So now I wait in this new man-made prison deep under their holy city, locked away in another prison.*

10

The Tour

Shepherd took Samyaza's journal with him everywhere
he went over the next month. Some travel plans for
The Shepherd were set to go on a short public relations
tour to a few international destinations. Shepherd learned
that the pope traveled in style but cheap. Meaning, he traveled
everywhere in a private jet, but it was a rental. The Vatican
didn't have its own jet, but it did charter private planes for
the Holy Father and certain special groups that traveled to
the Vatican for events and conferences. Shepherd had gotten
a kick out of the fact that, although it was a rental, they still
always designated the plane "Shepherd One" for its call sign
while carrying the pope. It was a tradition started by the flight
crews long before Pope Leo XIV, The Shepherd.

The Shepherd had become the new marketing brand name
of the Vatican almost overnight. The nickname had already
blossomed over social media, but when it came out that the
pope and his staff were showing support, it was suddenly on
t-shirts, mugs, hats, and many other tourist items being sold
by street vendors just outside St. Peter's Square. Believers

collectively began referring to him as "Our Shepherd" or "Our Holy Shepherd". His media attention before becoming pope had already gone viral, but once elected, Shepherd went from being a viral video to a regular social media tag. There was a podcast devoted entirely to him that three Catholic Priests out of Boston, Massachusetts, were putting out, and now *The Shepherd*, his call sign, was getting ironed onto sweatshirts.

The month-long tour had taken Shepherd and his small staff entourage to five different countries—through Mexico, Brazil, the Philippines, the United States, and back to Italy. Shepherd read through sections of Samyaza's journal when he could while traveling between events. Most of the time he could find for reading was on overnight flights or late in hotel suites. Samyaza's adventures drew Shepherd in when the sun went down. Stories of sailing across the Atlantic and meeting great, although brutal, explorers like Christopher Columbus stirred up longings for action and adventure from Shepherd's youth. It reminded him of his time as a boy, pretending he was an explorer traveling along the banks of a small stream that ran towards the coast below the hills of his neighborhood. He built a few rafts back then that held up well, at least under his slight frame, and pretended he was a great explorer looking for new worlds in his imagination.

The tour schedule was exactly how Shepherd wanted it to be, and he asked for each day to be packed. Every daytime slot during the tour needed to be filled. He told Marco when they were making initial arrangements one morning after coffee if he was going to spend a month traveling, he would make the most of the entire time at each stop. The tour was only intended for him to get his face out to the public more and do some big parades and large courtyard masses, but

Shepherd saw it as a wasteful expenditure of money that could be put to better use. He worked out with Marco what days and times he'd be in each city and built the itinerary to accommodate visits to local non-profits, humanitarian organizations, homeless shelters, food banks, and even some smaller catholic churches in need. Each visit drew more media attention and funding for the organizations. During his visit to New York, The Shepherd sat down for a podcast with *Tres Padres*, the podcast priests from Boston, and did an entire episode interview with them. It had become a habit of Shepherd's to listen to them while on the first leg of the trip.

The tour itinerary was posted online for press, fans, and people of faith to follow. The *Tres Padres* made a plug on an episode during the tour that, as one of them put it, "If the Shepherd would grace us with his presence, we'd love him as a guest anytime, especially since he's gonna be stateside."

Shepherd wanted to see St. Patrick's Cathedral while visiting, and he'd loved listening to those three priests talk about their church's issues and international concerns, and they were helping his cause anytime they discussed Shepherd's Flock website. He had Marco contact the *Tres Padres* email to see if they were interested in making the short drive and meeting him in New York for an episode. They urgently accepted and not only set up the interview exactly whenever Shepherd had a block of time big enough free on that stretch of the trip, but they also reserved for the podcast to be at a unique venue. *Tres Padres* booked a private rooftop courtyard overlooking St. Patrick's Cathedral in the city. There were also a select number of honored guests in a small audience area, and they recorded a special live video streaming episode. The venue was a massive step up from their usual recording studio, aka one of the three priests' offices. They were making the most of the opportunity to do a fully exclusive episode just for Shepherd.

The live interview episode of *Tres Padres* with special guest *The Shepherd* himself had over 100 million live viewers, just shy of a Super Bowl's average numbers. The whole recording was downloaded over 700 million times within a month. The *Tres Padres* priests helped promote *theshepherdsflock.va* during the show. Pointing out its already monumental success only furthered the website's exposure to the world through the podcast. Within two days of the broadcast ending, *The Flock*, as the website was now getting called, Shepherd's idea for sharing resources around the world and connecting people had over a billion members. The expressions "give to the Flock" or "join the Flock" were becoming commonplace. The episode was also quite a boost for the Tres Padres guys; it was definitely a win-win.

"The site has really been exploding! Hasn't it, Shepherd?" one of the padres asked Shepherd in his interview segment.

"Yes, according to Marco's last update, we've facilitated the changing of hands of over 1.6 billion dollars as of this morning," Shepherd answered, giving a thumbs-up to Marco, his now right-hand man, off camera.

"We understand the site has an option to click for an additional small percentage if anyone wants to give to the church itself. There's been rumors about what those funds are used for. Is that anything you can elaborate on?" another padre asked.

Shepherd replied, "Yes, I want to be transparent with that. First of all, we greatly appreciate the donations that have already been given. The option to add extra, to make sure we're not taking from any charitable causes, was something requested by my staff to help—keep the lights on, so to speak."

"Was the Vatican in trouble otherwise?" the third padre inquired next.

"Not in trouble, I would say, the church lacked the funds necessary to be as helpful and influential as it could have been for a long time. It seems that the church's agenda on the surface has been a mission of spreading the good word but mixed with human limitations."

"Human limitations?"

Shepherd explained, "Yes. From our perspective, we're limited by our vision. We can't see what's around the corner in the future, but we all want to get there. And we want to get there in one piece. The human factor of the church will always be a struggle. Greed will line pockets behind closed doors, jealousy, fear, desire for power, and the list goes on. The church has been dividing, breaking, weakening, splitting, reforming, changing, and adapting for hundreds—thousands of years. The Roman Catholic church has been so preoccupied keeping up with costs, demands, and changing times that nothing external is seeing growth. The church has strength, resilience, and longevity but has been dwindling over the years. The same thing happened in my hometown back in New Zealand when I lived there as a kid."

"I thought *The Shepherd* was from Australia?" padre one inquired.

Thankfully, padre number tres answered, so Shepherd didn't have to for once. "Well, he is from New Zealand but immigrated to Australia. Right, Shepherd?"

"Yes. Exactly," Shepherd said reluctantly. "As I was saying, parts of the community no longer wanted to follow our parish's strict, reserved teachings at the time, so a second church was established on the other side of town. You see—not because we were growing, which would be good, but because they couldn't get along. No one could agree on where money should be spent, where missions should invest efforts, what teachings were true, and which were being misconstrued. It was just bickering and stagnation. Eventually, a third and a fourth church were established, all smaller than the first, and all dwindling, dying, and damaging the community in the end. We were divided. It was a community of believers who didn't believe in each other. You see, padres, the Flock website isn't really about money. Yes, the money is helping put the church back on a stable base so that it can be a strong beacon for truth, assistance, and encouragement, but the real goal was to impact communities. To not only share resources from where they are in abundance to where they are lacking but also to show communities they're not alone. That neighbors can find and help each other. If you don't have someone right next door to help you, you might have someone just a click away in this vast population of our planet. We're all neighbors, and we need to help each other first. We've seen some of these non-profit groups not only receive the funds they require but then give BACK into *The Flock* when they have excess from what was received. Devastated communities now have the help and resources they need, and regular people, along with millionaires and billionaires, are getting up in the morning and checking *The Flock* to see if anyone new is in need. I believe we're finding as a human race that technology and connection can be used for something better. Not to get us more funny videos to watch while we sit and look at our phones on the toilet, but to help everyone either find what they can receive or what they can give." Shepherd got a good laugh from the small audience and the padres on that joke at the end.

Shepherd continued, "The testimonials from those donating and receiving have become a new section on the site. Sort of a social media posting board, if you will. We've seen several amazing stories shared already. One donor has moved to the community he connected with that needed a doctor. A surgeon in Omaha, Nebraska. His name is Don. Don was searching the Flock site for a worthy cause and found a group asking for money to provide some pay for a doctor in their village in the Sudan. Don was single and living in a small apartment in the city. After a few emails back and forth with the community leaders, he decided he was moving to Africa! Don arrived in the Sudan one week ago and has already performed several lifesaving procedures and surgeries for people in a community that normally would sadly wait for someone so sick to die with no other options. It truly is amazing how much more has already started to blossom from this endeavor. These stories are the whole reason for the Flock site, and we're just getting started."

The Tres Padres Podcast experience left Shepherd feeling reinvigorated at the end of his tour rather than wholly exhausted as he first anticipated. When the tour got to Italy for the final stops, Shepherd had more mental energy than ever. He stayed up late a few nights and finished reading Samyaza's journals in his quarters. He spent the last leg in Castel Gandolfo, the pope's official summer home known as the Pontifical Palace in the Italian countryside outside of Rome. Marco had set up a large outdoor public mass to be held for the first couple of days while Shepherd was there. The crowds were enormous for each mass, to the extent that a highway exit had to be shut down because the parking lot area had overflown and backed up the off-ramp. People parked along the highway since there was nowhere else at all for cars to go. The last days of the tour were like an Italian religious Woodstock.

The Shepherd's tour ended after two days of morning mass that were followed each afternoon and evening with other speakers and musicians. Shepherd reserved just a little time for himself on the third and last day in Italy. He figured that the trip could exhaust him when he planned the itinerary so packed. Shepherd knew himself and the importance of self-care well enough that he scheduled one day of vacation time at the end for recovery before returning to life in the Vatican. Being constantly surrounded for a month by others' voices, opinions, expectations, and needs, Shepherd had been renewed in spirit but exhausted in physical energy.

His plan for the last day was to allow himself time for relaxation, meditation, and restoration. He wanted some quiet separation for his thoughts, to process the tour experience, and to pray. Shepherd had planned for everyone in his staff on the tour to take a day off for themselves as well. Some of the staff refused and carried out a few daily tasks. They were too devoted and used to their routine to want to do anything else. Some leaped at the opportunity and were either gone before the sun came up or slept in late through the day to renew themselves however their personality type needed. Marco had decided to go for a brisk hike in the countryside by himself. As he put it, nature was how he connected to the Creator and collected his thoughts.

The Shepherd took a light breakfast alone in his room that day. He didn't want anyone on the staff to see him or to worry about him in the slightest, so he stayed inside until the noise of the morning scuffle diminished in the outside hallway. During his one-day vacation, he committed to setting aside any emails, social media updates, and Samyaza's journal. His suite in the Pontifical Palace had its own private balcony directly connected to his bedroom. Instead of checking his phone or opening a journal, he sat with a small cup of black tea, a little honey and cream mixed in, and leaned back in a patio chair, enjoying the quiet.

That morning, the choice of tea over coffee was intentional, and almost a ceremonial decision for Shepherd. Black tea was the Shepherd family's staple morning beverage when he was growing up. Any morning the weather was beautiful, as it was that day, his mother would take her tea the same way, with cream and honey, and sit on the back porch looking out at the sea that stretched to the horizon edge from the New Zealand coast just down the hillside their house nestled into. Some days, the view would keep her out on their back porch for hours if she could allow the time. Shepherd requested to change to tea after arriving and seeing the view of Lake Albano from his balcony. the view reminded him so much of the view back in New Zealand from his childhood home that his mother cherished.

The Thompson family were whalers during a time in history when that sort of thing wasn't yet frowned upon as a profession, and black tea had been made initially more popular and imported into New Zealand through the whalers. Whaling was so common there in the 1800s that hundreds of ships were in their waters alone. The practice died out over time, as did most of the whales, unfortunately, and Shepherd's grandfather was forced to reluctantly change to a different line of work to put food on the table for his family. Despite the change in catch, fishing and the love of the sea stayed in their blood as parts of tradition and always rang of nostalgia for Shepherd.

The balcony of the pope's quarters in his summer home overlooked the Lago Albano, or Lake Albano, an awe-inspiring volcanic crater lake that the Castel Gandolfo stood tall on the crested edge of. Shepherd sat there taking in the scenery and pretended for a little while that time didn't exist. He wondered if his mother had similar thoughts in her quiet moments when she sat on their porch when he was a boy. Shepherd imagined that those bits of peace were how she recharged her batteries when needed. He recalled seeing her motionless in her rocking chair, gazing silently out toward the sea. Her spirit floating over the breeze. As a boy, Shepherd had usually assumed she was upset at him, his father, or one of his sisters, and she was surely out there stewing about how to either confront or move past the issue, but those were the conclusions of a confused, rebellious child. Looking back now, Shepherd reflected more that those moments were a peaceful time for his mother, allowing her to let the appreciation of her life and love settle over her and take hold in her heart. Shepherd didn't even realize he had closed his eyes and let his head tilt back to rest at some point during that meditation on his past and his family. He opened his eyes to the blue sky and almost felt a sense of weightlessness for a second as if he'd tilted back in a chair and his equilibrium was off. He lowered his gaze to meet the horizon and dropped his foot off the patio chair he had it propped up on to reground himself. Seeing the break of the skyline across the lake and resting part of his body back on earth brought him into reality.

After his meditation on the balcony, Shepherd dressed in one of his regular afternoon pope outfits for leisure that was part of his standard wardrobe and took a late morning walk in the gardens. The Castel Gandolfo gardens were primarily open grass areas encased in different symmetrical patterns of landscaping lining circling stone pathways. Bushes of an odd oval, pointed upright shape stood segregating great tall maze-like hedges trimmed perfectly rigid surrounding the inner walkways. Between the walkways and hedges, waist-high stone walls stood as barriers for some of the more delicate landscape sections. Shepherd found a spot on a wall with a taller pillar cornerstone section that he could use as a makeshift armrest. He plopped down on it to relax after walking an entire circle of the main palace.

Shepherd gave himself another moment and found that he was getting bored with his day of meditation. He looked up to see the sun was about at its zenith and walked back into the palace. Shepherd headed for his room to come up with something else to occupy his time for the rest of the day since it seemed to him his deep thoughts were taking a day off from that point also. As he approached the hallway towards his suite, the two Swiss Guards, who refused to take off for the day, stood a little straighter. When they noticed it was Shepherd approaching, they relaxed. He had never busted the chops of any guard; they were more worried about a higher staff member like Marco catching them. It warmed Shepherd's heart to notice they already had that level of comfort around him. He said a hello and a thank you, nodding at each guard as he passed one and the other opened the door for him.

Shepherd closed the door behind him and turned into the large entryway of his suite. Lunch was laid out on a table with a few chairs around it in the center of the room. The lunch consisted of a myriad of sandwiches and finger foods, along with a variety of Shepherd's favorite sodas that he'd requested to be on the menu for the day. He grabbed one of the sandwiches and a soda while walking out onto his balcony again and kicked his shoes off. He looked back at the clock on a wall for the first time that day and saw it was half past noon. Thinking of nothing that really caught his interest, Shepherd looked back into his suite toward the edge of his bed, flipped around, and gazed back toward the lake below.

A few boats dotted the water; Shepherd held up his hand to shade his eyes from the sun and was able to confirm better what type. Some were sailboats, a couple were speed boats, and even simple row boats were closer to shore. Shepherd began thinking about his little rafts as a boy and fishing on the sea in small charter boats with his family and friends. He started to feel that his day of peace was beginning to boil up into a day of craving adventure. His mind had its needed moments of meditation; maybe his spirit desired to be revived in a different way, with something to make him get his hands dirty and remind Shepherd he was alive. Perhaps he needed to be reminded he was still... Liam.

Shepherd started to shift his mindset outward for ideas, and as he looked down below the balcony, an immature but glorious plan entered his mind. He stepped back inside the suite, mulled over a few details in his mind, and went through his clothes frantically, putting out another outfit.

Next, Shepherd went to his main doors and popped one open. The Swiss Guards were just outside, seated in the hallway. He called over to them as they looked his way, "This lunch was great. You guys want some before I send back the rest? I ate so fast I think I'm going to take my first late afternoon nap in—I don't know how long," he joked.

"No, thank you. The kitchen staff brought us some food when they arrived with yours earlier, Father Shepherd; very kind of you, though," one guard replied.

"Great, good. Well, if you don't mind, since I could be napping, when they come with my dinner later, could you ask them to be a little quiet? I may still be asleep, but I'll have my bedroom door shut." Shepherd was making sure the guards would be his *do not disturb* sign for the evening.

"Of course, get some rest, father," the second guard replied as they both nodded.

"Thanks, boys." Shepherd smiled subtly and waived good night as he shut his door. The stage for his evening plans was set. Shepherd jumped into the bedroom and closed the double doors behind him. He changed into the other clothes he'd picked out, which included some sunglasses and a fedora he'd been given at a shop in town on his first day in Italy. The pope checked his pockets, grabbed his phone, turned it to airplane mode, and disabled the GPS as he slipped it into a pocket. When he turned to go out onto the balcony, he had a final pause. Then, thinking, *why not*, he went back to his bed and tucked a few pillows under the duvet to make it look like he was curled up sleeping. It made Shepherd chuckle to imagine Marco peeking into the doorway, maybe later that evening, and thinking it was him fast asleep. The potential for that scenario made the feeling of adventure all that more exciting, and it began to take hold of Shepherd as he finally turned to make his escape off the balcony. Shepherd checked left and right, and the coast was clear below. He had a moment of clarity where he'd realized stretching would be a good idea but concluded adventures don't wait for stretching, and he grabbed an iron lattice to the right of the balcony railing and swung his legs over the side. He descended with surprising ease. Once he'd been two steps down, it became apparent that the trellis was shaped like a ladder, clearly designed as a safety precaution but hidden as a trellis for vines.

Shepherd dropped to the ground, tucked his hands in his pockets, and strolled towards the exit like a tourist without a care in the world. No one at the front gate recognized him, and they paid hardly any attention to someone leaving the grounds compared to a person entering. Pope Leo XIV sauntered down the street towards the village and lake below, ready to spend the rest of the day on an adventure as his old self, Liam.

11

The Old Man and the Sea

Shepherd, or for the adventure ahead, Liam, ambled down the winding hillside road from the Castel Gandolfo, looking to see what was around each corner. Liam kept attempting to display the persona of a casual tourist, but underneath, he was beaming with anticipation for something more exciting. Liam felt like a kid on an adventure walk in the wilderness. As he strolled along, he saw a few local cafés and shops, which he peered into on his way past. The hillside road was mainly lined with old run-down hotels and dilapidated villas that had fallen into disrepair since their glory days. Along the water were a few leisure craft rental businesses and lakeside patio restaurants. Once he'd reached the shoreline, Liam could see there were skinny docks, and out from those were kayakers and paddle boarders. Further out were some larger boats. It was nothing compared to the ocean, of course, but Liam enjoyed hearing the water hit the shore and lap against the pebbles at its edge. He stepped off the road and slid down an embankment to where he was at the cusp of the water's edge. Most of the shoreline was grit and rock, slowly being worked into sand as the light current tossed debris particles back and forth. Liam felt drawn to linger near the water. He took off his shoes and decided to walk along the banks till he found his adventure.

About fifteen minutes of walking and leaving footprints in the dark sand around the deep volcanic lake brought Liam to the beginnings of a marina. It wasn't any kind of high tourist or fishing season. At the time, the marina was mainly used for boat storage for private pleasure craft and a few small charter boats. Liam saw an old man taking the cover off his boat a few docks in. He stepped from the shoreline and slid his loafers back on, making his way out on the dock to say hello.

"Ciao! Parli Inglese?" Liam said hi and asked the man if he spoke English. One of the more critical Italian expressions he'd memorized even before coming to Italy.

"Well, hello there. Yes, I do, I do. How are you today?" The boatman replied.

"Very good, thank you. Liam is my name, and yours?" Liam stuck with his covert first name identity and stretched his hand to the man in greeting.

The boatman looked facetiously at Liam's hand and then grabbed it firmly with his callous, old, thin hand. The boatman had a firm grip for such an elderly fellow. "Elias. Elias Hofstein is my name. A pleasure to meet you—Liam. I'm just about off the dock here. Can I help you with something?"

"Ah, well, I don't mean to get in your way. I was hoping you might know where I could see about renting a boat for the day?"

"Well, the marina is closed for some work since it is the off-season. There aren't any boats available for rent besides some kayaks," Elias said with his eloquent Italian accent.

"Gotcha. Well, I was hoping for something more, well, like what you're going out on, but another time, I guess. Thanks for your assistance." Liam waved at the man and began to step away to walk back down the dock.

Elias called out, "You are welcome to come out with me if you're interested in a quick pleasure cruise with a little fishing. I won't be gone for more than a few hours. You ever been out on the Albano before?"

Liam turned back, beaming, "I haven't, and that's very kind of you, but I wouldn't want to put you out just for my holiday. I fished a lot at sea with my father when I was young; it's been a long time. His boat was very much like this one you've got here."

"It's no trouble at all, and it sounds like you may know enough to be of some use. I could use an extra hand out there. My wife would sleep easier tonight knowing I had someone along. It's my last trip out before putting this boat up for sale, and—I'd welcome the company," Elias stated somberly.

Liam saw the emotion start to build in the old man's face. It was apparent Elias was more than happy to have anyone along to give his old boat a sendoff. "I'd be glad to join you and see if I can lend a hand to earn my keep, cap'n," Liam said. He made Elias laugh, and with that, they shook hands again. Liam hopped on board and began checking where he could be of assistance to cast off from the dock.

The small outboard engine revved on, and they slowly cruised out of the marina past the outer wake buoys and into the deeper middle of the lake. As they cruised along, looking for a spot Elias was anxious to get to by a particular "magic hour" for fishing, Liam got to know his captain.

"You seem to know your way around the lake. Have you

always lived and fished here?" Liam asked.

Elias replied as he turned the boat to run parallel to the upcoming shore, "I have lived here in this village since I was a boy. I'm ninety-two now, and I've fished this lake my entire life."

Elias' voice was raspy, like a man who smoked most of his life but had given it up at some point to save his throat. "My wife and I have a small cottage on the east side of the village. It was originally her parents' home when she moved here after university with them. I was already living in the village and ran a café. She was a schoolteacher, retired now, and these last four years has been wheelchair bound. Her knees just aren't what they once were, and that's the only reason she isn't out here with me today. My Isabella loves to be on this boat on the water. The only reason I got it was for her," Elias said over the wheel as they cruised closer to the opposite shore from the marina.

"You just got the boat for Isabella? I thought you said you fished here your whole life, Elias, since you were a boy?" Liam asked, perplexed.

"It's true. I've been here all my life and fished here since I was a boy." Elias killed the engine and dropped out an anchor. The area along the shore where they stopped was overshadowed by a large rock wall with a few trees grouped at the top, overhanging the water below. It was a great spot. The trees overhead would entice fish down below to linger nearby, hoping to get insects and debris dropped from above. No one with a regular fishing pole on shore could easily drop a line from the rock wall into the water. It was the kind of place that could only be fished properly from a boat out in the lake beyond the rocks.

An excellent choice for a final voyage fishing spot, Liam thought.

Elias continued his thought after the engine died, "No. I wouldn't have gotten a boat if it wasn't for her asking for one for years."

Liam again sensed the emotion in Elias' voice when talking about his wife and the boat. He decided to just enjoy the peace and quiet and get into some fishing. Elias was already starting to break out a couple of rods with open-faced reels attached with fresh lines. Elias passed Liam a rig, and Liam quickly set his up, checking his drag, loading his line through the loops in the pole, and picking a lure from Elias' massive tackle box. Then, having to put that lure back and instead tie on the "right one for this spot," as Elias put it. Liam finally impressed Elias with his hook-tying technique, which he created on his own with a quadruple knot, looping back through the main hole and then tying off once and done!

The two men sat in the late afternoon sun, reeling lines in and out, hoping for a bite. The fish weren't giving them much. Elias started to look frustrated after close to an hour went by with only an occasional tug from a fish too small to even set the hook.

"Maybe we're not holding our mouths right," Liam said with a chuckle under his breath. It was an expression his father had used to say when the fish weren't biting.

Elias got the joke. He shook with laughter as he reeled his line back in one more time. Elias dropped his pole into a holster at the side of his chair and stepped into the small cabin up front. He returned promptly with two ice-cold beers, popped the tops from both on the side of his boat's windshield without even checking if Liam was interested, and passed one his way.

Liam grinned. "This makes things perfect, Elias. Cheers. How can I thank you?" he said, taking the bottle.

"Saluti," Elias replied as he tapped his bottle to Liam's and took a large swig in the sunlight. "No need to thank me. This is a big occasion. When I set out this afternoon to take this stupid boat out for one more little fishing trip—" he took another swig of beer, "—before I get rid of it forever, it was one of the worst days of my life, Liam. But now, I am helping someone have a relaxing day and enjoying a beer with *The Shepherd* on a boat on the Lago Albano."

Liam's brain took a split second to process Elias' last comment, revealing Elias knew who he really was. Once it clicked, Liam spat a little beer and nearly let his pole slip into the water but caught the falling rod with his knees. Elias laughed at the sight of the pope on his boat, fumbling not to drop his fishing pole. Some of his beer trickled down the front of his chin underneath his gray whisker as he grabbed his sides, watching Liam collect himself and try not to spill any more of his own beer.

Once he situated himself, Liam asked jovially, "Did you know it was me the whole time?"

"Your whole um—Clark Kent thing with the glasses, the clothes, and the hat may have worked, but you forgot to check your jewelry." Elias pointed with his beer bottle to the Ring of the Fisherman still wrapped around Liam's finger. He had forgotten to remove it, and anyone in Italy would know it immediately. It explained why Elias had given him a strange look when they first shook hands earlier that day. Elias had known Liam was the pope the entire time, just from the ring.

Liam set down his fishing pole and wiped up some spilled beer on his leg as he leaned against the side of the boat. "I hope you know I wasn't attempting to trick you or anything. I was just trying to make today about—today, and you just happened to be the first person I stumbled upon on my one-day vacation adventure around the lake. This has been a great experience. I'm so glad you brought me out here with you. Thank you for everything, truly."

Elias rolled one of his bony shoulders from under his suspender and let it fall to his side. Then he untucked most of his shirt and sat back down in his fishing chair. "You know, I'm not a man of your particular faith. A catholic, that is. I'm not a man of any faith, exactly. I have a hard time accepting beliefs that some others accept ignorantly. I think it's important to do good in the world as best as you can, regardless of faith, for all mankind, just like you said in your speech. I saw you on the internet that day you were elected, and I even attended your mass on the hillside here a few days ago."

"I'm still searching for what great thing I can do to help the world. The Flock website is a start, but it won't be enough. Elias, let me ask—you said you're ninety-two. You're the oldest person, honestly, that I think I've spoken with in private since I became pope. What wisdom would a man of your years be willing to offer to *The Shepherd*? You say it's important to do good in the world, and you've probably experienced a lot more life than myself, living almost twice as long. With all you've seen of the world, how would you change it for the better?" Shepherd asked.

The old man leaned forward in his chair. It looked like he had something on his heart, but he needed a moment before starting. Then Elias spoke, "Liam, Shepherd. Let me tell you what I know from what I have experienced. When I was a young boy, my father, mother, my sister, and I lived in this village above the leather shop that my father owned and worked in alongside his father before him every day. That is, every day of his life until World War II came to Italy.

Because Mussolini had made the Patto d'Acciaio Agreement with Hitler, Judeans, Jews, such as my family, were treated very differently all of a sudden. Stores owned by Jews were no longer getting business, like my father's shop. We were able to scrape by making a small living selling to more loyal families and Jewish customers for a short time. Then, in 1938, legislation was passed that began taking away Jewish people's rights within all of Italy. One such right was that of a Judean to marry a non-Judean, which was my parents' situation. My father was a Jew, and my mother was a gentile Italian. The government considered my parents' marriage invalid, and after the laws were enforced, no one wanted to come near our shop or to do business with our family anymore.

My father had to close the leather shop, which never opened again. All the leather goods in our shop that no one was willing to buy were either picked off one by one as people came through stealing or scrounging at night, or mice and rats ate them as they ran out of food like the rest of us.

For a while, we could stay at home in the village. It was against my father's moral judgment, but for our survival, he created the facade that he was getting work in the city while my sister and I stole what we could to eat and trade from the hotels and villas on the other side of the lake. We first stole clothes from a few tourists with children to have classier outfits that no one would ever expect on a street urchin thief. Then, we would walk into resorts with families or groups with other children. Once we knew the layout of the place, we would watch for opportunities to steal food, silverware, personal items, wallets, and cash laid out for tips; anything overlooked or walked away from was fair game if we didn't get caught. My sister and I looked like any other rich kid running around disobeying their parents without a care while the world was at war all around them. All of this was against my father's moral values and better judgment, but we were starving, and no one would buy or even sell with a Jew anymore.

My sister got caught stealing once, and I was able to help her escape. After that, my father had our family pack up anything useful, valuable, and mobile. We moved into the woods outside the village. We were out of sight of all the homes and roads; it was a pocket of heavy wood just on the other side of the crest of the lake that had more forest below it. Only an insane hiker or a lost hunter could find us or even see our fires at night. We lived like that in the forest for more than a year. My mother and sister would maintain our camp and supplies. At the same time, my father and I slipped down to the lake to fish, collect water, and scavenge what we could around the outskirts of the village and roads at night.

The entire village population grew poor and fished the lake heavily for their own food, just as we were. Many other families were using the lake for resources. There had been a drought that year on top of everything, changing the lake's entire ecosystem. The smaller fish died off with the lower water levels, being eaten by larger fish out where there was less cover. With all the fishing and starvation, the lake emptied of life. Winter came, and ice fishing became the only way to get something to eat unless you wanted to sip some pine tea. Blech! The girls collected firewood while father and I went out on the cold lake as often as possible, and we always avoided trouble with neighbors. Other families in the village moved away with nothing to eat, and no tourists came to the lake anymore until the war ended. Even constantly fishing, there were days that bled into weeks where we wouldn't get anything to eat."

Liam had been leaning on the boat, spellbound by Elias' story the whole time. He crouched down, letting his feet slide out from under him, and rested his back against the inside of the boat as he took another swallow of his beer. Elias paused momentarily to look over at the sun, which was starting to get a little low and take cover behind thin clouds. The old man's story was already more powerful than anything Liam had expected. He didn't want to say anything to interrupt, so Liam sat quietly watching Elias. They both sipped beer while he talked.

Elias took another drink before continuing, "I'll never forget, one day, I was out on the ice with my father. We hadn't eaten in four days, and I think the time before that last meal had been another three days. I pulled a massive perch from our hole in the lake ice. It was enough food that our family could ration two days' worth out of the single enormous fish at that point. It was close to spring, and the fish was filled with eggs, which was also part of why it was so large. Everything else we caught had been bony and starving like us, but this Perch had survived well enough to nurture hundreds of eggs to be ready for spawning in the coming spring. My father realized all this and explained to me, his young son, about the starvation and the eggs. He said that we desperately needed this food but that if we ate that fish, there might not be any new fish in the next season because of all the die-offs. His logic was that if we eat this fish now, we'll have food for a couple days; if we let it go, we may have weeks' worth of food in the spring.

I was too young and hungry to fully understand, and I begged and pleaded with my father to keep the fish. He'd said, 'The longer we kept it out, the less likely it'd survive,' and tossed it back into the hole. It vanished into the dark water, and we didn't catch another fish till the ice thawed. There were plenty of Perch in the spring; father was right, but he didn't live to see it. My father was starving much worse than my sister and I knew, and he only lived five more days after we let that fish go. I finally was able to scrounge some food and grab a few cans of condensed milk off a truck that was stopped at a checkpoint. By the time I got any of it back to my family, my father wasn't able to eat anymore; he was so weak, and he forced my mother to save the milk for us. My father died of starvation in my mother's arms while my sister and I sipped on condensed milk." Elias' eyes dripped with tears as he looked toward Liam. "We truly know the Creator is real after we have reason to feel hatred towards him."

Elias tossed his empty beer bottle down into the cabin of his boat. He didn't seem to care if it rolled around in the bottom of a boat that he wouldn't own for much longer. He looked back at Liam and said, "I was a child then. I didn't understand what my father was doing until I saw the fish in the spring, until I met my wife, and until I became a father myself. Until I saw my sister become a doctor and have children and grandchildren of her own. I didn't understand what beautiful lessons my father taught me in his last days. I was too hungry and mad at the Creator and too ignorant to understand everything at once.

My father sacrificed himself to save his family. If he hadn't, we likely all would have died that winter trying to keep him alive or later that spring from starvation, just like him. I'm thankful for everything he has given me, taught me, and made me choose to be in this life. I want the Creator to take it back! And that, Shepherd, is the thing that I wish could change about this life and this world for the better. I wish that the Creator that we acknowledge didn't put us in a life where we must see such horrible suffering to understand such valuable truths. Why did my father have to go through the pain of that ultimate self-sacrifice? Why am I a better person because of that? The Creator sent his son; my father sent himself. And if you could ask the Creator from your seat in the Vatican to give my father back, I'd appreciate it. Let him know we've learned enough lessons. We don't need another holocaust, or dead loved one, or terrorist attack, or war." Elias turned his gaze away from Liam back to the horizon as he finished his final thought. "We just need love. That was the message of the Messiah, his son. That was a rabbi I could get behind the teachings of. But this Creator who makes those he loves most, suffer most—I'll have a bone to pick with him when I see him soon enough. I would wish we never needed to learn the lessons that hurt the most."

The story left Liam speechless, sitting on the floor of the old boat. Elias turned around after he was done speaking and revved up the engine, signaling it was time to head in. Liam snapped from his trance and went to grab the anchor to be of some help. It didn't matter that Liam was speechless; Elias had nothing to say during the entire ride back. It wasn't awkward with the loud motor distracting from the lack of conversation across the water to the marina, and Liam needed time to reflect on everything the old fisherman said that day.

When they glided back up to the dock, Liam helped Elias tie off the boat and tarp everything over before leaving. The two sauntered to the end of the pier and stopped where it was best to part ways.

"This was a boat ride, I promise, I'll never forget, Elias. Again, I want to thank you for your hospitality. I hope all the best for you and your wife, Isabella," Liam said, reaching his hand out.

Elias reached out and shook Liam's hand. He had one last thing to add before they parted ways. Elias gripped Liam's hand hard and pulled him closer. He was surprisingly strong, "I do have some faith. Shepherd I—I have known two competing ideologies that have changed the world—power hungry selfishness, and sacrificial selflessness. Whichever is chosen in each life, self is at the heart of what changes the world. I hope you always choose what is selfless and not selfish and do the right thing. And if you could, please pray for this very old sinner before his time is through, if you don't mind." Elias wept again and looked up at Liam, who was also getting dewy.

With that, Liam took his hat off and asked Elias to pray right there at the end of the dock. Liam said a prayer over Elias and his family. The two embraced, and Shepherd turned to make his way back down the road towards Castel Gandolfo. If he walked fast, he might make it back before sunset. Liam took his hat and glasses back off as he rounded the last corner of the wall before he was in sight of the little guard house at the front gate. As he approached, the guards recognized Liam this time. They watched him walk past like he owned the place, seeing their completely befuddled faces.

Liam laughed, "Ha! Guess I'm Shepherd again now." He lightly jogged the last little distance to the area below his balcony. When he stopped, he felt way more out of breath than expected. "The food here is going to send me to an early grave if I'm not careful," he said, heavily wheezing.

"More likely, the fall off the balcony could kill you first," Marco said from above, making Shepherd jump out of his skin below. Marco was standing on the balcony watching Shepherd as he approached. Marco was leaning over the railing, wearing what looked like some hiking shorts, a windbreaker jacket, and hiking shoes.

"You're probably right, but I'm still coming up this way!" Shepherd yelled as he ran towards the hidden ladder and climbed up.

Marco dropped his head and shook it side to side, flopping his thick, dark ponytail while Shepherd plopped onto the balcony next to him. "You're not a teenager, Shepherd," he pointed out before he turned Shepherd's direction. "I enjoyed your little attempt at a ruse with your pillows. I've been checking in on your room off and on for the last hour and was about to have some staff sent out to look for you. Maybe next time, don't turn your phone off? Where have you been man?" Marco had never spoken to Shepherd quite so flippantly before.

Shepherd relented, "Marco, I apologize. I meant to be back before anyone noticed, and I had my phone on me in case of an emergency. I knew if someone discovered me gone, I'd be tracked, and the adventure would be over."

"The adventure? What did you do all day?" Marco asked, perplexed.

Shepherd sat with Marco on the balcony overlooking the lake till the moonlight replaced that of the twilight. Marco's day had been relaxing but uneventful, so Shepherd's story of the *Old Man and the Sea* dominated the conversation.

Marco was fascinated with the old man's story as much as Shepherd. He asked, "So what do you think Elias really meant by that? About what he wished could make the world better?"

Shepherd shrugged and replied, "I think—Elias wished he wasn't thankful for the things he wished never happened. I don't believe he was being literal, but I do believe he was trying to share some wisdom with me. I think he wanted to share that life lesson with me in the hopes that it could save me from having to learn the same lessons myself, which—maybe I haven't. But hell, he's got forty years on me!"

Marco reflected on the story, "What a painful way to start out in life."

Shepherd lightly nodded in agreement. "My parents died old, in nursing home beds, months apart. They had children in their forties, so—it was just their time to go. I was a middle-aged man myself already, and all my siblings too. Poor Elias, to see his father die in front of him as a child, I'm sure it affected all his life choices," Shepherd said with a bewildered tone. "I don't know. I don't know if I was Elias' father if I could've made the same choice to let the fish go. Sometimes, you can try to do the right thing with the most logical and honorable intentions, and it can still be a horrible choice to live with."

The two men sat quietly for a minute after Shepherd's last thought. Marco eventually made the first move to get up and stretch, signaling to Shepherd he was leaving. They hugged, and as Marco exited the room, he said, "You know, next time, you can just ask me to tell people you're sick, and I can cover for you."

Shepherd laughed, "Now, where's the adventure in that!"

12

The First Game

O n his first routine evening back in Vatican City, Shepherd found himself having a lively after-dinner conversation with a bishop visiting from the United States. Bishop Donelly was from Ohio and a professor at the local college connected with his chapel. The bishop had been visiting from the States for a lecture series at one of the museums in the Vatican and was invited by some of the staff for dinner that night. He was asked to join Shepherd as his conversational dinner guest. Bishop Donelly was studying theological origins for his lectures and was working on a book on the same topic. He was also part of a research project partnership at Boston College that was getting into A.I. theories of something called "predictive human history and prescience."

Shepherd was exhilarated to talk with an American about some of his recent experiences on the leg of his tour in New York and another bishop at that. Donelly quickly assured Shepherd he didn't know much about the big city. He said where he was from mainly was "cows, trees, and corn."

Shepherd was most curious to hear Donelly's perspective on his agenda as pope, one man of the cloth to another.

Shepherd asked, "If you had been the bishop that they elected pope, what would you think should be your primary driving focus for your work in this position? With this influence?"

Donelly answered in his plain American accent, "The world is becoming more and more connected. Anything you do now in any position can have global ripple effects. But in your position, ripples are almost guaranteed. I expect the weight of the world may be what you feel on your shoulders, and it sometimes actually is. If it had been me, I would think I should tell myself I was elected for a reason, and the Creator will work through me, just as he would through anyone he needed for his grand design. And I should trust my intuition because it's not mine, but the Creator's that guides me."

Shepherd felt Bishop Donelly's answer was well said.

Shepherd nodded and then inquired further, "Tell me more about this A.I. theory of yours. What does it have to do with theology exactly?"

Bishop Donelly smiled and said, "It's originally the theory of my associate, Professor Kozlov, who's developing a version of A.I. that takes his work into account in the construct of forming a consciousness for the A.I. In Layman's terms, how does an A.I. *see* events? Fate? Coincidence? Could an A.I. take a religious perspective? These are some of the questions Kozlov and his team I've joined are trying to answer. We see how A.I. fits with predestination, fate, free choice, etc. This research could find the ultimate answer to the question of whether the Creator has a plan for all of us. We believe science could help people see his plan and maybe figure out what parts are still to come."

After their meal, Shepherd made sure to get Donelly's contact information and committed at the end of their discussion to stay in touch. Shepherd returned to his personal suite for the evening and locked the door quickly behind him. He didn't take his usual time getting ready for bed that evening. He changed into his same evening pajama pants, flip flops, and a baggy hooded sweatshirt, but he skipped some usual hygiene evening activities. It was his first evening back at the Vatican since the tour that wasn't filled with meetings. Shepherd had read all of Samyaza's journal about his journey with Columbus and was chomping at the bit to hear more about what happened after he arrived in Europe. Shepherd grabbed his headboard key from the pope journals chest and popped it in to raise his bed, exposing the door to the secret hallway. There was a cardboard box with books he had prepared for the evening sitting on his chair that he grabbed on the way to the hidden entrance. Shepherd flipped the lights on and quickly made his way down the long winding hall to the underground security room below the square. Bruno was working that evening instead of Rossi. Bruno had been made aware from Rossi's reports of Shepherd's visits and that Shepherd knew the prisoner protocols.

"Hello, Bruno. Your watch tonight?" Shepherd said when he arrived.

Bruno looked up from his desk and wheeled around to walk out from behind and greet Shepherd. "Yes, father. You have something for me to inspect?" he asked.

"Yes, I have some books I'd like to bring the prisoner if that's alright?"

"Should be fine," he replied as he walked up and grabbed the box from Shepherd's outstretched hands. "Just need to make sure nothing in here is on the unapproved list."

Shepherd stepped around behind the security desk and peered at the monitors between the walk-through break in the circular counter while Bruno looked over the books. He noticed there were only four monitors, each with its own black-and-white stationary view. One camera was on the inside of the elevator, another outside of the security room hallway that led to the main Entity headquarters, another next to the small area in front of the elevator doors at the bottom. Shepherd distinctly recognized the phone on the wall on the old monitor. The last camera pointed directly into Samyaza's cell from the back of the observation room outside of the glass. It had a view of almost the entire space, except the far right corner where the old door was sealed shut.

"Just this one can't go," Bruno said, pulling a book aside and setting it behind the security desk.

Shepherd looked to see which book it was. "Why not *Catcher in the Rye*? Just curious, he had requested that one himself."

"I don't know those kinds of things, as you might already be aware, Shepherd. But if you'd like, I can submit a request with Janis—" Bruno pronounced it *Yanis*, "—and you can take it up with him. He's in charge of the protocols for the prisoner."

Janis Borgman was the Head Commander of the Entity. Janis was someone that Shepherd had very much wanted to sit down with ever since he found out about the Entity's involvement in keeping watch over Samyaza, but he hadn't yet been brave enough to set up the meeting. Janis was a Dutch former police detective. For years, he already had quite a reputation in the Vatican as somewhat of a stickler to the church's rules and those of his order. He was considered by most of the higher staff as an unnecessary relic of the church's more rigid past, but Janis didn't care and wore the persona like a badge of honor. Someone of such nature was very opposite to that of Shepherd. He could picture the clashing of opinions already if they sat down together, and Shepherd was waiting for an unavoidable reason to have to meet with such a man. Shepherd was the pope, but he was intimidated by Janis' reputation.

Shepherd once again made the nerve-wracking trip down the deep elevator shaft. *I have got to see if that second entrance can be opened back up at the stairs.*

Having only one way up from the lower room was getting to him. Shepherd determined he'd make an appointment soon with Janis to see about making some changes and updates to the prisoner access and protocols. At the bottom, the elevator doors slid open, and Shepherd rounded the corner with his box of books in hand. He flopped the box down next to the two-way drawer area by Samyaza's cell's glass viewing wall.

Samyaza wasn't in his chair this time. He was lying on the camping cot against his far-left wall corner, behind the same support column that slightly concealed his old TV. Samyaza appeared to be sleeping when Shepherd peered in at him.

"Samyaza?"

He didn't move an inch when Shepherd called out to see if he was alert.

"Sorry, I hate to wake you. I could come back tomorrow?" Shepherd didn't know what the etiquette was here. As far as he knew, Samyaza didn't need sleep, so he wasn't sure what was happening.

Shepherd sat down in the chair in his area and waited a bit. After a few seconds, Samyaza gasped out of nowhere and quickly sat upright. Shepherd reeled back, freaked out, and almost fell over in his chair when Samyaza lunged from his horizontal position.

"Sorry about that. I was—away," Samyaza quietly explained while he slid off his cot.

"Uh, hello. What do you mean away? Away where?"

"The phantom realm, or what your religious types would call the spirit realm." Samyaza could see the confusion on Shepherd's face. "I can still leave my body and pass from this realm to that one if I choose to. I usually do not; the perception of time moves much slower there when one enters voluntarily, but occasionally, I like to stretch my legs, metaphorically speaking, and I shift over, leaving my body lying here, motionless. It is the closest thing I have that reminds me of taking a swim—feeling weightless, and drifting through an alternate realm. Again, my apologies if seeing me in that state alarmed you, Priest," the Watcher said.

"Oh, no, it's fine. I see people laying around having out-of-body experiences all the time," Shepherd stated. He was teasing, of course, but Shepherd's sarcasm was lost on Samyaza.

Shepherd smiled, "I just returned from a trip and finished your journal, Samyaza. It's good to see you again."

Samyaza glanced at Shepherd and then looked off to one side with a head shake.

Shepherd realized when he went about with pleasantries as if this wasn't a warden and prisoner relationship, it probably seemed more like a joke than anything else to Samyaza.

Samyaza brushed past Shepherd's statement. "I suppose you have some more questions after getting through all that reading. I have been curious, where are you from originally?"

"I'm originally from—" Shepherd paused, realizing what he

was about to say again, and continued, "—originally, I'm from New Zealand, but I immigrated to Australia as an adult. I do have some more questions, quite a few more actually. I have some books for you first and brought your journal back, of course; thank you again for that." He passed the journal and the box of books through the drawer for Samyaza.

Samyaza walked over to check the books out. "*The Swiss Family Robinson?*" He read one of the titles aloud.

"One of my favorites. I got some of the ones you'd asked for, but I thought I might add a favorite or two of mine. Have you read it?" Shepherd asked.

Samyaza looked at Shepherd with puzzle, again, at his casual nature. "No, I have not, but thank you."

Shepherd could tell that things were getting awkward again. Samyaza didn't seem particularly open to his attempts to connect. Shepherd looked over at the chess table sitting on his side of the glass. "Would you care for a game?" he said, motioning to the board.

Samyaza looked up from the books at Shepherd. There was a slightly awkward pause where Samyaza kept eye contact with Shepherd for a bit of a linger, and then he looked at the chess board, then back at Shepherd. "What about your questions?"

"Let's add it to the game; I take one of your pieces, you answer a question," Shepherd said.

"And vice versa!" Samyaza shot back.

Shepherd liked that he was getting some enthusiasm, "Of course! Game on?"

"Game on, Priest!" Samyaza retorted.

Shepherd was even less of a fan of being called "Priest" than Holy Father, but he felt that accepting the nickname was a chance to start to connect with Samyaza, and he suffered it to stick.

Shepherd sat down in the small wooden armchair at the chess board beside where he'd been standing and glanced over the table. He would have to move all the pieces for both players since he was on the side of the glass with the physical board. The chess board was covered with dust, and so were the pieces which sat untouched for who knows how long. Shepherd concluded they'd play on a dusty board with nothing to wipe it off this time, but he would bring something to clean it on a future visit. Samyaza scooched his green armchair over next to the glass on his side. Shepherd blew a swift of dust off the board to clear it of most of the debris.

Shepherd picked up the black king to examine it. The chess set was ancient, maybe hundreds of years by the look. The board was made of wood and built into a small two-person tabletop, but the pieces were made of ivory for white, obviously, and onyx for black. The board itself was standard-sized, but the pieces were enormous, much taller than any Shepherd had played with before. The round base of each piece filled an entire square. Each rested edge to edge, with just a little point showing at each square's corner tip underneath. For each back row, the higher-value pieces stretched tall, while the pawns were much shorter and somewhat stumpy by comparison. The larger oblong pieces made it a tough board to navigate, and if you had any sleeves, you'd surely knock them left and right. Shepherd's board back home, and the one from his childhood, were simple, cheap plastic and wood piece sets. This set had been made long before there were any size standards and looked to be carved and honed entirely by hand.

"White or black?" Shepherd asked through the glass, indicating with his hands he could turn around the table if needed.

Samyaza replied, "It seems fitting that I should be black. Would you not agree, Priest?" with a smirk.

"I suppose I can't argue with that. Is that how you see things? The Watchers are part of the dark, and the church is part of the light?"

"That is a question, and I do not see any pieces moved or captured yet, Priest," Samyaza pointed out.

"Right, right, sorry." Shepherd moved one of his pieces, starting as white. After a couple of moves back and forth, he said, "Knight captures pawn. Alright, back to that first question about you Watchers' thoughts on the light and the dark. Good and evil."

Samyaza replied with a move, "Rook to A6. I do not suppose any spiritual being sees it the way you humans do, with light and dark, good and evil, right and wrong. We Watchers would not think in the same ethical dimensions. We have existed much longer and in different states of reality. We do not have the same consequences or life cycle as humans, so we are entirely outside those ideas. Think of it as more of a difference in philosophies on what would best shape the world. When looking at large-scale global situations, with any cause comes inevitable effect. One person getting a promotion means another will not get a job. One region getting the rain it needs for its growing season could mean drought for another entire civilization. There is a balance to the world, and that balance can shift light or dark, I suppose, from your perspective, based on those global-scale changes. The weather can be good, and the weather can be bad, but would you ever say the weather is evil?"

The gameplay continued, and Samyaza captured a piece, "Rook to A3 takes bishop. Tell me again, Priest, why is it you were elected, do you think? As Holy Father? You are not the usual type. Take it from the only being alive who has met more than a few popes that have come down to have a look at their prisoner in the dungeon."

Shepherd nodded, "You're right about that. It was very unexpected. I think everyone is hoping for a big change in the world, and I've always spoken from my heart about my desire to make a difference. It seems my message has taken hold of so many that they felt encouraged to elect someone with my qualities, who was a little younger, hoping there could be time to make a lasting impact." Shepherd captured Samyaza's rook and was able to get in another question of his own. "Can you explain why you're not to be touched? From everything I have read, you're strong, but you don't have super strength, and you're not dangerous to touch. Is it some kind of sense you have when you touch someone? Do you—do you read their mind?"

Samyaza huffed, holding in a chuckle. "Not so invasive as that, no. If I touch any person's skin in any way, I can intuit their emotions, intentions, desires, or how they might be leaning towards a decision. I can see what is in someone's head right at that moment and observe what character of person they truly are."

Shepherd snuck in another question, "Just from one touch?"

"Any one touch, yes, Priest," Samyaza clarified. The game seemed to be slightly disarming Samyaza.

Shepherd made another attack on his next turn, "Queen takes pawn. So, if you did get out of here, I remember you mentioned you'd go find this Sword of the Cherubim, and do what with the sword, exactly?"

Samyaza glared at the chess board through the glass as he answered. "The Sword of the Cherubim is probably impossible for a human to find. Yes, some of the details of the sword's origins are in the Vatican Archives, but, being written in Watcher, only myself or one of my brothers could ever translate it in this age. The only other writings in existence that are in that language would probably be some of my journals from my time in the New World before it became the Americas. I had several journals then, mostly written in Watcher. They were quite precious to me but were lost after arriving at the European port. My luggage was lost somehow, and I was forced to make do with the clothes on my back after the journey. But I would say, Priest, the sword is most likely deep underground. Otherwise, I am sure someone would have discovered it again over the millennia. The sword is not discussed much in myths, legends, or folklore. One would think humans would know by now if anyone ever found a giant fiery sword sticking up from the ground. The King Arthur legends were close, but no fire, and certainly the wrong location. The Cherubim Sword stands taller than a man, but when wielded, fits the balance and length needed for whoever swings it. Its power is so immense that only an angelic being can touch the hilt. No human, not even one possessed by a Watcher spirit, could wield the Cherubim Sword. It would turn anything unworthy of its power to ash at just a touch. Queen to F5," he said, calling out his next move.

Shepherd made his move in return and asked another question. "Bishop takes rook. You were brought to Europe by Columbus, and then you got him to take you to Italy and get an audience with the pope?"

"Nice move, Priest. Yes, I was brought before Pope Julius II those many years ago. I knew his language well by the time I arrived, and we talked at length about who I was, where I came from, and how I might be of service. I knew if I came asking for favors, I could be more scrutinized, but if I came offering assistance in some way, I could gain influence with the leadership of the time. The church seemed to have a good seat of power already in the society I observed for those few months. I was allowed to walk free in the streets of Rome outside the Vatican. I was especially impressed with the great Colosseum. I was saddened to learn how much of its history is bloodstained. What horrors mankind continued so many centuries after those great modern achievements, it sickens me still," Samyaza answered.

"In what way did you offer to help the pope?" Shepherd asked.

"I offered to research and form an expedition to recover the Cherubim Sword and the Garden of Eden. Now that there was a Watcher available who could wield it, finding the sword could help humanity. With the sword, I would regrow my wings, great, dark, dragon-scale-like wings. With the ability to fly, as an immortal, and with a weapon that could split anything, physical or spiritual, I would be once again the greatest weapon this world has ever seen or will ever see. I took the sword up in the Bekori Wars once long ago to end the most horrible conflict the world has yet to see. With the sword, I regain my true Watcher form from long ago, before we descended to help mankind." Samyaza paused here, lowered his head, and continued. "I swore that when that deed was done after the last battle had been won, I would return the sword to the angel keeping guard at the garden entrance.

I kept my word, and the sword has stayed in that place since, undisturbed."

"And so, what was Pope Julius II hoping you'd be able to do? Lead the armies of the church—or Italy? Take over and unify the entire human race under one church? One religion?" The gameplay continued, but Samyaza and Shepherd continued to ask questions unencumbered by their former rules.

"Not exactly, though, that was the hopeful plans of several others down the line." Samyaza winced, "All of which were unsuccessful."

"What do you mean exactly? Other popes tried to use you later?" Shepherd asked next.

"You have the chest of journals up there, I presume? Find the journal of Pope Clement VII and look at around 1524-1527 A.D. That should help you get the idea. I would rather not relive those moments, but the details will surely be there if you must know. It was read to me once from the journals a few hundred years later by another pope. Julius II, my original captor, was not interested in global domination. He was interested in furthering the profit and world influence from the church and his seat. He had asked me once what my motivations were for finding the sword. I explained to him that I wanted to find the sword of the Cherubim, to end my and all the Watchers' existence once and for all. We had become a virus on this planet, it seemed, taking over other creatures, manipulating the course of history here and there, causing pain and death on massive scales, whispering diseased thoughts into the consciousness of humans, only spreading pain and misery. The Watchers lost their purpose, and their minds have gone as well. I told Julius II if I found the sword, I would fall on it. By doing so, I would take my life and the spirit

158

of all Watchers back to join with the Creator to whatever end but to be gone from this world forever. Julius II, at first, saw this as an opportunity to do great good, but then realized what it might mean for his church."

Shepherd inquired, "Ending all evil influences in the world sounds like a good thing. So then, how did you end up down here if you were essentially free and working under the pope?"

"Julius II and his advisors realized that if all the Watchers were gone, and all evil was wiped out, they could be putting themselves out of a job. No one prays for sunshine if it never rains. No one would look to the church for their salvation anymore if they no longer felt the tug of what they called 'the devil' on their left shoulder. They were worried their tithe profits would decrease and their influence worldwide would diminish, so I was kept as an insurance policy. I was lulled into cooperation for a year, all while my prison was being constructed down here, built to the specifications that I was so willingly advising them on that would be necessary to contain a Watcher. After explaining how possession works, the distance we can travel, and my knowledge of the spiritual realm, I realized that it was all used to build this place deep down here, where I have been held indefinitely. Even if I went back on my vow to not possess another being, there's no one to possess that's not a *believer*, as you call them, for over a hundred meters in any direction," Samyaza explained.

Samyaza called out his next move and continued. "Pawn to C3, Priest. After I was tricked down here, with the promise of a new archive section for my research looking for the sword, I was trapped to ensure *evil* was kept on a leash. A leash that was just long enough that it would cause a little trouble out in the world and create in people a need to look to the church for salvation and guidance. However, the leash was also tight enough that the world balance was under the control of the Vatican. They would ensure that evil would never prevail and that it would never be snuffed out. And so, I have been somewhat of a *pet*, I would say, these last five centuries."

Shepherd made his move in reply on the board, "Check. Did you ever get close?"

"Did I ever get close to what, Priest? To that sycophant Julius II?" Samyaza raised his voice slightly, showing his anger.

"No, to finding the sword. How close did you get to finding it?" Shepherd asked solemnly.

Samyaza replied, "I was able to translate some of the archival texts, but I kept most of my work in Watcher so that only I could read it. That was MY insurance. Julius II knew I had never found the true location, but he also knew I narrowed it down to a hemisphere and then a continent, and I was beginning to break down the actual longitude and latitude. I was stuck on some continental drift mathematics, and I indicated last to Julius that I may be unable to find the location after all. Julius then decided I should be put here for safekeeping. After that, I would assume any attempts to recover the Sword of the Cherubim were fruitless without my assistance. Bishop takes queen if you don't mind."

"What if we could find it?" asked Shepherd, moving his next piece, paying little attention to the board now and more on the conversation at hand. "If I could get some people, professionals, with modern technology, search engines, supercomputers, translators and scientists—historians! What if we could get you the sword? Would you still want to—go through with your initial plans?"

"It is not possible. I do not see any way, but if the sword

were found, I would go and finally do what must be done to end the blight the Watchers have been on mankind. I would have to be released to recover the sword myself; no human could touch it, and no object could move it. The sword must be pulled from its resting place by the hand of an Archangel or a Watcher. I could pull the sword and then use it to end the Watchers, but again, I see no way to do it. Also, why would you let me go? Would that not be your own *job security*, as they call it, going out the door?" Samyaza pointed out.

"I want to change things!" Shepherd was paying no attention to the chess game at that point, and he felt insulted by Samyaza's insinuation. "I don't want job security! I want to change the world for the better! I could have someone find the sword. Shouldn't we try again? I'm sure there have been discoveries and new technologies invented that can take you further than you could with the limitations of the sixteenth century!"

"To what end?" Samyaza said emphatically. "You will not let me out." Samyaza laughed louder suddenly than ever before in front of Shepherd. "HA! And even if you wanted to let me out, the Entity will enact their protocols to override you, and they will keep me down here anyway. No, why bother finding the sword since I am the only one who can wield it? It is useless to the church, or anyone for that matter, without me, and here I will remain."

"I could let you out. If it was truly the right thing to do, and the best thing for humanity, and it was something that I felt was God's will—"

"The Creator has nothing to do with it, Priest!" Samyaza interrupted and yelled at Shepherd for the first time. "I was already imprisoned by the Creator once! Do you not think the Creator could have imprisoned me forever the first time in the ice if he wanted things that way? I got out! I was always eventually going to get out somehow, and I am tired of hearing humans saying what they think might or might not be 'God's will.' Keep those silly notions to yourself, Priest." Samyaza was extremely off-put and annoyed, "I have seen what you humans have decided to do when you think something is *God's will*. Your peaceful and Holy Roman Catholic Church had its crusades in the Middle East hundreds of years before I even arrived at your shores, and then it took seven hundred years for one of you to apologize for that genocide! Do not talk to me about what your kind has declared God's will again," he stated firmly.

Shepherd was sitting in shock, wide-eyed, as Samyaza yelled at him through the glass.

Samyaza realized he was actually scaring him. "I apologize. Sometimes, I forget I am talking to *The Shepherd* now, not someone else. Regardless, I will never be allowed to leave this prison. The point is mute, Priest. Bishop to H5," he said.

Shepherd moved the piece as requested. "No, it's alright. What you're saying makes sense based on the account that I read. I didn't think of it that way before. Sorry to bring up a sore subject, but I must say, if I did truly believe it would be for the good of all humanity, I'd find a way to get you out of here, Samyaza," he said plainly.

Samyaza looked at Shepherd, and one of his eyebrows shot towards the ceiling. He replied, "I have heard similar promises before, Priest. And those popes either did not keep their word, changed their minds, died, never returned, or just got told 'no' by whoever was the Entity Commander at the time and got scared. Julius II created a perfect system—one way in, one way out. There are security layers by the dozens before I would set foot outside of Vatican City. On top of all that, a checks and balances system of authority that has what is essentially a loop built-in—the pope has ultimate authority, except in the prisoner protocols, the Entity supersedes the pope's authority and is, in the end, still required to keep me here indefinitely regardless of whether or not the pope allows it."

"Just so I understand, the protocols are—rule one—the Entity will never let you go. Rule two—the pope can decide if he wants to let you out. Rule three—if a pope tries to let you out, an Entity guard will see rule one."

They both laughed a little. Samyaza added, "Yes, essentially. A perfect loophole to keep me here enacted by Pope Julius II in the original Entity agreements after I was placed in this cell." He was waving up at the ceiling.

Shepherd felt his sense of adventure kick in. He wanted to inspire Samyaza. "I think we could figure out a way."

"A way to what? I have you in a few more moves, Priest," Samyaza said, assuming Shepherd was referring to the game.

"A way to get you out of here. If it ever was what I decided, we should have a plan, Samyaza."

Samyaza started to look less like he was enjoying himself and more like he was perceiving Shepherds words as a cruel joke. "You're not serious? Please. I don't have the stomach for mind games anymore." He stood up from his chair, turned his back to Shepherd, walked over to his desk, and leaned over, resting his palms face down and arching his shoulders. Shepherd watched Samyaza as he stood there holding down his desk for a few seconds.

Shepherd then had an idea. He jumped up from his chair and looked at the small cylindrical airholes that cut through the glass. "Touch my pinky!" he called over to Samyaza.

The Watcher pulled back upright from his lean at the desk and turned halfway back to look at Shepherd with the most befuddled face he'd offered up yet. "Say again?"

"Yeah, touch my pinky! Through the airhole. It's just big enough, look." Shepherd stuck his pinky into one of the holes about shoulder height in the glass barrier. His pinky went in just over halfway through the thickness of the glass. "If you put your pinky in the hole from your side, you can touch my finger. Touch my pinky Samyaza!"

Samyaza almost looked uncomfortable, as if the idea had made him feel vulnerable for the first time in hundreds of years. "I am not going to poke my pinky in there and touch your pinky! What would be the point of that? Plus, could the guards not see us on the monitors? You will get us both in trouble with the Entity!" he said quizzically.

"You'd believe me. You'd see my true intentions and know that in my heart, I truly want to do the right thing for humanity, and if that means helping you, then I would at least try to get you out of here and find that sword. I checked the monitors up there; they can't see this area well," Shepherd said, moving closer to the side with the concrete-encased doorway.

Samyaza's eyes got a little wider. His face went stoic. He moved up to the glass again with the quick pace he used due to his tense, rigid Watcher frame. "Alright, Priest. You are the one breaking your own people's protocols, not me." With that, he stuck his pinky into the tiny airhole, and connecting with the tip of Shepherd's pinky from the other side for just a second.

Samyaza pulled his hand back and grabbed his arm that he'd just raised to the airhole with the other like he had gotten electrocuted. He lurched forward, and his eyes dashed back and forth like they were reviewing a reel of information at high speed.

Shepherd pulled his hand down and stepped back from the glass, in a bit of shock, seeing Samyaza in such a trance after just touching his fingertip for what was barely a second. Shepherd felt nothing but cold skin; the connection hadn't affected him, physically or otherwise.

Samyaza closed his eyes and slowly rose upright. He corrected his posture as he breathed out and let his hands drop to his sides. He opened his eyes and looked directly at Shepherd. "You really would help get me out, Priest. If you were sure," he proclaimed, like a revelation. Shepherd could see hope coming into his eyes.

Samyaza turned as if shaking off a feeling, realizing he was showing some emotion. "Apologies, I have not seen another's heart and mind in—a very long time."

Shepherd nodded, stepped back to the glass, and lifted his arms to rest his palms against the surface. "I would, but I would have to be sure, Samyaza. I would seek outside counsel. I'd consult with the Entity first and reason with them, but—"

"You cannot reason with the Entity, and no one will counsel you in favor of my release!" Samyaza interrupted Shepherd again, "The Entity Commander will be the most devout clergy member! His life mission would likely be to keep me here. If anything—if you do want to help me, the Entity is going to need to be the last to know. Otherwise, they will certainly bolster security around here, as a precaution, to thwart any escape plan you might concoct."

Shepherd turned and paced in front of the glass. "No, you're right, we should do the opposite. We'd have to lull them to sleep. Make them think you're my favorite pet or something down here. Get them to relax, lighten their guard, then we can more easily find cracks in the security!"

Samyaza smiled a little. "That is a good start. But there is still only one way in or out, cameras everywhere, not to mention no working door to my side of the glass." He motioned to the far wall that had a sealed-up old door with boxes stacked in front of it.

"Don't you have any other skills or abilities? Strengths that can help?" Shepherd asked.

"I have my mind, an immortal and impermeable body, and perceiving the minds of others I touch. I will not break my vow and possess someone. That is my rap sheet, so to speak, Priest. This is all I have to work with. Hence my being here for the last five hundred years!" Samyaza lamented, tossing his arms in the air slightly.

"One thing at a time, but it's not as simple as just getting you out. We'd still need to find the sword, get you to it, and then—you just kill yourself, and all your men? I mean, your Watchers?"

"Yes." Samyaza went stoic.

Shepherd realized his adventurous spirit was getting too much of a dopamine boost from the idea of planning a heist to get a prisoner out of the Vatican dungeon. He took a deep breath and sat at the chess table to stare at the board. "I don't know if I want that to happen. To sacrifice your entire— species to end evil on Earth feels wrong. This feels wrong."

Samyaza could see Shepherd was hesitating. "I saw in your heart you want to help humanity. My Watchers would gladly sacrifice themselves with me to have one last positive impact on this world, and then we can finally be at peace. The sacrifice would be a gift for all of us and the world," he insisted.

"I fear instead of your jailer—I'd become your executioner, Samyaza," Shepherd said with concern in his voice.

"Call it mercy, Priest! Mercy for me. Mercy for my Watchers! Mercy for the world, to no longer suffer our existence. And for the church! So our evil,as they have called us, may no longer burden the world, and they can focus on other important tasks that you know well can help mankind. It's a zero-sum game if I ever saw one, Priest!"

"I'm very sorry, Samyaza. I'll have to take time to think about this. The concept and result appear one way, but the actions are devious, deadly, and feel—wrong. I don't know yet what is best or what to trust. Right now, my gut says think, don't act just yet," Shepherd said.

"Of course, I understand. I have been here a long time." He laughed painfully and motioned around him. "Not as if I will be going anywhere in the meantime!"

Shepherd saw this as an opening to return the subject to the game. "Your move next, wasn't it?" he spoke.

"Knight to F3," Samyaza said, requesting his move. He continued his stance and wasn't even looking at the board.

Shepherd leaned back in his chair and looked over the board for a minute. "Oh. Wow, it looks—it looks like you've got me in a stalemate with that one."

Samyaza looked back towards the board. "Indeed, it does. Not a bad first game. Sorry, I cannot shake your hand, Priest. Any more questions for this evening?" He seemed suddenly indifferent and dismissive.

Shepherd read the room. "I think my human body needs to turn in for the night. Thank you for answering my questions and for the game. I will try to find what I can do for you,

Samyaza. I truly will."

"I believe you might, Priest."

From there, they bid each other good evening. Samyaza turned to his new box of books like he was checking for another to start fresh, and Shepherd strolled back to the elevator to make his trip to the Vatican above.

13

The Journals of Pope Clement VII

The following excerpts have been taken directly from Pope Clement VII's journal entries 1523-1534 A.D. These accounts are cataloged and transcribed verbatim.

March 2, 1525

I have decided to put this prisoner to some use. My predecessors had either little interest or, perhaps, ill-understood the power that lay in our dungeon, but I do not have such misgivings. I see the tool that our prisoner really can be for advancing the interests of the church. I have begun to question the prisoner at length most evenings. The creature seems reluctant to provide me with answers to some of my more in-depth questions on the origins of mankind before the flood, what it knows about the Creator and his plans for mankind in the future, this Sword of the Cherubim, and the journals scribed in the Watcher language in the archives. The prisoner does not trust its captors. I will have to find another way to motivate it to be forthcoming. The simplest way I can see to try and coerce this creature is to offer it something it desires. I have asked it multiple times, and the only thing the creature will give me information in exchange for is its release. Obviously, it will never be released, so I question and inquire further, and it gives me nothing. I will try to offer it a few luxuries and pleasures on my subsequent inquiry to perhaps make some headway in persuading the creature.

April 18, 1525

The bastard gives me nothing! I offered everything I could think of, and the creature spit in my face! The prisoner has not cooperated as I had hoped with my recent efforts to indulge its more, possibly, human side. I paraded everything I could think would tempt it down that damn spiral staircase.

First, I started with comfort items. I offered the creature finer linens, blankets, cushions, and pillows. The prisoner wanted nothing to do with such luxuries. I questioned it about the comforts it might like, and it said that nothing in the world would induce it to speak with me anymore on the subject of the Creator, the past, future, or even the present for that matter. I offered it still any furniture or writings I could provide for the beast's education and entertainment, and the creature did not give anything so much as a look—stubborn thing.

I went further, and had our chefs and kitchen staff provide a full menu for the prisoner. The creature examined the menu and tossed it aside on the ground as if it were a useless trinket. I persisted, thinking if it indeed does have a man's stomach in there, then the aroma of something delicious could get the best of it. The chefs prepared their most aromatic, exquisite cuisine and I had it paraded down to be laid out on a long table in front of the bars just out of the prisoner's reach. I wanted the beast to see, smell, and almost feel like it could taste the food. When the food was in front of it, I could see that the creature was somewhat tempted. The prisoner was easily able to resist the temptation, but the aroma agitated it. I progressed further in pushing the temptation by eating in front of it and then asked the guards to sit and eat in front of it as well. Hearing the bites being taken, the moans of elation from the enjoyment of each bite of something new and delicious, the smacking of lips and licking of fingers, something finally got to it.

The prisoner yelled for us to leave it be and that nothing could be done to tempt it into helping "such deviant hypocrites," as the prisoner described us.

I made a final attempt to sway the creature with one more temptation of the flesh. I had a servant fetch a few girls from a brothel near the outskirts of the city. I had them sent to the dungeons with instructions to tease and torment the man they found down there with their bodies on display for it. They were paid well for their silence and to do any number of pornographic displays with each other for the prisoner to tempt it that evening. When the whores came back up the stairs, they said the man barely looked at them. They said they did everything they were asked and more, and the prisoner sat in the corner in a chair, staring off into the stone wall at nothing, completely ignoring them.

My methods of tempting the prisoner have all failed. It pains me to have to do this in order to get results, but it is for the greater good of us all. Since these other crude methods of temptation have failed, I shall have to move towards other, more painful methods to get what is needed. The preparations are already underway.

May 22, 1525

The prisoner has given me no choice. The beast gives us no insights about itself and its abilities, no information about the fellow "Watchers," as it calls them, that possess our kind from this other realm it sometimes speaks of. I have had the Entity guards working day and night to prepare machines, cranks, knives, saws, a kiln, water tanks, and pulleys outside the prisoner's cell. It has had to sit and watch them construct everything; I have wanted it to see all that's being prepared. Hopefully, this will help build fear of what is to come. We will have our darkest torture guards from Rome's prisons break the creature apart until it speaks. I will get the creature to tell me what I want to know! I need to find out what it knows to help me gain some other type of leverage over the cardinals. The Vatican treasuries have all but run dry in the last year. I have nothing left to pay them off. With what the prisoner can reveal, I am sure there will be new ways found to gain power for the church so that I can regain the wealth needed for my plans. The treaties I have strategically aligned to increase our military potential rely on my control over those greedy bastards. If I cannot find something else to control the cardinals, I need something I can use to get more coin to buy them off longer. If I cannot increase my political influence abroad, I fear my grand plan for unifying all of Italy and faiths under my papacy will fall to pieces.

April 29, 1526

The prisoner is genuinely a fantastic specimen. I am infuriated that I have still been unable to gain any new information from the creature. Still, I have learned much from the—experiments that the dungeons of Rome's best floggers and scourgers have been implementing to break it.

They have already tried stretching it on the racks for days on end, and the creature is firm in its silence. We have learned that its body is unbreakable by any means we possess. We have tried cutting, breaking, bashing, burning, and nothing will tear the creature's skin. Its bones cannot be broken under the crush of heavy cranks. The creature is unable to be stretched, and the racks have broken under the unshifting power of its form. It is unlike anything I have ever seen. One torturer crushed glass and, using a grotesque muzzle, forced the shards down the creature's throat. It screamed in agony for two days, passing the glass, and still it offered no information. The beast's body, inside and out, is entirely impenetrable.

I traveled to the dungeon myself several times to see these miraculous findings. As far as we can tell, this Watcher creature's body is immortal. It has also been confirmed from testimony in stories and other journals and by observation that it does not age in any physical way we have detected. The prisoner needs no food or water, nor shall it get any without giving up more information! We cannot seem to break its body or its spirit. There is a human part of it that must be feeling the pain. The screams are blood-curdling. The creature's body does not break, cut, or bruise, but it reacts as though it feels every slash, blow, and crank from the different tortures unleashed on it. If it does feel the pain, this begs the question of whether, if continued, the creature could eventually break. If we cannot break the beast's body, perhaps we could break its spirit. Attempts have been made around the clock for days to find this creature's tipping point but with no solution in sight.

June 27, 1526

I thought I had the bastard! I had found something I thought would get under the prisoner's skin momentarily. I found reference and testimony of another Watcher possessing a human who had come from the New World with the prisoner. I had my investigators in the Entity track that traveler down. He was in France. The possessed man was captured and brought here by true believers it could not possess. The demon was strapped to the racks and tortured in front of our prisoner. The prisoner called the demon in the man's body Yekun.

This Yekun called out from inside the man, begging its leader, Samyaza, the prisoner, to do nothing for it. At one point, the demon, Yekun, said something about Samyaza, "finding the sword." The demon asked Samyaza to give nothing, to say nothing to help save it. But then, this Yekun's last words before leaving the poor sailor on his death were, "Samyaza! You promised us all! You swore to bring back our world!" When the man finally died, the demon was released from the dead body into the spirit realm to wander again. Hopefully, it will be a long time before it finds another poor, lost soul to take over. The prisoner screamed and wept for days after that but still refused our questions.

September 16, 1526

I have not been able to find the Sword of the Cherubim. It is the only possibility to come from these attempts to gain information from the Watcher, and it seems the sword will never be found. The demon, Yekun, mentioned a sword, and we found writings of a Sword of the Cherubim in some of the prisoner's journals. There were also references to this sword and its possible location in the archives. Still, even our most learned scholars and linguists have not been able to translate the texts to attempt an expedition in search of such a weapon. I will have them continue to attempt to decipher and scour the archives for more information and clues of this sword's resting place. If it is as powerful as the Watchers have indicated, it could be the weapon that turns the tide for our cause.

November 4, 1526

I have nothing left to barter with. The treasuries have run dry, and I have debts with neighboring countries and lords that have begun to ask for return payment. The cardinals are beginning to push back since their pockets have started to become light, the greedy sinners. If they only knew the true scope of my plan, what I am trying to accomplish. If Italy can be unified under my authority and have its own military force, we can begin to take back the empire that once built this great church. The Watcher prisoner is the key to everything; though I have nothing else left to use to persuade the creature. I have resorted to every final measure concocted by mankind for pain, suffering, temptation, and desire. The dungeon masters plagued it with every gadget and weapon that they could find in existence. They even shot a canon at the bastard! None will cause even a scratch to the Watcher's body.

January 11, 1527

There has been an exciting discovery with the prisoner today. Most recently, the dungeon workers have concocted ways to render the Watcher unconscious. It cannot be burned except for the creature's hair, which grows back quickly, but it can drown and it can be frozen. Every time it drowned, no matter how long it was left underwater, it would always revive on its own once taken out of the tank. The torturers came up with a plan to drown the Watcher when winter came and freeze its body with snow and ice pack. It is currently sitting on ice now. We are leaving it till the ice melts, but I fear the creature will stand up and brush off the snow once spring arrives.

February 3, 1527

I have sent everyone away and cleared the entire dungeon torture chamber area. The place was foul and disgusting. The prisoner is on ice for now. If the Watcher revives, I will leave it. I have no more use for the creature. It has provided nothing; thus, I will offer it nothing: no comforts or conversations. I will keep the Entity guarding from the post above the stairs, but there will be no need for further trips into the depths below the Vatican to speak to that creature. It will rot in there, forgotten for eternity as far as I am concerned. Now, I find myself forced to beg for more support and scrape for other sources of credit. I fear I shall soon have the emperor knocking at our gates if I cannot maintain sovereignty. The protocols will be such that only these journals are left as a reminder of these events. If this Watcher were ever to get out, may my successors beware the creature's vengeance on the Chair of Saint Peter. May the prisoner be left and forgotten, lest it be unleashed and wreak havoc.

14

Passing the Centuries

S hepherd exited the elevator 120 meters below the center of St. Peter's Square, at the cell of Samyaza the Watcher, imprisoned deep beneath the Vatican. Shepherd was in his usual evening pajama attire: hoodie, flip flops, and plaid pajama pants. He walked to the glass wall between his room and the cell that had kept Samyaza prisoner for half a millennium. Behind the glass, Samyaza was sitting in his chair, watching something on the television in the corner towards the elevator. He was wearing a pearl-colored Panama hat with a black band on it.

Shepherd had to ask about the hat first thing. "Trying a new look?" he said sarcastically as he approached the glass to greet Samyaza.

Samyaza reached for his remote and paused whatever documentary he was currently watching. "Ha! Not exactly, Priest. It is these damn lights. They are always on."

"I brought you some more books." Shepherd passed the books into the two-way drawer between the glass. "There's seriously no switch down here? Anywhere?" he added.

Samyaza motioned above at the lights as he walked over to pull the books through and examine them. "There is no switch for these lights as far as can be found, and I have checked high and low. The lights occasionally go out during maintenance or power outages, but never for long. When a bulb goes out, the Entity guards notice it on the security cameras and come down and replace it within the day. The lights are always on to keep me visible on these old cameras they have down here. Thanks for getting me *Don Quixote*, by the way. What is this one?" he said as he held up a second book.

"*The Count of Monte Cristo*?" Shepherd read the cover through the glass aloud. "I added that one. Thought you might like it. It's about love, betrayal, and a prison escape."

"I am surprised a book about an escape is even on the approved Entity list for my reading." Samyaza handled the books back and forth with a quick juggle between his palms. He dropped the books with a thud on top of his short pile of the next ones he planned to read.

"It's a classic. I think the Entity is more concerned with ensuring you don't consume more modern bits of information and ideologies."

Samyaza nodded and motioned back at the lights. "The fixtures are also sealed and only accessible through slots in the ceiling in your adjoining room. I cannot even pop out a bulb if I wanted to. I wear this hat, I have a few others or a hood, or cover my face with something if I need a break from the constant watchful light that I am kept under."

Shepherd moved to his small agenda for the evening, "That is one of the things I wanted to ask you about tonight, Samyaza. I'm putting together a list of changes to request to make your cell more comfortable, along with some improvements for my concerns, like having another way to get out of here if the power goes out and the elevator shaft is my only escape. I have a meeting with Janis at the end of the month. He's the current Commander of the Entity and is in charge of the prisoner protocols. Do you have any requests for changes down here? Besides a light switch?" Shepherd was half joking but jotted down *light switch* all the same.

They talked at length about the different improvements that either thought could give Samyaza some chance to feel more human. Shepherd made some suggestions based on his more modern world knowledge, and Samyaza shared a few things that he thought might make existing in his cell more palatable over time. After they chatted at some length, the two found themselves sitting down in front of the chess board again. Samyaza asked this time if Shepherd wanted another game.

"Fancy a game, Priest?" Samyaza asked.

"As long as I get another question for each capture?" Shepherd requested back.

"If you must, Priest."

Shepherd began the game of chess with his tall ivory knight. The two had gotten a good rhythm for their play, with Samyaza politely calling out his moves from behind the glass while Shepherd fumbled with the odd-shaped pieces on the board.

Shepherd waited till he got his first capture this time before saying anything. "Rook takes pawn. Samyaza, I read the journals of Pope Clement VII." Shepherd paused to see Samyaza's reaction.

Samyaza was sitting in his tall backed, green chair. He had his chin resting on his one fist propped upright on his elbow, sitting on his knee. He reached back and scratched the back of his head and twitched. It was like he was recalling a painful memory, and the psychological trauma was causing him to tense up. "Yes. I appreciate you taking the time for that. It was something you needed to understand, but I did not have any desire to be a part of the retelling. I knew what was in those journals, and it was detailed enough for you to learn what that time was like for me from his awful words."

"Samyaza, it may not mean much, but I apologize for all the pain, torture, and brutality that has been brought upon you by those men. And for Yekun. I feel there are not words enough to apologize for the horrors visited on you all those years ago. I have to know, what has happened since that time? The journals tell very little from what I have found of the last four hundred years. Why didn't all the other popes write about you?"

Samyaza answered, "Very soon after my time with lovely old Clement VII, Rome was sacked. I suppose political powers struggling and shifting high above had no time for journals in a chest or to get to know some relic in the basement. I became like a bad penny, occasionally getting noticed, looked over, and then just as casually discarded as a burden, a shameful reminder, or a quandary that no one had the stomach for anymore."

"When did the elevator get put in? And the phone? The modern lights?" Shepherd rolled a few questions into one.

"John Paul II," was Samyaza's answer. "He figured out the entrance in the late 1980s. Found his way down here, and he was the last pope to sit at this table with me and share a game."

"When was that?"

"I think it was 2003, if memory serves. John Paul had the elevator installed in the late nineties since he was having trouble with the stairs and wanted a way to get down in his weakened condition as he got older. Like you, he was elected younger than most but did not find me down here for about a decade. He had drawn the same conclusion as all the others who had taken the time to crack open the journals and find their way down—that I was best left here, contained as the potential lesser of two evils in their perspective.

My presence weighed heavily on John Paul. There were times he questioned whether to have the doorway excavated to be able to let me out, but he died before ever taking any action. He had the bars changed to glass to give me more of a sense of 'being cared for, rather than imprisoned,' as he put it. I was given my own small library to draw books from, and from time to time, new books that the Entity approved were brought down. John Paul II was the only one willing to go against the Entity's protocols. He and the Entity Commander at the time had come to the compromise together that if the information I was getting was reviewed and approved—what harm could it do? As long as I could not leave, and if there was only one way in or out, there were no issues. I got new furniture just before the door had been walled up. Losing the door was a condition for the Entity to allow construction to be done on the elevator shaft, and the stairs were sealed up with rubble from above to maintain the single entrance or exit protocol. The Entity liked the idea of having me in a big glass box with no holes, but John Paul was able to get the drawer added so I could get personal items and books."

"Where did the television come from? John Paul II, too?" Shepherd asked.

"That was a final gift from John Paul II, yes. He made a final request with the Entity that I be given access to any new forms of mass entertainment that the Entity could approve. It was added as part of their protocol, after much debate in his later years, that I would be allotted new forms of entertainment to 'maintain a connection to the present world' as he put it in the language of the request to the Entity. He did not know how long I would be here or if other popes would read the right journals to find the entrance. The protocols require journal entries to be vague and leave out certain details. Otherwise, those sections are omitted and not enclosed in the chest after that pope passes."

"The Entity reviews the journals before they become a part of the collection? I've wondered about that. Why hasn't any pope ever included a clue of sorts to finding you down here?" Shepherd asked as he captured another piece, trying to keep the game going in the background of their conversation.

"The Entity has clear instructions that on the death or retirement of any pope, the Ring of the Fisherman key, the chest, and any evidence of the prisoner is to be removed and placed under the guard of the Entity immediately. Julius II wanted me not just safeguarded by the Entity but forgotten as much as possible. As far as what gets put in the chest and why, I do not know more details. I am unsure if the Entity always thought it best to continue the tradition or if they chose not to bother, so the secrets stayed buried sometimes. There have been several popes that either never got around to the journals, never figured out how to get down here, or were not curious enough to investigate. I have had stretches of decades with no one entering the observation room other than to change a light bulb or do some other maintenance. One time, a man came down, in plain clothes, looked in, and walked back out. Still, to this day, I have no idea who that was or if he was supposed to be down here, but it was years before I saw anyone else, and no Entity guard ever came to explain."

"Someone just waltzed down the stairs, took a look at you, and then walked away?"

"I swear. No idea who it was," Samyaza said as he threw his hands in the air in dismay.

"So then, you got a TV and online streaming—because John Paul II made sure that those protocol options would be continued after his death, and they approved streaming TV for you?"

"Yes. There was a—softer Entity Commander at that time, I suppose. It is only incoming information. I prefer to learn what I can from reading, but it is truly wonderful to see some of the things going on in the world today. Some of the new visual effects you humans have created to show your stories are enjoyable. I had to learn quickly about how not everything on television is real. I am confused as to why there are so many programs about murderers and serial killers. Are these popular out in the world?"

"It's something of a recent—I'd call it—unhealthy societal trend to watch these killer documentaries. It's quite morbid."

"Priest, even I know from down here that humans being entertained by murder is not a *recent trend*," Samyaza said. "Remember the Colosscum?"

"Fair point," Shepherd agreed. He fit in another question, "I know Clement VII mentioned stopping giving you food—has no one offered you food this entire time?"

Samyaza reluctantly answered, "No one seems to want to bother with the second half of that equation. I stopped eating and drinking water after I was first put down here, and I soon no longer needed a bucket for my—excrement. Since that time, the Entity has yet to be convinced that there is a good reason to give me an unnecessary luxury that would create a new chore for the guards. No one wants to clean up my shit, Priest. Knight to A3, check."

Shepherd had begun to lose focus on the chess game. He had one more question he'd been holding on to. "Queen takes knight. Has anyone come close to letting you out?"

Samyaza focused on the board but continued the discussion, "There was one time I almost left this prison; the only time really, it seems. It was during your World War II. Pope Pius XII was the pontiff at the time."

Shepherd was entirely off the chess game now and focused on the story. "Did he want to let you out to find the sword so that you could be used as a weapon like what Clement VII wanted?"

"No, he did not think they could find the sword, and the Entity still would not let me work on the Watcher language texts in the archive to finish my research anyway. Also, the Entity was still sworn not to let me out. Even if Pius XII had decided to let me go, with no sword, there was no point."

"So, Pius thought you falling on the sword and killing the Watchers could be enough to end World War II immediately? How?" Shepherd was on the edge of his seat.

Samyaza replied, "It seemed that way to Pius XII once I advised him that Azazel, one of my Watchers, was at the head of the Nazi Regime."

"A Watcher had possession of someone in Nazi leadership? Like a general?"

Samyaza looked up from the board to meet Shepherd's eyes, "No Priest. Azazel was in the body of a human called Adolf Hitler."

Shepherd couldn't care less about the chess game at this point. He moved pieces carelessly, more focused on what Samyaza had to say. "A Watcher possessed Hitler?" Shepherd asked next.

"Yes, Azazel. He was one of my chiefs in the time before the Great Descent when we arrived here on the physical plane of Earth. Azazel was the holder of the Watcher's collective cruelty, greed, and desire for power. He also had the ability, in Watcher form, to manipulate minerals. He learned this gave him the ability, on Earth, to influence the chemicals in a human's brain on touch, and later, when a human was nearby, he could alter their minds, influencing their hormones, their serotonin levels, and their very consciousness. He was, and still is, a master of manipulation. Us Watchers are all connected. He carries the burden of our awful traits throughout his entire existence, still to this day.

Pope Pius XII was one of the few in the last century to crack open most of the pope chest journals. He had already been visiting me before the war with Germany started. He brought one of Hitler's speeches down here, typed out soon after the war had begun. I reviewed the speech word by word and recognized my old friend Azazel in the writing. It was in a new language, but it was the words and agenda of the Watcher Azazel, who I once thought I had killed, ending the Bekori Wars, the battles of the nephilim, before the time of the flood, but I was mistaken. Azazel was the first Watcher to be detached from his physical form by the Sword of the Cherubim long before the Great Deluge. He is how we first discovered that something tied us Watchers together and connected us through the phantom realm. Azazel's spirit was still in the phantom realm, and my body linked him here, in the physical world, allowing him to possess others, as all the Watchers do up there now." Samyaza motioned to the surface above. "He has been floating from one host to another since that discovery longer than any other Watcher. Azazel has caused more chaos and cruelty in this world likely than all my other Watchers combined. It is difficult to blame him for these things if you consider the fact that he genuinely never acts on his own. He bears the burden of all two hundred Watchers' malice, greed, power-mongering, and heartless traits. If Yekun was correct, Azazel may not even be aware of who he is or what he is doing. I'm sure this Hitler would have been awful enough on his own, but being possessed by Azazel gave him access to knowledge and powers that made his warpath many times more potent because of the grip he had on the Nazi party leaders and their minions.

I do not know where Azazel has been since the time of that great war. I am the only Watcher with a physical body, so I have not lost my mind. The rest of my Watchers are out there wandering leaderless, with no idea who they are anymore—lost in a fog of overlapping consciousnesses latching onto them as they drift from body to body, mind to mind. I was the anchor that the Creator left on Earth to hold their spirits in a purgatory that would only wreak havoc on humanity. I wish so much that I could end it for all of them, to end this for myself, to end the pain that we Watchers have brought into this world."

Shepherd sat quietly for a minute after listening to Samyaza. "Your move, Priest." Samyaza broke the silence.

Shepherd moved a piece and captured another one of Samyaza's pawns. "Check. Samyaza, what is the Creator like? Can you describe him? Also, could you explain more about

Watchers and Archangels and what connects all this? What can you tell a mere mortal like me to make sense of spirituality?"

Samyaza looked puzzlingly through the glass back at Shepherd. He said, "Alright, let me give you sort of a rundown, Priest. You've been patient and an enjoyable new companion these last few months." Samyaza aggressively stepped up from the board and paced the room with his hands crossed, holding one wrist in his other behind his back. "The Creator is not what everyone here seems to believe now, and that is honestly the best I can say about that. He does not talk to anyone anymore like everyone always says in these movies and books. It's all in their heads. You would not believe the power of your own brain. You cannot understand the Creator any more than you can interpret the wind. I suppose that is a good analogy though for it—wind. A man hears and smells something in the wind and—perhaps with his senses, can feel the flow of it, but a dog smelling the wind can tell much more from the same sniff of air. If the energy of the Creator, energy is the closest word you have, is like the wind, the Archangels would be like bloodhounds. They can interpret the wind better than anyone. Us Watchers once had a general grasp, but the Creator cut us off from that ability when we first fell to Earth."

"So, Watchers observed humans, and then you came to Earth to help them, but what is the function and purpose of the Archangels?" Shepherd asked.

"They don't do anything you would perceive as interference, I suppose. They influence nature and spirit; they are much more powerful than us Watchers in the phantom realm. They can influence the physical realm through possession or a whisper in an unsuspecting ear with an idea." Samyaza sat back down and glanced over the chess board.

"Archangels possess people too? I thought only demons—or Watchers did that?"

"The angels can do anything we Watchers can, but they are not bound to the physical realm like I am. You could not trap an angel in a cage like this."

Shepherd made a move on the board and continued, "What purpose do the Archangels really serve then? Are there different ranks?"

"There are the projections, which you humans call angels. They're simply glimpses of Archangels placed through space and time at moments predetermined by the Archangels. Since they have some power of divination, they have the ability to project themselves and appear to be in many places at once. Their real purpose would best be described as memory. Archangels are the memory of this universe. They are the servants of the Creator, the gatekeepers of the past before and after this realm. They have observed all that is and ever will be," Samyaza replied.

"Do the Archangels want anything?" Shepherd asked.

"They have no souls, and they are hollow shells of armor lining the corridors of a realm that the Creator and humans have not tapped into for thousands of years. Does a hollow object want for anything?" Samyaza said disdainfully.

"I guess not," Shepherd lamented. "What about the one referred to as Satan, Lucifer?"

"That name has been tied to many different beings and creatures across the lifetime of this Earth. But the angelic Lucifer was cast from the phantom realm long ago. Yes, he is in hell, as you would probably put it, but there are no real devils, demons, or angels there. Lucifer had all his desires and dissent removed from his consciousness by the Creator and was given the task of turning the engine of the Earth at its core. He toils and turns moving rock and molten metal deep in the planet's center. His legend was attached to all manner of evil throughout history, and to my Watchers, but no *Satan* is sitting on a throne of hell with a pitchfork, or boatman, or Hades. Even according to your own legends, what did Lucifer do exactly? He made one suggestion to one woman, to eat one apple. Was that serpent to blame? Or would you blame the Creator who planted the tree in the first place? This is where the details get confused in human logic with all the blame tracking back to the Creator, but it is not that simple."

"This is a lot to wrap my head around. The Archangels don't sound very important."

"The Archangels are the equivalent of security guards at a mall now. They have some influence but do not really use it for anything of value anymore. They probably would not even notice us Watchers dropping off the face of the Earth. Knight to D5, check." Samyaza finished his explanation as he called out his next move.

"Do the Creator and the Archangels know you're down here?" Shepherd asked next as he moved Samyaza's piece. Samyaza was moving towards a checkmate now. It was going to take a lot of practice for Shepherd to get even close to Samyaza's undoubtedly master skills.

"It is not as simple as that, Priest. There's nothing the Archangels and the Creator don't know, per se. It is more of a question of—whether my being here is something they intend to do anything about. We Watchers first thought the Creator only knew what we reported, but we soon learned the one thing you humans did get right, which is that the Creator does perceive all space and time. He does not have a hand in

189

everything, though, and we are all a part of this universe of his creation. So essentially, yes and no."

"That makes—sense. Doesn't explain much though," Shepherd deduced. He retreated his last piece, seeing already what Samyaza was planning on the board to finish him off.

"Queen to B1, and I believe that is checkmate, Priest. These details will never make sense in any human terms. The picture is too large, and you cannot zoom out far enough to perceive it. The closest approximation might be—this chess board. The Creator made the board and knows where everything on the board can and should move. It has rules, but it has trillions of options. Picture you and I playing chess as the Archangels and the Watchers. The Watchers manipulate, while the Archangels influence. We are moving pieces on the board while the world keeps spinning. In the end, the game plays out one way or another. Some moves are obvious, others are unexpected." Samyaza sat back and peered at the finished game he'd just won. "Good game, Priest."

"It was. I think my chops are coming back to me. I haven't played in so long. Maybe if I keep practicing with you enough, I'll become a formidable opponent," Shepherd said as he pulled the pieces back to their original position.

Samyaza moved his green chair back to his TV viewing position and plopped down.

Shepherd recognized his queue to leave. He stood up and adjusted his hoodie over his pajama waistband. "Well, I'll be meeting with Janis soon, the Entity Commander, about the improvements we want," he said.

Based on the records in the pope chest, Samyaza seemed to be opening up more comfortably than in any of his previous histories. Shepherd wondered if it was him or if Samyaza maybe just didn't care anymore.

"I look forward to hearing how that goes. Take care, Priest," Samyaza casually called out while flicking on his TV.

15

The Shadow

J anis Borgman, The Head Commander of the Entity Organization of the Vatican, age seventy-one, was a retired Dutch National Police Detective from the Netherlands. Janis was a tall, lanky man with jagged features that gave him a *Lerch from The Addams Family* kind of look. He had a cumbersome Dutch accent, was always clean-shaven, and had a buzz cut he kept neat. The man hadn't been at the Vatican long before becoming somewhat of a staff urban legend. He was nicknamed "The Shadow" after it was once brought up in a gossip cluster of the staff. He managed to always linger up behind people when they were talking. Janis towered over people like a stretched shadow on a wall opposite a low-hanging light. Janis was a giant, but he seemed to have a skill for moving in and out of rooms and conversations without others noticing how he came and went.

A church leader at the parish he attended in the Netherlands recommended Janis as "the perfect man for working within the Vatican Entity."

His family had tragically died in a drunk driver accident

shortly after his retirement. He was in mourning and needed a purpose in his life; he found it in the Entity. Janis was a man of the most vigorous devout faith. The loss of his family was the catalyst that incited him to devote his life entirely to the church. He had no need for money or desire for power, making him incorruptible. With no family ties left that could sway his judgment or be used against him as leverage, Janis, indeed, was the perfect man for running the Entity.

Shepherd had scheduled a meeting with Janis several weeks in advance. He'd researched in the pope journals and on the protocols, directives, and authority of the Entity to prepare for rebuttals from the commander, and so the delay was put to good use by Shepherd. The location for their rendezvous was Janis' office, where he held all his meetings if he could help it; controlling the atmosphere and the space was very important to him. One of the Entity guards in training, who was working at the headquarters as an assistant, led Shepherd to Janis' office. Janis popped from his seat behind a small, practical office desk to shake Shepherd's hand. Janis had recently started using a cane for some arthritis issues, and he leaned on it as he rounded his desk to meet Shepherd.

The two greeted each other with a handshake and a mutual nod. Janis motioned for Shepherd to sit in his guest chair across from his desk. His office was simplistic; the desk had a small '90s tube TV in the corner facing Janis. The rest of the office resembled what you'd expect in any police station bullpen. The surface of the desk was spotless, besides a large notepad and pen in the center. The dark, green painted room was dimly lit with wall sconce lights, like in a movie theater hallway, and a small lamp on the opposite end of the desk from the tiny tube TV. The chair Shepherd sat in leaned back far, too far. He felt more like he'd have to lean forward since tilting back left him staring at the break in the ceiling above Janis' head. Shepherd wondered if Janis had chosen the chair because of its obvious discomfort.

"I know we met briefly on the day of your appointment, but I am glad to be finally sitting down one-on-one with *The Shepherd*," Janis said, with a coy emphasis on Shepherd's nickname as pope.

Shepherd thought, w*hatever respect he has for the church, it may not extend to the pontiff's seat.* He was having a last-minute, panicked moment of self-doubt about whether this conversation would be fruitful. *Janis at least jumped up to shake my hand. Maybe he respects the office, not the man?*

Shepherd shook the feeling as best he could. He replied, "I've been looking forward to this as well. I've been making it a point to get to know everyone on Vatican staff and guard."

Janis sat back down at his desk and flipped open his notebook. "I take notes for all my meetings and interviews. I hope this is acceptable?"

"Yes, by all means."

"I hear you are originally from New Zealand, but you immigrated to Australia when you went to university, is that right?" he queried, fumbling his pen towards his notepad's next blank page.

Shepherd glossed past the frustration of hearing his catch-phrase for the thousandth time with a sigh before answering. "Yes, I stayed in Australia. Since then, I've been back home many times for visits with family."

"Could not quite place the accent otherwise, but that makes sense now. I'm Dutch, but everyone always thinks I am German. Well, Father Shepherd, since you set this meeting, how can I be of service to my church?" Janis asked, folding his hands at the edge of his desk closest to his chest.

Shepherd began, "Thank you. I appreciate the time. I've been wanting to discuss a few things with you about the Entity guard and some of their protocols, specifically the protocol for the prisoner, Samya —"

"Ahem!" Janis cleared his throat and waved his office aide, who was still standing at the door, out of the room. Once the door was closed, he said, "Apologies, please continue, Father."

"Yes," Shepherd became unavoidably quieter after the aide was rushed out conspicuously. "The uh—prisoner had some concerns I would like to help with, and I have a few of my own to speak with you about. There may be a need to make more modern changes and approaches to these protocols," he said, waiving the protocol notebook.

"I have reviewed the logs from your visits to see the prisoner. Pope Francis never went down. He reviewed the journals once and had a few questions, but I guess he never figured out the entrance to the security room from his chamber. I'm aware of some of the prisoner's concerns from previous commander logs. I also have logs with details from many previous Entity Commanders. You say you also have concerns of your own, Father Shepherd?" Janis asked.

"Yes, for simple starters, we should be able to get the man some newer, more modern clothes, toiletries, and facilities to make his—uh—stay more comfortable," Shepherd suggested. "I prepared a list of some specific items for you. I mixed his requests and some of my own, too, if you approve, of course." Shepherd handed him the list.

Janis took the list and tucked it between a notebook page, "I'll review it, and we'll see what we can do," he stated firmly.

Not even going to look at it in front of me? What a power move. "Next, I have some bigger items that I think we should consider," Shepherd said, flipping to a page of notes he'd prepared.

Janis raised an eyebrow and flipped the list from the notebook back onto his desk. Something on the list caught his eye and made him lurch back. "Bigger requests than a modern full bathroom?" he said with a raised voice.

"There really should, at the very least, be a second way to get up from that—that dungeon! What if I'm down there and the power goes out?" Shepherd posed.

Janis pursed his lips, "There are generators and backup redundancies."

"Fair, but what if it's mechanical failure? What if I am stuck down there for days waiting for a crew to fix something, and I have no food or water?" Shepherd pointed out.

Janis was impressed with Shepherd's passion, and that he had been giving this some serious thought. "I'll see what we can do about the stairs being opened back up, but why does the creature need modern plumbing? A sponge bath basin, some soap, and a safety razor have always been the standard protocol, and they've been sufficient, in my opinion, and that of previous Entity Commanders. The Chair of Saint Peter originally made these protocols, but they cannot be so easily changed. There must be cause and moral obligation. I appreciate your concerns for the prisoner's comfort, but this is not the Hilton, father."

Shepherd noted that Janis called Samyaza a *creature* just as Pope Clement XII had done in his journals. "No, you're absolutely right, commander. This isn't a fancy hotel. This is the Vatican. The most holy city of this most holy church, and we have a prisoner. We are not a hotel, and yet we have staff, meal service, and guests. We are not a prison, and yet we have a prisoner, security, and guards. And just like we accommodate guests as if we were a modern luxury hotel, we should accommodate our prisoner the same as a modern prison. Should we not?"

Janis seemed slightly taken off guard by Shepherd's clean cut rebuttal. He couldn't refute Shepherd's remark. "We should—that is humane and appropriate, Shepherd," Janis agreed reluctantly.

Shepherd's firm *take charge* approach tactic worked so far, but he knew Janis might be picking his battles.

"So, along with updated *amenities*, you're asking for a second entrance? That goes against one of the primary protocols for the prisoner. There cannot be a second entrance to the prisoner's quarters. This rule was part of the original protocols and will not be amended by us. That is actually out of my hands," Janis explained.

"True, there can't be a second entrance, and there won't be," Shepherd corrected.

Janis's expression moved to irritation. "ONE elevator and ONE set of stairs make TWO entrances, my dear Shepherd," he condescended back, counting on held-up fingers.

"But they both meet at the security room upstairs, don't they?" Shepherd rebutted back.

Janis pondered that comment for a minute. Shepherd did have a point. Although both entrances led to the security room, in essence, only one entry point needed to be monitored. It was a gray area, but it would fit the protocol. "Yes, that's true. If we cleared the stairs and repaired the old sections— ahem—it's going to be costly and would be over our budget," he said.

"I've taken a look at that. I'm glad you brought the budget up. The budget for the prisoner protocol chapter of the Entity hasn't been enough in centuries. It's time to make up for years of neglect with this program. John Paul II made several changes, but poor Samyaza—"

Bang!

Janis aggressively flipped his thick notebook shut. He leaned forward in his elbows and folded his bony, dry fingers together in front of his chin. Shepherd's body language shifted him back into his chair slightly in response.

"Father, I know very well your reasoning. It's just like your mission, *save your neighbors first, save the church later*. I understand you want to save the world and your neighbors, but why do you want to save this creature? Surely, the church comes before the creature? I have a different prerogative than you, father. I say, my Creator comes first, church second. Why should the resources of the church go to some demon prisoner's comfort? If anything, let me have some funds for the Entity to hire a few more guards so we can have a stronger security rotation. Once, a guard had to use the restroom for too long, and a tourist got through and somehow used the extra badge to the elevator. He went down and saw the prisoner and came right back up, but the security is too light as it is for me to do my job effectively."

Janis was a devout man. From his seat, the church came first. His perspective of the world and concerns about its salvation were checked at the entrance of the Vatican when he took up his post as commander. The man had one mission—to serve the church and to do that by keeping the prisoner locked up tight. He didn't care about the world or his neighbors; the world took away everything he cared about, and one of his neighbors killed his family. The Creator's church saved him. Shepherd wasn't going to convince Janis by appealing to his humanity or mercy for a *creature* like Samyaza.

Shepherd persisted, "This isn't comfort. This is penance for what has been done to Samyaza."

Janis Scoffed. "Penance? For what? Do you know what that creature is? He is no man! Have you not learned the lessons of the chest? Because I've read some old logs that tell a thing or two. Some things that should be kept secret. I'll keep them well enough and use them to do what good I can. But that thing in the dungeon and its minions out there roaming the world are why this church is so important and necessary! Some demon lord lurking in the basement is of no concern for the funding this Entity receives other than to bulk up security, as far as I'm concerned."

"It's not only up to you, Janis. I do have some authority here as pope. And this penance I speak of is for his cruel torture and imprisonment over the centuries."

"What is it you speak of, Shepherd? Please do not reveal too much; consider the protocols. What can you tell me?" Janis wasn't sure what Shepherd was referring to.

"It's in the chest. In a former pope's own hand, the man was tortured endlessly in ways no human could ever withstand!"

"Well, there you have it! He isn't human then! So, how do we even know the creature was harmed at all? Could have been a ruse to elicit pity!" Janis' words were cold. "We both have to agree on any changes in the protocol. Look, I'll consider reopening the stairs. Any broken sections are getting ladders; we're not pouring concrete down there. And if you find the funding for more guards for me, then we may have a compromise."

Shepherd perked up at that olive branch. "Before you agree—you probably should read the section requesting that the door be reopened and updated with modern security."

Janis stood up and grabbed his cane, leaning to the side of his desk. "Absolutely not!"

Shepherd grabbed the protocol booklet again, "I've checked, and the door being removed isn't even in the protocol! I've read this cover to cover, and there was originally a door and a key, even when there were iron bars. They just blocked off the old door when the stairs were sealed shut. If we install double modern doors with everything reinforced to meet the requirements to hold Samya—the prisoner, then we are still in protocol guidelines." Shepherd felt he needed to add more to convince Janis. He lumped in, "And it would give the guards a chance to check the cell for contraband if we set it up with a holding room and—"

Janis interrupted as he looked at the list again, "But there's still the matter of this plumbing request and the budget!"

Shepherd turned his notebook to another marked page. "I have a plan for that, too. I've worked with Marco to find some local contractors that do pipe and equipment assembly work for private bunkers and bomb shelters. They have a whole kit and system that we can put down there. The system has pumps that work to move the freshwater down and the gray water back up. We can have your approved staff trained on how it gets assembled; the company makes the system to specifications, delivers it, and your Entity staff will install it. No plumber should have to even set foot on Vatican soil for any of this," Shepherd said as he grinned, pleased with himself.

Janis wasn't giving up without a fight, "There's still the

matter of the budget, Father Shepherd. As you said yourself, the prisoner protocol budget is already minuscule."

"Yes, I have a plan for that too. We'll be selling an art piece from the museum to cover the cost. The gallery curators will decide which piece will be easiest to part with. As for the continuing expenses, until I develop a better solution with our accountants for a permanent change, some of my salary that I've already refused to receive can go to the prisoner's caretaking and well-being."

"I'll have no such thing! I will not accept funds from the sale of church property or the Vatican coffers used for the creature's comfort."

Luckily, after working with Marco, Shepherd anticipated Janis would draw a line there, and Shepherd had one move held back, "Fine then, I have full authority over a portion of *The Flock* fund from the new website. I'll supply funds for the prisoner protocol maintenance updates and security changes. As I said, this is long overdue, and we won't be doing any half-measures."

"What about the board to oversee the direction of the funds?" Janis asked.

"That hasn't been established yet, though it is in the works. I have control over what special projects I deem worthy should receive some funding here and there," Shepherd clarified.

Janis sat back in his chair, looking somewhat exhausted, "Why do you insist on taking such good care of this forgotten, evil creature?"

"For just that reason!" Shepherd found himself almost yelling across Janis' desk in his face. "Samyaza should never have been forgotten down there, and he is not some *creature*! Samyaza is an intelligent being. You're letting a 500-year-old booklet tell you he's dangerous and evil! Those labels have been played up and stacked against him from the beginning. These protocols are designed to keep your order obedient and bound by your faith to a secret. Aren't you curious? You don't have more questions? Don't you want to know more about these secrets?"

Janis was unfazed by Shepherd's intensity. "Speaking of secrets, father, I must urge you to refrain from saying more about the prisoner or what you've learned from your secret chest. These are also part of the protocols I am obligated to enforce. To refrain from speaking with anyone about the creature. We enforce the protocols, watch the prisoner, keep the lights on, keep it there! That's what we do. That is what the holy church of my Creator has entrusted me and the Entity to carry out. You will not persuade me otherwise, father," Janis stated firmly.

"The Creator didn't give you these protocols. Most of them were dictated by Pope Julius II," Shepherd commented. "I read—something in the chest—"

"I'm assuming this is something from your chest that was delivered by agents Rossi and Bruno on your first night? If that is true, I must urge you even further still, Father Shepherd, to refrain from speaking with anyone, including myself and the Entity guards and staff, about matters we do not need to be aware of. The protocols of our order insist. You must understand."

"Yes, I understand. But Janis, if you knew who he is—"

"I know enough to be aware that this thing you call 'Samyaza' is guarded by one of the most devout and secretive organizations on the planet. It has been here for centuries, is declared evil by our holy church, and has been put in a prison that any mortal would have perished in without food and water within a month. And yet, it lives on. For centuries now, it has lived on! It's the most unnatural thing I've ever heard of, and it won't be getting out on my watch! Not while I have breath in me. That inhuman, twisted piece of evil will stay put!" As Janis said his last words of that statement, he flipped the small TV monitor on his desk around to reveal Samyaza on screen, in black and white, sitting at his chair in his cell far below, reading a book.

"You mean you've only watched him from here?" Shepherd yelled.

"And occasionally, the security desk, yes. Entity Commanders are forbidden from entering the lower prison in the protocols."

"You've never been down there? It's almost as if your job demands ignorance, and you're just happy to accept it!"

"I need no explanation for why to serve the church, Shepherd. It's part of the oath when you become part of the Entity. It's been this way since the beginning, to take the assignment completely on faith. These cameras made it so we could view him without visiting, but we never meet face to face, as protocol demands."

Shepherd took a breath and continued, "You keep a being prisoner for eternity on faith and choose ignorance over information because of a protocol that some greedy, politically driven pontiff 500 years ago thought would be a good idea at the time? That's ridiculous!"

Janis stood up and folded his suit jacket in front to button it before grabbing his cane again. "Everyone in this city does every job they do on faith, for their faith. Including you, father. Why should mine be any more or less 'ridiculous,'

Father Shepherd?"

"You don't even know why you're supposed to keep him down there in the first place!" Shepherd's calm composure was faltering.

"I know that the creature is evil! I know that it's evil enough to bury deep beneath the holiest dirt in Europe. This is the lesser of two evils as far as I understand, as far as my oath dictates, my church requests, and my faith in my Creator demands. And even you do not supersede that authority, father. I'll admit I greatly respect that your character demands action, but you must accept mine equally requires I resist. I'll grant updates on goods and toiletries. The facility update will take more time and planning, but if your budgeting comes through, I will support the changes. Except for the doors!" he added at the end.

"The doors are for the furniture! You can't move anything bigger than a breadbox through that drawer down there!" Shepherd shot back.

"Double doors, the key is only at the security desk when not in use, and the security station will have a monitor and button access to the doors remotely. That holding room idea of yours will be mandatory. I'll oversee its structural engineering personally," Janis replied.

"We have a deal commander—and three meals a day," Shepherd slid in at the end.

"No! One meal a day, from our kitchens," Janis counter offered.

Shepherd was getting somewhere, "One meal a day from our kitchens—and—"

16

Small Victories

S hepherd stood once again at the elevator doors, ready to bounce out with a smile on his face. The doors opened, and he laid down a box he was carrying in the corner of the entryway and made his way around to greet Samyaza. That day, Samyaza was writing something at his desk in a journal when Shepherd arrived deep underground at his cell.

"Some new *Chronicles of Samyaza* in the making?" Shepherd prodded casually to break the silence as he walked into Samyaza's view.

"Yes. 'Dear diary, today I watched the episode of my favorite show where Matthew dies driving his car into a tree outside the abby'—riveting." Samyaza pretended to read sarcastically over his shoulder.

Shepherd couldn't help but bust up laughing. He saw Samyaza let out an actual roll of laughter for the first time. After a minute, the energy settled.

Samyaza said, "Come for another game already, Priest?"

"No, actually. Well, I'd go for a game later, but I've got

something better for you on this visit today."

"Some more books from the list?" Samyaza stood up and walked toward the glass in front of Shepherd.

Shepherd grinned, "I have something new for you today. One of your other requests. One of the requests we made to the Entity," he said facetiously.

Samyaza's eyes lit up. "Already? They approved a few things?" He said, beaming.

"Janis approved almost everything, Samyaza," Shepherd revealed plainly with a smile.

"You are having me on for a laugh, Priest! You cannot be serious!"

"I'm serious. Some will take longer to get arranged, installed, and scheduled, but I brought you something small that I could at least arrange for today."

"What is it?"

Shepherd returned to the door and grabbed the large box he had left there. He set the box on the floor in front of the glass so Samyaza could see it. He lifted the lid to reveal the contents and tilted the box for a better viewing angle. "I got you your fast food order, my friend!" he chirped.

Inside the box was a trash bag on one half side and a fast food takeout bag with a drink carrier on the other. Samyaza fell to his knees on the other side of the glass. "I am going to enjoy food today?" A tear came to the Watcher's eye as he knelt with his hands on the glass.

Shepherd lifted the food bag, opened the top, and wafted the open end of the bag at the airholes.

Samyaza could smell it through the holes, "Do not be cruel, man! You cannot send that through without something to help me take care of the—waste later. Remember the Entity protocols."

"That's the other part," Shepherd said. He put everything back in the box and put it into the drawer, passing it to Samyaza. "Take a look," he added, pointing at the box.

Samyaza opened the box and first smelled the food again. He paused and closed his eyes. "That aroma is incredible," he said as he pulled the other items out of the box to the side of the food. It was a small bucket with hefty trash bags inside, and at the bottom was a roll of two-ply toilet paper. "You did think of everything, Priest," Samyaza smirked.

"Hope it will help you manage for now. Best I could find on short notice anyway. I figured you would sacrifice a little decency for a meal." Shepherd said.

"You thought right, Priest."

"I have my own meal. I'll join you. Please don't wait for me, Samyaza, dig in," Shepherd said, retrieving his own bag from near the elevator.

Shepherd bowed his head quickly to pray to himself over his food like he always did at the table. As he started saying his blessing in his head, he heard Samyaza speak.

"Baruch ata Adonai Eloheinu Melech ha–olam ha-motz-I lechem min ha'ar-etz."

It was spoken in Hebrew. Shepherd had heard parts of the prayer before. It was a traditional prayer of thanks and blessing over bread. Shepherd looked up to see Samyaza opening his eyes and raising his head. Samyaza grabbed the bag and opened it up to see what was inside.

"Samyaza you—pray?" Shepherd asked curiously.

"Yes, I pray," Samyaza replied. He wasn't interested in talking anymore. He grabbed a few french fries and took a bite. His reactions were that of joy and elation, a beautiful version of pain even sometimes in his eyes as he chewed and savored each bite.

"Sauce is in the bag. And that's a cola."

Samyaza looked at the large plastic cup, "I have never used a straw before," he said. Samyaza grabbed the drink and put it to his lips to take a sip. It made him cough and sputter at first, and then he almost couldn't stop drinking it. The best reaction came when he bit into the burger.

"Thank you, Priest," Samyaza said as he chewed and wept.

To see the oldest being on Earth brought to tears over a fast food meal was quite a sight for Shepherd. "You're welcome, Samyaza. I'm glad I get to share this moment with you and could help make it happen. Again, I'm just sorry it's been so long. You've been through so much."

"Nothing you could have done about that, Priest," Samyaza said between some fries.

"Still. So, you pray? I have to ask you about that; come on." Shepherd dunked a chicken nugget into some barbecue sauce and shoved it into his mouth.

The two sat on the floor and talked through the airholes in the glass as they enjoyed their meals. Samyaza answered, "I take a moment out of respect and reverence anytime I can enjoy a satisfying meal. And a meal of any kind, for the first time in this long, is worthy of a quick word of blessing and thanks."

"But who are you thanking exactly? You thank the Creator?"

"Who else should I thank?"

Shepherd swallowed hard so he could enunciate better, "It's not that I think you should be thanking someone else; it's that you're—doing it at all! Being thankful for a meal, yes, I understand. I just never thought I'd see a *demon* pray."

"Demons are a name and idea made up by humans to try and make sense of something they cannot ever fully understand. To explain to you how we see the universe and the spaces between, please take no offense, but it would be like you trying to explain color to someone color-blind. You can tell them something is purple, compare it to other purple objects, help them recognize what shades are purple, but that color-blind person will never fully experience what you describe and will never actually see the color."

"I can understand that well enough, but you can at least take a stab at it. Not to bribe you, but I did get something else!" Shepherd said, pulling another cup from the bag and holding it up. "For a chocolate milkshake, would you try?"

Samyaza burst out, "You bastard! I cannot believe you held that back! Pass it through, Priest. I will answer your questions."

Shepherd uncrossed his legs and jumped up to pass the shake through the glass. He was happy to hear someone speak to him like a regular person again. He'd been *The Shepherd* and *Holy Shepherd* so much it made him feel alien, and these talks with Samyaza brought him back to baseline. The feeling was one of the parts Shepherd began to appreciate about his chats with the Watcher.

"Wow!" Samyaza exclaimed after his first swig of milkshake. "Alright, allow me give this a try. Why do I pray to the Creator? Besides the fact that he is THE Creator. In many ways, I am a spiritual being, the same as you humans, though not as independent. There are other beings I am connected to, my Watchers, humans, my physical body to an extent. I beg the Creator daily to let me be at peace, to let my Watchers come home—he does not answer." Samyaza took another bite of the burger and chewed a bit slower for a moment.

"Well, has he ever?" Shepherd asked.

"It does not work like that. I am not asking because someone is listening, but I am being heard. And it is not an answer one looks for, so much as trying to put a request out in the universe that I want to influence an outcome, if that makes more sense."

Shepherd was somewhat following, "I don't quite understand. It doesn't sound particularly dissimilar to any prayer, I guess, but can't you explain more?"

"More what?"

"More about prayer, spirituality, and the Creator."

"Well, I can tell you some now, Priest, but not as much as you might expect."

"How so?"

Samyaza rolled his eyes and chewed down a bite before continuing, "Think of it this way—you are the pope, but just because you are the pope that does not mean you naturally know more than others. I am a Watcher, but that does not mean I was given some wealth of knowledge at my creation other than what my Creator deemed necessary. And he did not consider much necessary for us to start other than to know a little about the Earth and humans. Most of mankind's advances in understanding have given you knowledge of things close to what we Watchers knew. You humans, on your own, through research and modern science, rediscovered much of what we Watchers taught your ancestors. It is incredible how far you have come without much help from the Watchers this time. Not as strong or wise, we created more advanced technology, but humans now have far more electronics than any pre-flood civilization, and most are used for war or strangely—entertainment. Anyway, I am trying to say that you are asking many questions about many things that I have been out of the loop on for roughly three thousand years, so there is little knowledge I have that is relevant to how things work today."

"So, what makes you evil then? Can you answer that?"

"We have been over this, Priest. Those concepts are yours, not mine. I cannot explain them for you."

"Sorry, what makes you a problem to the Creator?" Shepherd reiterated.

Samyaza stopped short of a bite and sighed, then said, "I will not speak of this much. Anything before the flood, consider it off-limits, Priest. Nothing is left of any use from that time, nor would that be of help to you in this age of man. The Creator imprisoned me in ice because—I tried to stop his flood. I loved the world as it was despite all its imperfections at the time. The Creator wanted to wipe the slate clean, start over, and Noah was the only one with a pass to the new world."

"You knew Noah? The Bible Noah?" Shepherd couldn't help but look fascinated at hearing a more in-depth version of a Bible story he'd known since he was a child and hearing it from a first-hand account at that.

"Know him? I was present at his birth! Red eyed little shit. In the end, I tried to stop him when the flood was coming."

"You didn't want him to build the Ark?" Shepherd inquired.

"I assumed if there were no Ark, the Creator would have to stop his flood," Samyaza said with a shrug.

"You tried to stop the Creator's plan, and so he killed all your Watchers and trapped you in ice for thousands of years. Why keep you trapped like that and not destroy you like the others?" Shepherd asked, closing his fast food bag and wiping his hands on his pants.

211

"According to the Creator, I was expected to suffer greater, and my Watchers had a part to play yet in this world. Sorry, again, it is hard to explain. As if the words do not even exist to convey the right concepts." Samyaza was finished eating and wiped his mouth. "Please, do you mind at least asking about something else, Priest? Another subject perhaps."

"Um—you talked about Lucifer and hell some, but—is there a heaven and hell, and what do you know about them?" Shepherd asked.

"Hell is more a state of consciousness after death with ties to a being's past, and heaven is most simply explained as a blissful ignorance of the past with no concern for the future. Time has no meaning in those realms, but again, I am using apples to explain oranges. These answers do not all translate into human terms," Samyaza said.

"Why are you Watchers so misunderstood and misinterpreted in history? You're not even in the Bible; how is that? And why are you and your Watchers nothing like the demons that ARE mentioned in scripture and stories?"

Samyaza looked perplexed, "That is your bloody religion and your book, Priest. Why are you asking me? I had nothing to do with such things! The losing side does not write history. Noah did. The losing side, which was all of us Watchers, was cast aside and left to suffer. Man moved on without getting a leg up from us after Noah. You got as far as you could without us. Now, all you do is fight over whose idea of the Creator is better, over whose religion is the most 'peaceful.' The stupidity of the wars you humans have fought in our absence, the atrocities you have caused, I fail to see what is better in this new world. Indeed, some acts were influenced by the Watcher. They are now like rebellious, leaderless children throwing firecrackers at passing cars! However, humans take too little convincing for Watchers to hold all the blame. Mankind created this new world. Watchers are just—watching you all burn it now."

Shepherd was reeling from the blunt revelations from Samyaza. "Wow. Alright, fair enough on that one. Can you talk about Adam and Eve at all? The Garden of Eden?" Shepherd asked next.

Samyaza looked sternly at him. "I will not talk about anything else before the flood, Priest. You can forget about it! My past is mostly outside your history books, and I should like to keep things that way."

"I understand, but I hope you can appreciate my natural curiosity about such things, the origins of life and the beginning of—everything," Shepherd stated.

"Even if you could know and understand some of these things, they would most likely not change or enrich your life. I find, with humans, often the more knowledge one acquires, the more one realizes they have yet to understand. Do you not agree, Priest?"

"I guess that can be true at times. Can you tell me more about the phantom realm you can go in and out of that your Watchers use? Do you ever see them there?"

"One at a time, please." Samyaza was trying to savor a few french fries. His stomach started to make some foul noises. "Must be filling up for the first time in a while," he said.

"Oh no! I didn't think of that! Greasy food may have been a poor choice for your first meal in so long. Who knows what it'll do to your digestive system after it has been unused for so long!" Shepherd pointed out nervously.

"You said you did read Clement XII's journals, right?"

Samyaza reminded him. "Remember the glass?" he added.

Shepherd cringed at the reminder of Samyaza's suffering, "Yeah, sorry. This is probably a cakewalk."

"What is a cakewalk?" Samyaza asked, holding his stomach.

"It means something is easy, but I think it used to be a thing people did around a wedding cake. I'm not really sure."

"Hmm." Samyaza slurped up the last of his chocolate milkshake through his straw and sat the cup to the side. "Angels, Watchers, demons, Archangels, and everything in between are really just different attempts at turning energy into existence by an artist who tried to improve his work with each new effort. Each version of being is essentially a different art project by the Creator himself. There were the Archangels, then us Watchers and humans came soon after, then—"

"Who has more authority?"

"The Creator has all authority. Things do not work quite like that. I would advise you not to think of the structure as leaders, generals, and authority. Think of it as—ability, and connection, and what comes naturally."

"Are the Archangels in the phantom realm or the physical realm more?

"The physical realm did not exist when the first angels were created, and they never had a need for physicality when they were formed. So they mostly reside in spirit."

"Where were the angels formed?"

"Again, I am using apple context to describe oranges, but it does not fit all."

"Right, sorry. Do angels talk directly to the Creator? Is it like when we pray? Or a more direct line?"

"How their communication works is difficult to describe. The Creator is outside all dimensions and time. The Creator does not so much dictate and have a voice as he—reveals the shape of our destiny within his design. Words that the Creator says do not need sound to be heard. Actions he wants you to do are not choices you perceive yourself to be making. If the Creator wants you to do something, he will make it seem as though that decision is the only choice. Or, it will simply be the inevitable choice he already perceives you will make." Samyaza stood up from the glass and walked to his chair.

"Because the Creator knows the future? Even though we have free will? And why do you call the Creator 'Him'? Is he of a specific gender?" Shepherd asked as he moved to his chair by the chess table.

"Remember, apples and oranges, Priest. Some details cannot even be described in your terms."

Samyaza's stomach began to groan and growl ferociously. "This may feel like a cakewalk, as you put it, but I may need some privacy soon to deal with the side effects." His stomach groaned more aggressively this time, making him lurch forward slightly and hold his belly. "Very soon, actually, Priest; I would appreciate you taking your leave so I can deal with this alone. Thank you again for the meal."

"Of course. Yeah." Shepherd replied awkwardly. He could tell he was being politely asked to leave so Samyaza could use his new makeshift camp toilet. "I'll come back for the bucket tomorrow." Shepherd turned toward the elevator to leave and give Samyaza privacy.

17

The Shepherd's Journal

The following segments are separate excerpts taken from the Journals of Pope Leo XIV, The Shepherd, from 2023-2040 A.D.:

December 2023

I started writing my first Christmas homily as pope today. I'll be expected to say a lot for my first year, but I'm told it becomes less of an ordeal after that. I have begun work on several of the projects I launched during my time on tour. The Flock funds will help make a lot of what I have planned possible.

I've been making sure I take time to visit Samyaza regularly. I usually visit on Fridays when the Entity brings him his takeout meal for the week. A quick update—all Samyaza's clothing and toiletry changes were approved through Janis after a few debates on mouthwash and whether deodorant was necessary for a "creature behind glass." The budget issues were resolved by including a ten percent oversight of general Flock donation funds by the newly appointed board managing the Flock organization. That means I'll be getting control of a portion of the funds for whatever I deem worthy.

With the funding and details in order, it won't be too long before the construction of some of these more significant improvements to Samyaza's cell is underway. I've already got Entity agents taking measurements to get contractors' information for estimates on the stairs and the sectioned plumbing that will be installed later.

The meal service we've set up for Samyaza is quite simple, and it ended up not costing anything within the budget except for the one takeout meal a week. The kitchen puts out dinner every night as usual, and there is always extra that goes to staff and nearby organizations. Along with their usual dinner cleanup routine, the staff now takes a tray with a little of everything to the Entity headquarters. Entity staff then takes the tray to the security room above the prison. Then, usually Rossi, inspects the tray, takes the meal down the elevator himself, removes the old dinner tray from the drawer in the glass wall, and slides the new tray in. I have volunteered to help handle Samyaza's you-know-what bucket when it needs to be changed out until the plumbing is installed. Bruno has been generous enough to volunteer and help with that chore whenever I travel.

I sometimes request a particular order for Samyaza's takeout dinner, but he otherwise has a rotating schedule that he can request periodical changes to if Samyaza learns of something new he'd like to try. It's been great to see him have something to enjoy and look forward to, even if it's as commonplace as having a peanut butter and jam sandwich for the first time, like when I gave him mine the other day.

August 2024

I had my meeting with Bishop Donelly today! It was great to visit with him again. He flew in early this morning, and I tried to get the man to rest before we talked, but he insisted on wasting no time. We just finished reviewing the finer details of the plan and funding for him and his team before I came to my room to write. He's very excited about this new mission I've given him. He'll be selecting his own team, other than the experts and linguists I've recruited already. The A.I. project will receive extra funding from us alongside the Watcher project.

October 2025

The old text Donelly's team turned us onto is the key to launching everything on the Watcher project. My hope is that Donelly will soon find out if the mission will be worth continuing past research and moving into expeditions. I can't wait to see how this pans out. Funding shouldn't be a problem anymore if it goes that far. The Flock site has already brought in more funds in my purview than I could ever ask for to see this thing through. However, I can't sacrifice too much time for this side project of mine if it doesn't bear any fruit of its own. Hopefully, I'll have good news on that front soon.

July 2026

The remodel to Samyaza's cell is done! The construction crew put the last finishing touches on the interior doors just this last week! I celebrated by using some money left over in the security system updates budget to get Samyaza a larger-screen television set! Another protocol loophole is that you don't have to ask permission to get him a larger version of an amenity he already has. Samyaza had been watching everything on a 13-inch old little TV. The last amenity the Entity Commander had allowed after John Paul II's final request was to keep the prisoner's entertainment at a modern level. I got him a 70-inch LED UHD 8K TV, whatever that all means, and even had Bruno come down and mount it on the wall with me for him while Samyaza waited in the new holding room, which was a fantastic addition to the security updates. Janis was only willing to compromise on the doors if there was space in the budget to construct a third door to a small reinforced holding facility, which Samyaza would need to enter voluntarily to stand in while anyone enters his cell. It was a clever way of ensuring he was 100% secure while accessing his room and facilities with no problems. As if Samyaza would do anything, I highly doubt it. There's still the elevator and the desk upstairs with a guard, anyway.

Samyaza loves nature programs on the big screen. He said it makes him feel like he has an actual window now, like he's flying again but from his chair. The green chair and his desk were the only two pieces of furniture he kept. He insisted on those two things staying, but we updated almost everything else. His books have been given proper shelves and his boxes given an appropriate wall of shelves and drawers. Everything that is allowed down there is reviewed, approved, and cataloged, but the extra procedures merely gave a few Entity members something to do during their guard duties.

I got my emergency exit staircase leading up to its new reinforced security door at each end! The plumbing went in right after the stairs but with incredible difficulty. Eventually, Janis' arm had to be twisted to allow a couple of construction workers, already on other Vatican contracts, to assist with a few parts. Otherwise, the Entity guards did their best to erector-set the piping and plumbing together. Samyaza got to enjoy his first EVER shower. He didn't even care that we never got anything worked out for a hot water system. He was just glad to be done with getting sponge baths only once every decade or so. We couldn't get enough electrical changes approved through Janis to add lighting updates, and an entire stone wall would've needed to be removed to replace the old lights above.

The cell would have been buried along with the current open space in rubble, leaving it a nightmare to excavate and to keep a prisoner in that environment would have been impossible. Eventually, all agreed that the current lighting and electricity in Samyaza's cell would have to stay as is with what was installed in the '90s. I think it's wild we did all this work modernizing the doors, the TV, the plumbing with toilet, shower, sink, all that, and we can't get a switch installed for the lights above his cell.

I left the cameras untouched on purpose. I saw no need to be able to see a higher resolution, more modern picture of Samyaza in color, and Janis couldn't agree more that another expense wouldn't be necessary.

September 2028

I had a video conference call with Donelly and the team this morning. They think the geology team has found it! I'm packing right after this to leave on a flight this weekend. Marco will be clearing my schedule for the next couple of weeks so that I can go and see for myself. I think it's time to tell Marco I feel a case of the flu coming on.

(Portion of September 21, 2028 entry REDACTED)

I don't know if I'll ever make use of it. I don't like keeping Samyaza in the dark, but I must see this through. I need to see the truth with my own eyes and know I have options if there's ever such a dire need.

(Portion of September 22-30, 2028 entry REDACTED)

January 2030

I just got back from visiting Samyaza downstairs this evening. I call it that now, downstairs, but I usually take the elevator. I mean, it's easier.

Janis was asked last month in our quarterly staff meeting if he'd like to retire soon. Janis said he'd "retire when the Creator ends his term," making his proclamation of sticking to his post till his grave. The man will be in a wheelchair soon enough. His legs have gotten so bad.

I've been feeling that everything has gotten too commonplace, especially during my visits to "the prisoner" in the dungeon downstairs. I keep thinking about old Elias on his boat that he hated, telling me his wish of saving humanity from pain; about the stories Samyaza told of the flood, the great wars, the holocaust, all these things that have happened that maybe could have been averted if other popes had gone through with what I question now. Is this the lesser of two evils, keeping a being like Samyaza locked up? Couldn't he do more good against the bad that's happening now? What concern is it of ours if he chooses to leave this existence behind? To let the demons, Watchers of Earth, finally rest, to give the Watchers peace, and to allow Samyaza to leave his physical prison once and for all. The burden weighs heavily on me.

I see only benefits and no harm in releasing Samyaza. I dwell on this moral dilemma day and night. Don't I need to live by my own mission statement—save your neighbors first, and the church comes later? I can't choose to keep my neighbors in the world suffering to save the church. That's Janis' philosophy, not mine. I don't see how Samyaza being kept downstairs could be the Creator's plan. At the same time, I know there are worse things that could happen. Samyaza explained how Pope Clement VII saw him as a weapon. I don't think we have anything to fear from Samyaza. He just wants to be gone, to be at peace. I'm sure no being, human, creature, or anything really could handle living for eternity. At least, not on Earth suffering in pain as a wandering solitary immortal.

I do wish to see him free, but Janis had one point, keeping

Samyaza in the cell poses no new risks. I trust Samyaza, but there's much I still don't know, and I haven't found a way around the Entity. I wish I had all the facts; everything is on faith. I never thought I'd say this, but I see why Pope Julius II hesitated in trusting Samyaza. I have a feeling that Samyaza may yet have some part to play in the Creator's plan. Why else would the Creator allow him to exist after the flood? But again, even if I decide to let him out, I haven't completely figured out how to get him past Janis and his men.

I have told Samyaza that if I ever found a way to release him, I probably would, but he has little faith. He knows my heart but also sees the task as impossible and seems to waste no energy entertaining the idea with me anymore.

April 2038

I've been away some. I was in and out of the hospital a bit this last month and hadn't found too much time to write. I just haven't had the energy for it. Ever since my heart attack two months ago, my health just hasn't been the same. I was always fit and felt like I would live longer than most, but this knocked the wind out of me in more ways than one. I got too soft after becoming "The Shepherd." My doctor kept telling me to cut back and exercise, but I didn't listen, and I quickly lost that spry, energetic step I used to have. Now, I'm stuck for a while in a hospital bed.

My sisters, Emily, Clare, and Beth all flew in from New Zealand to be at my side the moment they heard. Emily just turned seventy and couldn't believe I had a heart attack first! I think she had already been looking for a reason to finally come to the Vatican. Emily would never let me have her flown out. That was Em. She had to wait until there was a crisis. She carried with her a container of lamingtons the entire trip from back home. She had the same *recipe our mother used, and as far as my memory could tell, she pretty much nailed it. Em hadn't made any lamingtons in years, ever since her kids moved out. She used my health as an excuse to make something special again for me and to pay a visit. She was very sorry about the circumstances.*

Beth was in awe of everyone praying and gathering in Saint Peter's Square. The entire square was packed through the gates for the first week right after my heart attack. I had been running ragged, doing several events daily, and the stress must have finally caught up to me.

Clare thinks I need to remember the importance of self-care, and to "stop trying to sacrifice my health to change the world" like I keep telling everyone I'm trying to do.

She said last night, "Better a 100-year-old Shepherd doing a little, than a dead Shepherd before seventy who tried to do too much at once," or something like that. Not too eloquently put anyway, but true. I need to care for myself just as much as I'm trying to care for everyone else.

I haven't been able to visit Samyaza at all in my weakened state. I look forward to being able to see him when I get some of my strength back. If anything, I know he's taken care of, and there's a system in place long after I'm gone.

I need to complete my mission. My life's work is not yet finished. I have too much I want to accomplish, and there's too much in this world that needs help for me to stop anytime soon. I worry about that at times, more times than I'd care to admit in the last few months, that I may die, and Samyaza will be down in that deep hole forever. He may be forgotten again, left to wish for scraps from the Vatican table while hoping a new series comes out to watch on TV because he's seen everything ever made already. What sort of cruel joke of an eternity is that for one of the most unique and ancient beings that ever walked the Earth? Why would the Creator make a being so magnificent only to lock him away to be forgotten?

18

A Crisis of All Faiths

S hepherd entered the long board room in the main administration building of Vatican City. He was seventy-one years old at the time. It was early August 2041, and on that day, a meeting was called together by all of Shepherd's advisors. Cardinal Johns was there; he was partially retired, eighty-three himself, but staying at the Vatican, occasionally advising Shepherd and helping him keep in touch with current events. Marco and Bishop Donelly from the States were also in attendance. Marco's long ponytail had recently started to transition from a shiny black to a matted silver, showing his age.

Shepherd made sure he greeted each of them with open arms as he made his way into the room to find a seat at the table. The Shepherd was moving on his feet more quickly those days, being a few years out of physical therapy from his heart attack back in '38. Ever since his sisters gave him a wake-up call, he'd made his health and longevity of life more of a priority. Shepherd had cut a lot of things from his diet, even his beloved sodas. More often than not, he was using the stairs on his trips to play a game or two of chess with Samyaza while they discussed current and past historical events. Samyaza had become somewhat of a secret advisor to Shepherd over the years. It was one of the ways Shepherd found a silver lining to give Samyaza purpose in his situation. Shepherd felt this arrangement kept Samyaza's spirits up at times, based on his comments and reactions. If nothing else, Samyaza seemed glad to have a regular companion.

Over the years, the Flock website had worked its way further into more aspects of society for the greater good, thanks to Shepherd's continued efforts. The church—the entire church, now not only had zero debt but was the largest non-profit charitable organization in the planet's history. For most of the last decade, many denominations had united under one single banner. A congregation now calling itself just members of *The Flock* or *The Shepherd's Flock*. Shepherd wasn't a huge fan of that second one. He wanted the corroboration to continue long after he was gone and figured the less his name was tied to different pieces of the organization, the less they'd need re-branded after his time ended. It was sort of a United Nations of religious denominations. All had their separate structures, but were strengthened by many unified core beliefs and unanimous agreements. The mission of the establishment's part of the organization agreed to always align with the indoctrinated ideology of *The Flock*, *"Save your neighbors first."* *The Flock* and its funds had all but eliminated world hunger in the last few years. Shepherd had used Flock resources to fund research and patents, which were under the Flock ownership, not himself, in the areas of botany and famine relief. *The Flock* also purchased vast tracts of land in the Sahara Desert under the Vatican's stewardship. The land was cheap, and the research was fruitful. What had once been the largest desert on the planet, and growing, had become the fastest-growing agricultural mecca of the world. The botanical research Shepherd funded found ways to grow crops in the desert through a soil conversion bacteria mutation in the roots of common edible plants. The bacteria nurtured growth in the extreme heat and would trap moisture and nutrients underground. It reacted with the sunlight above the top layer of sand, causing the sand to have a chemical reaction, crystallizing it almost like a glass roof greenhouse effect above every single plant root system. This top layer then rotted when the plant died, restoring the nutrients into a new super-soil. Shepherd had all but done what he set out to accomplish from his first day as pope. The world was a much better place than it was when he got started.

Among those gathered at the meeting were several science specialists, advisors with international political connections, professors with more acronyms after their names than most, several religious leaders, and some from religions outside Christianity. Many were attending via video conference on screens lining the conference room. Janis was also asked to attend, still holding his post, even from a new hover wheelchair. He was there with his notepad tucked on his knee under his lanky aged fingers. The room was mic'd for sound, and cameras were hidden away, capturing whoever was center stage in the physical room to broadcast to others around the world. Several introductions were made, a few sound and response checks were done with the video group, and Shepherd was asked to lead everyone in a blessing before the day's events and discussions.

Shepherd gave his usual blessing, which he kept on hand

for such occasions, with a few additions regarding those attending, and the meeting commenced.

After some more pleasantries and thank yous, Bishop Donelly stepped up. "Professor Alexander Kozlov and I called this meeting today. He's a colleague of mine in the States, and he has something to say that, once I heard it, I knew needed to be shared. Some of you on video now and here already know what Professor Kozlov is about to share, but I'll let him take it from here. Alex."

Professor Kozlov stood up so everyone could tell who he was before speaking. Kozlov was an old Russian immigrant literature and religious theology expert moonlighting as a professor at Boston College. He was a man always looking to grow in wisdom. He spent his time researching, studying, and learning when he wasn't teaching. The man was a Russian brain sponge. He looked like Winston Churchill right down to the balding head and cane. Kozlov was the kind of man who read historical novels about lost warship journals for leisure, took a class on astrophysics in his free time, and built clocks as an additional hobby, as if he had so much extra mental space after everything else.

Kozlov started, "Thank you, Joseph. Gentlemen and ladies, there's no simple way to put this, but every scientific, astrological, and religious community on the planet must be informed of our findings—that the world as we know it will be ending within the next seven years."

The room and the video feed were silent.

After a pause, Kozlov stepped from his chair and began pacing with his cane, shuffling behind the other attendees at his side of the table. As he paced, he continued, "We have seen astrological signs, issues with the balance of the planetary climate, the war in Israel, political shifts, the list goes on. We will get into some of the specifics within the discussion today to cover all evidence, A.I. findings, and testimony, but without a doubt, across all religions, ideologies, sciences, and understandings, we must confirm and spread the data. There are all manner of signs, predictions, scientific proofs, omens, and conflicts coming to a head. The world is on the brink of imploding. The new A.I. systems that our department in Boston partnered with MIT to maintain have been processing everything in preparation for announcing this data today. The data concludes that there is a 98.99% probability of world events colliding in an apocalyptic or extinction-level event in a seven-year time span, and so far, there is not a damn thing anyone can figure out to stop it."

"What do you mean? Now that you're telling us, why can't something be done to stop—whatever is is you're talking about?" One of the other religious leaders on video feed chimed in.

Kozlov answered, "We have already attempted to avert this crisis, and you are not the first group of influential people to whom we've presented these findings. We have political affiliates from around the globe on with us live who will be giving testimony today explaining that these facts and figures with all the supporting data have been presented to the leaders of countries around the world, including the United States, Great Britain, The New Russian Republic, and the Mediterranean Alliance members have all seen the same information you'll be witnessing today. No plans are being laid, no preparations are being made, and no information is being shared. In fact, we have been told by our governments to stay silent under threat of execution. My team and I are risking our lives to bring this news to the leaders of religious communities around the world today."

"You said nothing could be done," Shepherd interjected. "Why then take this great risk to tell us if nothing can be done?"

Kozlov replied, "It's true, nothing can be done, that we know of, and we didn't expect the political leaders to DO anything exactly. We believe humanity should be aware of its impending doom as our responsibility to our species. We should at least all be informed to prepare for what is to come in any way each man and woman sees fit. And maybe, just maybe, if everyone knows, we will have a chance to stop some of the coming disaster. There is that 1.01% chance that the A.I. has not been able to account for. Maybe there is something from collective knowledge that even our advanced A.I. is unaware of, and can't fill in the gaps. Maybe one of you, in your religious places of authority, is aware of something on the supernatural level that could be of use at this time. That is why we are here today. The world political leaders laughed us out as 'superstitious,' so now we are coming to the *superstitious* leaders of the world as our last hope to get the word out about this impending global crisis."

As he listened, Shepherd was having a thought, *Samyaza! Samyaza might be able to do something if he had the sword!*

As the thought was completed in his mind, Shepherd noticed Janis was looking in his direction. He must have known where Shepherd's mind would go first. Janis tilted his head at a downward angle and shook his head the way you tell someone the answer is already, *no, don't even think about it, pal.*

Shepherd put the thought out of his mind for a moment and tried to listen to what the experts laid out.

"Where are these percentages of probability coming from predicting a crisis? I don't understand." someone on the video feed called out.

"That is a new scale. We're calling it the Kozlov Scale," said Donelly.

Cardinal Johns asked, "Are you sayin' you want us to pray? Or are you asking if we know of some 'oly weapon? We can pray to our Creator and ask for guidance an' wisdom, but are you sayin' that even our own beliefs validate these findins? That's science fiction to you academic types, innit?"

"Not anymore, actually." Bishop Donelly stood up to begin his impromptu portion of the meeting, which was welcome since Kozlov had all but butchered the delivery so far. He was an academic, not an orator. "My research team and I have been working on translating ancient texts within the Vatican Archives for many years now under the direction of *The Shepherd*." Donelly motioned to Shepherd and continued, "One of the other projects we've worked on of our own choosing was the A.I. we developed with professor Kozlov, now known as Omega. We have been working on modeling this new A.I. to predict future events. The Omega-AI has a subroutine that is unique from all other A.I.s in existence. We get conflicting data from general computing and high-level analysis A.I.s; they also point to an apocalypse but have conflicting levels of accuracy across historical timelines, making them less trustworthy in their predictions. They tend to land more in the 55-62% range on the Kozlov Scale. The Omega-AI has been given the subroutine allowing its synthetic consciousness to believe in a higher power. This was never written into any previous A.I. system as a part of what makes the A.I. an individual thinking unit. Beliefs can be developed and discovered over a human individual's lifetime, but the Omega-AI operates under the assumption that there is a grand design to all things as no other A.I. could. Removing the perception of chance and replacing it with the construct of predestination for all outcomes and algorithms, Omega has not only accurately predicted all events in the last year of testing, but when we turn it to look into the past, every major world event since the beginning of recorded history is found with pinpoint precision."

"How on Earth is something like that even tested?" one of the leaders on the video feed asked.

Donelly answered, "Basically, in layman's terms, we give the A.I. all the information we can, all the capacity available. It uses every event that has already happened in history and based on that data creates an algorithm under the assumption that all events are interconnected rather than random. After the algorithms and new subroutines are mapped out we duplicate the A.I. on our servers with a blank slate, no event data, and we are currently running near full capacity on version Omega-AI-227. Once the algorithm is developed, the new update of Omega-AI is given no knowledge of human history, only the general knowledge and algorithms developed with the previous versions' construct data. We then begin to feed current world news information as it unfolds into the A.I. in real-time from all sources.

The A.I. then uses the 'Alpha-Omega' subroutines, as they've been nicknamed, to not only guess what already happened in the past but also predict the future. The last 132 adaptation runs of Omega have come back with perfect historical record matches after the initial gaps in our programming were worked out by the A.I., and it has now been successfully predicting future world events within 98-100% accuracy. The only reason we've seen fluctuations in accuracy is due to errors in the data we're comparing it to—fake news and bad facts, some of which have unearthed new truths. We find the A.I. moves us closer to 100% accuracy each time these outliers are fact-checked and corrected. According to the Omega-AI's predictions, all roads lead to the end of civilization in seven years. It's not just right most of the time—it's right all the time. And it doesn't just guess close—it guesses spot on. We don't have anything to explain it simpler for everyone to understand other than to say—we've made an intelligent crystal ball that believes in a higher power, and it's telling us our time is ending soon. Whether that's through war or some cataclysmic event—we still do not know." Donelly sat back down and wiped cold sweat off his forehead with the back of his sleeve.

Shepherd looked around the room at all the grief-stricken faces. Everyone was having the same revelation, but only Shepherd knew he had something he could do about it. He was the only person alive who did know. Janis was aware of Samyaza but not of all his powers and what could happen if he was let out. *Letting Samyaza out would be worth trying if we only have seven years left!* Shepherd didn't know if Samyaza and the Watchers being removed from the board would change the endgame that the A.I.s were predicting, but he had the thought, *If the world is ending anyways—isn't it worth a shot?*

The meeting continued with testimonials and presentations shown on hologram in the center of the table, along with historical findings, astrological charts, A.I. model predictions, and simulations. The Omega-AI showed the world engulfed in fire with no information other than a vague end date roughly seven years in the future. Omega could only predict with certainty three years out at the time but had enough information to know that something unstoppable as far as seven years out was generally inevitable on a global scale. The Omega-AI team was hoping some other data could fill the gaps in the odds and get their statistic closer to 100% as soon as possible to see beyond the three year event horizon at what might cause the actual apocalypse.

No one seemed to have anything to offer to satisfy the professor's request, and the meeting fizzled out to a bunch of sidebars and exchanges of information. There were commitments to help with cases where asylum was needed for protection for going public about the A.I.'s findings. News outlet contacts were already being called before the room was cleared. Shepherd waited till he saw Janis hovering out of the room towards his office, and he stepped up alongside him, making their way down the hallway together.

Shepherd waited till Janis noticed him by his side before he spoke. "You know what I'm thinking, Janis."

"I'll never allow it, Shepherd," Janis retorted in a raspy voice.

"The prisoner, maybe if we let him out—there's things I know—"

"The protocol, Shepherd."

"Forget the protocol man! The world is ending!"

"Exactly!" Janis stopped his hover-chair and turned aggressively towards Shepherd. "The world is ending. Say goodbye to what loved ones you have. I'm going back to serving my church till my time comes. I suggest you do whatever best suits you for the next seven years. If you want to retire early or—"

"Why are you talking like this?" Shepherd turned to look

around and whispered, "Samyaza could end all evil on Earth. That might make a difference! Even if it doesn't, why not try?"

"Try and stop the apocalypse? Be serious, Shepherd. It still doesn't change the fact that nothing in the protocols says *in case of apocalypse, throw all the protocols out*! No, the apocalypse is inevitable, and the Creator knew that when the creature was put away and placed under guard by his church. I will continue to keep my oath till my last breath! Perhaps that is my purpose, and why someone such as myself has been put here during this time. Maybe that Omega-AI has something to say about that!" With those words, the old Dutchman hovered off back to his office.

19

Deeds of The Shepherd

S hepherd made his way down the hallway behind the
door in his headboard as he'd done hundreds of times.
Bruno greeted him at the security desk as he opened
the back door to the winding hallway. Bruno was a little old
for the security post then but liked the quiet. He'd gotten used
to sitting and reading some of the books left at his stand and
kept from going further down due to the protocols. Shepherd
usually left the unapproved books with him to finish. Not
much in the guard post had changed except a few new buttons
for buzzing doors open and new keys for manual access. The
extra guards Janis wanted were recruited and trained to help
take extra shifts. Shepherd had ensured there were updated
chairs and a mini fridge put into the security desk when the
remodel took place to make even the guard station more
comfortable.

Shepherd walked to the elevator as Bruno made his way
around the desk to give him access with his keycard. Like
always, Bruno waved the key over the door panel, and
Shepherd stepped inside. The doors closed with a *clunk*

behind him. Shepherd reached the bottom to the sound of recently added elevator music and rounded the corner, finding Samyaza watching one of his usual nature programs on the television. Samyaza was sitting in his favorite green high-back chair. He hadn't aged a day in the last eighteen years, and was wearing his old tattered black saturno.

"It is not even Friday," Samyaza said. "Did I somehow lose track of time and miss a day down here in my sunless dungeon?" He asked jokingly.

"No," Shepherd sighed. "I got some interesting news today and thought I might talk about it with you over a game, if you're in the mood?"

"Always in the mood for a game, you know me, Priest," Samyaza shot back.

The two old friends sat down at the same table they had been using since their first game years ago. Samyaza sat in his greenback chair as he always did on his side of the glass, while Shepherd on his side rolled up his updated, more padded, lounge chair.

After progressing a few moves into the game, Samyaza pressed, "So, Priest, what news do you have that requires a chat with your old demon in the dungeon downstairs?"

Shepherd talked as he made his next move. "There was a meeting today, and in that meeting—it was agreed by all the experts and scientists that the only logical conclusion to all the evidence and information being provided—was that the world is ending. According to Professor Kozlov and the A.I. they're working with, the apocalypse is just around the corner, within seven years. The worst part is—there's nothing anyone can do about it," he explained.

Samyaza sat back from the game. He looked into Shepherd's

eyes to see if he was genuinely being sincere. He leaned forward and whispered, "Touch my pinky, Priest." Samyaza put his hand up to the glass and slid one of his fingers through the airhole to get a sense of what was happening in Shepherd's mind and what he had seen.

Shepherd put his hand up to the glass the way they had done once many years

ago for him to show Samyaza his true intentions and thoughts. He allowed Samyaza a glimpse into what he had viewed earlier that day in the meeting with a touch through the tiny airhole. Shepherd also felt he conveyed the situation with Janis since it was fresh in his mind at the time.

Samyaza spoke up, "I cannot believe you are serious! The time has finally come. But the plan will never work, Priest. We have gone over this a dozen times. You cannot get me out without someone in the Entity discovering us. There are too many variables that could go sideways. I shall say this, the scientists do not know for sure what they are looking at. The A.I. is not going to help change anything."

Samyaza may have gotten a clear picture, but it seemed Shepherd needed clarification on what he was saying. Shepherd asked, "Wait, you understand what they're talking about? All this information is coming from the Omega-AI. What could you possibly understand about that?"

Samyaza nodded, "That is true. I don't know much about these new sophisticated A.I.s, except for what I have seen in documentaries and popular movies. But what I do know, is that what they are describing in their discovery, or the algorithm as they call it, is what is known to us angelics as the Ether-Net."

"The Ether-Net? Like an old ethernet cable?" asked

Shepherd.

Samyaza shook his head, "No, come on, Priest, nothing like that. I mean the Ethereal Network that moves time and space in the way that humans perceive existence. It is one of those concepts with no words to explain or to help humans understand. I tried explaining it to you once long ago. We talked about how it was like a river or wind, but it does seem like this Omega-AI, as they call it, has found a way to interpret or read some of the Ether-Net. Through that interpretation, the A.I. has come up with algorithms that helped it predict the rest of the future unfolding pattern. The Ether-Net is something very few angelic beings have the ability to understand and fully interpret. The skill takes centuries of dedication. We can all perceive it flowing around us, but the Ether is not easily read in a way that can be used to predict future outcomes in the physical realm. My understanding has been that the Archangels can view the Ether-Net and make course corrections to it but cannot alter or adjust its overall directional flow. This Omega-AI seems to have a similar ability with which it can view parts of the Ether-Net in the recent past and the near future. The A.I. is using what scientists taught it to come up with predictions of the future, but it seems the A.I. is missing something it cannot understand."

Shepherd was in awe, "My God, man! You agree they really did come up with a way to closely predict the future of the world? Even from a spiritual perspective?"

"Seems that way, Priest," Samyaza stated plainly.

Shepherd felt the weight of the world building on his shoulders. "Well then, that settles it. We need to get you out of here!"

"What would be the point?"

"Exactly! It doesn't matter at this point, do you see? The apocalypse is just around the corner. What's the worst that could happen? They catch you, put you back down in here, and you just wait it out over the next seven years like the rest of us!" Shepherd said flippantly.

"They could do something to you, Priest, and then it could affect your position as Holy Father. Who knows what might happen? The cardinals may have you removed if they find out you have done something so egregious—like let me escape against the Entity!"

"No one would find out until it was too late anyway."

"But again, there is no point," Samyaza said. "We do not have the Sword of the Cherubim, and no one has finished my translations. There is also the incomplete geographical analysis of the new Earth after the flood. Even if this plan of yours does work, and you get me out of the Vatican, I can do nothing to stop this impending doom. I have seen this much in the Ether-Net from my prolonged time in the phantom realm during my first ice prison."

Shepherd pulled his journal from his hoodie pocket and moved to a page he had marked with a ribbon. "I think it's time I share with you a little bit of one of my journals from my earliest years as pope. I know I spend a lot of time down here, but I've been doing a few things on my own time up above to try and help—prepare for the worst; To make things easier. If ever the time did come when I needed to let you go, or I thought it would be best, I wanted to make sure it would be for a greater purpose. I will read this for you, Samyaza, so you can get up to speed on a few projects I've been running over the years."

The following is from the redacted portion of Pope Leo XIV's journals from September 21-30, 2028

September 21, 2028

They found it! Last year, the research team found the location of the Garden entrance. I had Donelly working with a few of his colleagues and students at the university, along with several language experts, historians, archaeologists, astronomers, a couple experts on ancient cultures, geologists, and a several interns. It was a pet project of mine. I had set up Donelly as the leader of a task force with one intention—translate the Watcher texts in the Vatican Archive to find the location of the Garden of Eden. Of course, the main goal was to find the Sword of the Cherubim, but I couldn't let Donelly and his team know that. I certainly couldn't tell them about Samyaza and how a prisoner is in the secret dungeon under the Vatican. Donelly and his team set out to translate the Watcher texts in the archives right away once they were able to make copies into their computer systems.

They had little to go from when they started. Samyaza had left his notes, but he also wrote them in the Watcher language. A few pieces were needed to possibly translate the whole text into a human-discernible language. The team had a significant breakthrough when one of the research assistants mentioned during a brainstorming session that the Watcher language most closely resembled Romanian. This made Donelly think of another manuscript that had similar-looking but untranslatable texts. It's called the Voynich Manuscript. It is a type of journal that dates to the fifteenth century that has drawings and writings of things entirely not of this Earth as we know it. All the text is in a language that has never been able to be translated, even though the manuscript has been sold between collectors for hundreds of years. When compared to the samples available online, it was clear that

241

the Voynich Manuscript was written in Watcher.

Donelly wanted to not only view the texts but also acquire the original, so he got me involved in that part. Trading art for art, from dealer to dealer, I got the accountants, museum curators, and archive librarians all involved to acquire the Voynich Manuscript for the Vatican Archive, with a hefty contribution from my Flock funds. The manuscript arrived by a three-man security team that flew undercover in coach with the leather bound texts and delivered them personally, requiring a signature and fingerprint scan. Donelly had studied the Voynich Manuscript years ago for a college paper. Once his intern commented on the Watcher text, he connected the similarities, remembering it appeared closest to Romanian.

The team scanned the text into their computer systems as well as analyzed every bit of biological and carbon data. The languages were identical when compared. With the extra information from the Voynich Manuscript combined with Samyaza's notes and the Watcher texts from the Vatican Archive, the code was cracked. Donelly and his team became the first humans in over 4,000 years to be able to read Watcher. All the texts were translated and loaded into a new database. PDFs were printed for me and a few other research teams already chomping at the bit to get the data and begin looking for the garden location. That was the next step, and the Watcher texts were going to lead us to the geographical location of the Garden of Eden. The Vatican texts were, in fact, the Journals of Noah and his grandfather Methuselah. The journals gave Methuselah's account of the construction of the Ark as he observed it and watched over Noah and his family in his final days. Noah's journals accounted for the location of the landing of the Ark, his logs of the new Earth, the works of his ancestor Enoch, and the recalculations of the last known location of the Garden of

Eden. His calculations were based on the adjustment of the new continents under the stars at a specific date and correlated the new tilted rotation of the Earth.

While the navigation team worked out the charts, data, and astronomy of the Watcher texts, Donelly and his team took a closer look at the Voynich Manuscript. It turns out, as it was very obvious to me and then later to the whole team, that the Voynich Manuscript was one of Samyaza's journals. He had lost some on his arrival in Europe in the 1500s. I remembered Samyaza said several times he'd lost a few journals after sailing with Columbus. Someone had found this one, traded it, sold it, it got purchased by a collector and got more attention, and sold again and again, and now here it was. Donelly and his team learned a bit about Samyaza, but the journal was from before he arrived in Europe, so there was no evidence to lead the team to the fact that the author of this text was hidden under my bed. They didn't know his name, so he was simply referred to as "the Watcher Writer."

The journal seemed to be all Samyaza's old medicinal logs, herbal formulas, astrological charts, and a catalog of plants that are mostly extinct. Also, some detailed measurements appeared to be his survey notes while he laid plans for a new city in Central America when he lived with the Mexica people that we call Aztecs. The last notes in Samyaza's journal were a few logs of the conversations with Yekun during his journey across the Atlantic. Samyaza already rewrote some of these in his more recent journals I was allowed to read. Samyaza's memory was incredible. When I secretly compared the two texts one night in my room, it was as if he'd transcribed his original journal practically word for word nearly 300 years later.

Two months after translating the texts, Donelly's team found the exact longitude and latitude for the garden. An expedition was mounted, and Donelly was reluctantly asked to sit the excavation part out once they found the site. I had to keep Donelly from seeing the sword. If the excavators found the entrance and saw it, it was not a big deal, maybe a few thousand dollars hush money to some diggers, but Donelly would recognize the sword and realize what was really going on, and so would anyone on his team. As far as the researchers were concerned, it was mission accomplished, but this has to be covered up for Vatican Security. The team took their fat checks, signed NDAs, and disbanded. Donelly continued to work with another professor, Dr. Kozlov, on an A.I. project that The Flock is also funding.

Meanwhile, the excavators were chipping away at the deepest part of a cave. The dig was inside a deep cavern hidden high in the Bale Mountains of Ethiopia. The excavation team has been reporting weekly progress updates directly to me. Today, I got the update that they found it! They found the entrance to the Garden of Eden!

My head digger, Ahmed, called to tell me they opened a chamber that shined so bright that they "all received second-degree burns" just from standing in the light of the entrance for a few seconds. The area was closed off until they contacted me to find out what they should do next.

I advised Ahmed to keep the area closed off and under security 24/7 till I arrive. I'm on the plane now. I'm going to see the Sword of the Cherubim for myself!

September 22, 2028

I arrived at the dig site today after a short jeep ride down a dirt utility trail from the main road. Ahmed was waiting at the path to walk the final stretch with me up to the cave. I have never done cave diving before, but I was determined to go as far as needed to see the entrance and the sword. I had Ahmed bring protective gear, goggles, and sunscreen. We packed in the protective gear and some supplies deep into the cavern. We had all the professional safety equipment needed. I wanted so badly to repel off something before I was too old to go on any kind of adventure. This was my last chance, I felt, to look off the edge into the abyss, and a few times in the cave I did just that. I wanted to feel like Indiana Jones, but I fear I looked more like one of those nerdy archaeologists in bright blue helmets and Patagonia t-shirts on the a nature channel.

The caves were remarkable, with stalactites and stalagmites everywhere—rivers and crystal ponds, glow-in-the-dark fish, and bioluminescent worms lighting the way. We got to an area where the cavern became tighter and tighter, so much so that we had to crawl on our stomachs and push our bags in front of us the last few meters to squeeze through. Once we passed through the previous tight passage, we came to a large cathedral-type open chamber. In the middle of the cathedral, on the floor, what looked at first glance to be a bottomless pit was actually a twenty-foot drop to another level. I got to repel into that lower chamber! A few hundred meters more walking, and we were at the last cavern before the scalding hot new opening. The light started to become blinding the final few turns back into the cave.

We unpacked our protective gear and adorned our goggles. Ahmed and I smeared our faces with sunscreen. Once we were all covered up, hooded, and goggles shielding our eyes, we continued toward the intense, blinding light ahead. Our goggles had the same strength as a welder's mask, but the light was still coming through. Our eyes were having difficulty adjusting. Ahmed told me he did not want to continue any further when we were just a few meters away. It was where the digging crew had burst through into the lighted area and turned back. I let him know I would continue the rest of the way on my own and that it was fine if he just wanted to wait there for me. The suits we were wearing should have been able to withstand being right next to a lava flow, but the heat was still extremely uncomfortable for me.

When I rounded the corner—there was the Cherubim Sword sticking out of the Earth! Fifteen—maybe twenty feet high it stood. The blade shined like the surface of the sun. The hilt was golden, shining brightly at the top. The blade appeared dark, yet it illuminated the cavern with its glow. It was like trying to stare at an eclipse. I could feel it burning at my retinas. Nothing could be seen past the light if there was anything of a garden behind the sword. I turned back around the corner and headed to where I had left Ahmed. I knew the sword existed now. I knew exactly where it was and how to get to it if ever needed.

September 27, 2028

It felt strange to travel so far and go through such an ordeal to return with nothing in hand other than some charts, printouts, and photographs. Ahmed and his men were well paid to seal the last part of where they dug back up, and Ahmed will be periodically checking the cave for any intruders and report to me if anything ever appears disturbed.

September 29, 2028

I'm on the plane now, crossing over the Mediterranean Sea headed back to Italy. Marco probably won't be able to keep up the ruse that I have the flu for much longer. I should be back in the Vatican before tomorrow morning. I've been able to keep this discovery a secret so far. I think I'm going to have to keep it that way—

"You have known where the Sword of the Cherubim was for the last thirteen years, Priest, and you never told me?" Samyaza burst out, interrupting Shepherd's journal reading.

"I had decided it was the route to take at the time. I was about to read this last part to you, where I talk about my reasoning for not releasing you just yet," Shepherd tried to explain.

Samyaza yelled, "I knew you never could release me! No one is ever going to release me! Every now and then, one of you wants to let me go for some reason, but here I stay! And now here is another priest, teasing me that they have known all this time about the sword, and apparently, one of my journals has also been discovered and kept from me!" Samyaza was livid with his old companion.

"I'm sorry about that, Samyaza. I thought ignorance would be bliss in your case until the information was actually of some use. Here, touch my pinky again." Shepherd said, moving towards the glass and sticking his little finger in the airhole once more.

Samyaza tapped into Shepherd's thoughts quickly again through the tiny airhole. He slid back in his chair, disgruntled. "If the world truly is ending in seven years—I can see why you have decided now is the time. It is up to you, Priest. The decision has always been yours."

"You've seen what I'm thinking of for the next steps over the coming weeks?"

"Yes. I doubt your plan will work, Priest. No harm in trying I suppose, at least, not to this immortal," Samyaza said lightheartedly of himself. "What do you suppose Janis will do when he finds out?"

"I don't know, but if the apocalypse is here, we may as well try. And if there's a chance you can help stop the coming crisis, it'll be all well worth it. Either way, you'll have freedom to do as you wish like the rest of us," Shepherd said.

"I know not what to say, Priest. I shall miss our games. What made you decide it was time? Other than the apocalypse, really?" Samyaza asked.

"I think it was the Creator's plan for you to be here, with everything prepared, right now, in order to avert this future tragedy. I can't sit by and let everything I've worked for die at a seven-year expiration date! That can't be the Creator's plan for everything I've worked so hard towards. I think he sent those Vikings to help you get out of the ice when you did. I believe it's no coincidence that you bumped into early travelers to cross the Atlantic, and as painful as it may seem—I believe you've been here waiting for this moment to make a difference. To help me make a difference for all humanity," Shepherd said confidently. "Let's get another game in right now, and we'll go over the finer details a little more this evening." Shepherd reset the board after Samyaza's apparent checkmate he'd achieved in the game they played while talking.

20

Sleight of Hand

hree weeks later, Bruno was sitting at his security post like usual for a Friday night. Shepherd had been bringing a few new dishes lately with extra food for Bruno on his Friday take-out night visits downstairs. It had become a more regular occurrence for Shepherd to visit on Friday and have a game with the prisoner. Bruno was looking forward to it so much that evening he noticed his stomach started to growl. He looked up from his current read, one of the books kept from making it downstairs due to the protocols. Bruno reached down and grabbed his stomach, checking the clock to see it was half past eight. The hour was a little late for Shepherd, but just as Bruno had that thought, *The Shepherd* burst through his hallway door.

"Bruno, my friend, I got you some great local fair tonight! I hope you're still hungry. I know it's a little late." Shepherd was wearing his usual flip flops, plaid pajama pants, and sweatshirt with the hood up. Not uncommon, the early fall nights had been chilly, particularly downstairs, as they now called the prison to seem less *dungeon-esk*.

Bruno was delighted to see Shepherd. "Thank you so much. I held off on dipping into my snacks too much, hoping you were coming down with dinner this evening."

"I told you I would, didn't I? Hey, is that box of books good to go down? I'll have Samyaza go in the holding room if you don't mind buzzing me in down there in a little bit," Shepherd said, motioning at the cardboard box from his last visit. Shepherd stepped behind the guard desk and grabbed the box.

"Yes, it is. Of course, and thanks again." Bruno started to organize his plate, enjoying the aroma.

"I wanna get this down there while his food is still hot. Do you mind if I use the card to take the elevator?" Shepherd asked. He had started retaking the elevator the last few weeks.

Bruno replied, distracted by hunger, "Yeah, no problem. The elevator card is in the same spot as always; drop the card off when you come back." Bruno was opening his food tray as Shepherd grabbed the keycard, slid it over the door panel and into his pocket, and headed down the elevator shaft.

Bruno sat back down at his guard post to enjoy his dinner. He set his book aside and dove into the dish Shepherd brought him. It was Italian—exquisite, authentic Italian. Bruno twirled some pasta up and took a bite as he watched the old security monitors at the desk. Even in 2041, Janis had never allowed church money to be wasted on updating the monitors or cameras for the prisoner's cell. Bruno watched Shepherd and Samyaza sit and eat while starting up a game of chess without audio. Samyaza was sitting with his hat on to avoid the light as usual.

After finishing his meal, Bruno turned back to his book, periodically glancing back at the monitors watching the ending of the chess game downstairs. After Samyaza and

Shepherd finished, they talked for a little while. Then Bruno was startled out of a reading daze by a loud *buzz*. It was the indicator that Samyaza was in his small holding room. Bruno looked at the monitor. Samyaza was in the little room between the double doors per routine cell maintenance procedures. Shepherd was out of sight by the door, waiting to be buzzed through with the box he'd taken down.

Bruno reached under the counter and pushed the door release button. The outer door clicked open along with the inner door to Samyaza's cell. Bruno waited for Shepherd to walk into the cell, drop off the large book box, and return to the observation room, locking the doors behind him. When Bruno saw Shepherd back by the chess board, he released the lock on Samyaza's holding room so he could make his way back to his cell. Bruno had expected the two to chat a little further into the evening, but the minute Samyaza was back in his cell, Shepherd was already in the elevator headed back up. As Shepherd reached the top, he popped to the side towards his door, heading back to his bedchamber.

"Good night, Shepherd. Thanks again for dinner. It was great!" Bruno said.

Shepherd gave him a wave and went for the door.

Bruno called out, "Oh, wait! Don't forget the elevator keycard."

Bruno turned his attention back to the monitor as Shepherd slipped the keycard onto the counter in front of him and headed through his door back to his bedroom for the night.

The following day, one of the newer Entity guards, Roberto, headed down the long hallway to the security room to relieve Bruno from the night owl shift he was finishing. The newbie entered the room in pristine uniform to relieve Bruno with his untucked shirt and untidy collar.

"Long, uneventful night as usual," Bruno said as he stepped from the desk. "The Shepherd came by but didn't stay long after he and the prisoner ate. I finished that book, by the way, if you want to check it out next. Pretty good."

"Yeah, maybe," Roberto replied sheepishly while reviewing his shift change checklist. "Bruno?" he called out.

Bruno stopped just before stepping out the door towards the Entity headquarters. "Yeah, what's up, poco?"

"You logged the elevator key out and back in, but you never logged the extra lower door key out," Roberto said.

"That's because the extra lower door key never got used last night," Bruno answered confidently.

Roberto looked up, perplexed, "Well then—why isn't it on the hook?"

That morning, Janis got to headquarters five minutes before the hour as he always did. He hovered over to his office, asking his current recruit assistant to bring him his morning coffee along the way. As his hover chair rounded his old simple desk, Janis cracked open his current logbook on top to check his agenda. He had a digital recorder that transcribed everything for him these days and a personal A.I. assistant, but he liked to take the occasional important notes with his own hands while he could still use them. He knew it wouldn't be long before arthritis and carpal tunnel completely took over. He scribed in the date and arrival time in the top right corner of the new page. The office recruit brought Janis' coffee in and placed it steaming on top of a small saucer in the middle of the desk.

Janis grabbed the coffee and took a sip, wafting the flavor. Right then, Bruno and Roberto burst into his office, and the

Entity recruit jumped back.

"Sir! You need to come see the prisoner!" Bruno yelled in a panic.

Janis nearly dropped his coffee. "Bruno, calm yourself, man. You know the Entity Commander never goes down there."

"No—Commander—you don't understand. Look!" Bruno yelled, pointing at the monitor on Commander Janis' desk.

Janis looked at the prisoner sitting in his chair. "See, he's right where he should be. What's the problem?"

"No sir, take a closer look!" Bruno yelled.

Janis looked at the screen and dropped his coffee and his jaw. The prisoner sitting in a chair on the screen took off his saturno and smiled up at the camera. It was *The Shepherd*.

Entity Interview Record 2873- October 4, 2041-Transcribed Via Desk Mate A.I.

Interviewer: Entity Commander Janis Borgman

Witness: Entity Agent Johan Bruno

Subject: The Shepherd, Pope Leo XIV

COMMANDER JANIS: This is Commander Janis Borgman of the Vatican Entity. Today is October 4, 2041. I am interviewing our Holy Father, Liam Shepherd Thompson, also known as Pope Leo XIV, also known as The Shepherd.

AGENT BRUNO: Also known as Our Holy Shepherd!

COMMANDER JANIS: Not—yes, also known as Our Holy Shepherd. I am accompanied by witness Entity Agent Johan Bruno for this interview. Bruno will be acting as a witness ONLY. Shepherd, can you please explain to me, and for the recording, how you came to be in the prisoner's cell below the Vatican last night? And how is it that the prisoner, also known as Samyaza, escaped undetected?

THE SHEPHERD: Yes, Janis. But first of all, I must apologize. I'm very sorry I had to deceive all of you. I had no choice. Of course, you would have all tried to stop me, but I had to get him out.

COMMANDER JANIS: I'll deal with the why later. Right now, I want to know how, and where the creature is!

THE SHEPHERD: Janis, Samyaza is gone. Long gone. You're never going to find him. He had a—what was it—a six-hour head start on your people? He might even be out of the country by now.

COMMANDER JANIS: How could he leave the country?

THE SHEPHERD: I got Samyaza a passport and travel documents, Janis. I've been planning this for a very, very long time. Again, I really am sorry, but the protocols being the way they are—if I ever was going to let Samyaza out, I had to do it without you knowing. I tried to talk to you about this when the Apocalypse Conference took place, and you wouldn't listen! Don't you see we have to try anything we know of to save the world? We can't let everything we've worked for end in seven years.

COMMANDER JANIS: We'll still get Interpol and our international agencies looking into this and find where he might be going. I know you had that little pet project with Donelly going on. Nothing goes on around here without me knowing!

THE SHEPHERD: Donelly had nothing to do with this. He only did research for me.

COMMANDER JANIS: Alright, well then, who helped you with the escape?

THE SHEPHERD: It was just Samyaza and me.

COMMANDER JANIS: Explain.

THE SHEPHERD: I figured it out mainly on my own over the years, but Samyaza had a few ideas and suggestions along the way. When we did the remodel to the cell I made sure to avoid adding costs to upgrade certain security aspects like the monitors, the cameras, and even some of the lighting. This kept the area in front of the new double doors as a blindspot. Once Samyaza and I decided it was time to start preparing, I filled him in on my plan. We began making other small changes; I started wearing my hood up more when walking past the guard desk at night. Samyaza made sure he kept watching TV late at night in his chair with his hat on. I began making Friday dinner a more regular part of my routine. Also, bringing Bruno some food was a part of the plan. Sorry, Bruno.

AGENT BRUNO: It's alright Shepherd.

COMMANDER JANIS: Witness only Agent Bruno, please! Go on, Shepherd. How did you get the door keycard?

THE SHEPHERD: Bruno was smelling his food when I grabbed the elevator key, so he didn't notice I also took the spare door key. I rode down to the basement, and Samyaza and I had our usual meal and a game of chess. Then, when I moved to take his books to the doors, I had Samyaza come to the doors, and I used the keycard to open both in the blindspot. I gave Samyaza a quick hug in the entryway. We swapped outfits, and I put on his hat and stayed in his cell while he went out into the observation room. I sat with his clothes and hat on in the holding room while Bruno buzzed Samyaza back into the cell, thinking it was me. For a moment, Samyaza was already free, but he had to go back into his cell one last time to drop off the box of books to keep up the ruse. He then walked back out the double doors, shutting himself into the observation room, where he headed to the elevator with his hood up, pretending to look and walk like me. I waited to get buzzed back into Samyaza's cell, where I walked back in, keeping my head down, hiding under the brim of Samyaza's hat. I sat and watched TV all night. It was fun; I haven't done that in years.

COMMANDER JANIS: You just sat there all night till we discovered you in the cell the next morning? How did you know the creature would make it past Bruno at security?

THE SHEPHERD: As I said, I'd been keeping my hood up more and walking directly back to my door without much more than a wave to Bruno lately. As long as Samyaza did the same, I figured no one would notice that it wasn't me.

AGENT BRUNO: I wondered why you'd been acting so differently when leaving recently, Shepherd.

COMMANDER JANIS: Bruno, please. So, you chanced the entire escape on the hood hiding his face?

THE SHEPHERD: It worked, didn't it?

AGENT BRUNO: I even had him drop the keycard, and I still didn't notice it wasn't you, Shepherd.

THE SHEPHERD: Don't beat yourself up, Bruno. I've been planning this for over a decade. I even planned the security for the cell with this escape in mind. I'm too much of an overthinker. I'd already devised this plan years ago before submitting my requests for a remodel. The updates and doors made it all that easier to pick and choose my own perfect escape plan, and now I finally got to execute it years later. What a retirement gift.

AGENT BRUNO: Retirement, father?

THE SHEPHERD: Well, yeah, that was Janis' suggestion.

COMMANDER JANIS: We were joking!

THE SHEPHERD: No, I think what you were saying made a lot of sense with everything happening in the world. Might be good for me to let someone else step up, and I can go back to my old home village and take care of my neighbors and family a little bit in my final years. Before I'm hovering everywhere like you, Janis.

COMMANDER JANIS: You can't be serious! You let the Watcher go! You can't just leave!

AGENT BRUNO: Watcher?

THE SHEPHERD: Yes, Bruno. The prisoner's name was Samyaza, and he was the leader of the Watchers. Now, he's making a beeline to the Sword of the Cherubim at the entrance to the Garden of Eden. There, he will fall on the sword, taking himself and his Watchers back to the Creator, leaving the Earth free of all evil influences and possibly averting what's coming.

AGENT BRUNO: You're trying to stop the apocalypse, aren't you, Shepherd?

COMMANDER JANIS: Bruno, keep quiet! I don't know what this sword is, and I don't care. You can't keep breaking protocol like this. Stop talking about the prisoner!

THE SHEPHERD: His name is Samyaza, and he's not a prisoner anymore. Therefore, no more prisoner protocol.

COMMANDER JANIS: You don't make the rules!

AGENT BRUNO: He's right, I think, isn't he? There's no prisoner anymore. Am I going to have to get a different position since there's no one to guard anymore?

COMMANDER JANIS: Shut up, Bruno! It doesn't matter! That creature isn't going to save the world. The A.I.s would've seen this coming.

THE SHEPHERD: The A.I.s didn't know about Samyaza.

He isn't in the Omega-AI database. He's the only thing that can account for the other 1.01% it was off on the Kozlov Scale. Maybe he can use that little chance to save the world.

COMMANDER JANIS: This is not the Creator's plan!

THE SHEPHERD: What do you know of the Creator's plan? How do you know this isn't exactly what the Creator wanted all along?

COMMANDER JANIS: You were there at the Apocalypse Conference. You heard the same prophesies and predictions as I did, with all the supporting data from the Omega-AI. The Creator has let us know that this day is coming, and there's nothing you or some Watcher can do about it! Does this sword really exist?

THE SHEPHERD: I've seen it myself. It's like looking at the sun. You want the world to end, don't you, Janis? That's what this is all about for you. You want the apocalypse to come.

COMMANDER JANIS: Of course I do! This world killed my family! This world killed my beautiful child. The only good part of the world is this church and the order it brings to mankind. If the Creator has seen fit to end mankind, I doubt there's anything you can do to stop it!

THE SHEPHERD: Janis, the Watcher's imprisonment was never part of the Creator's plan in the first place. Samyaza was put there by a pope who was scared he might lose his job if he let the Watcher get rid of the evil influences in our world.

AGENT BRUNO: That's who we've been guarding this whole time? I thought it was like—some demon.

COMMANDER JANIS: It is a demon! And it's clearly poisoned the mind of our Holy Father, making him release him from prison, falter the Creator's plan, and step down from his position in one fell swoop. Shepherd you—you fool! You stupid—stupid fool!

AGENT BRUNO: Can the Watcher stop the apocalypse?

COMMANDER JANIS: Of course not!

THE SHEPHERD: Samyaza might! Once all evil influence is removed from the world, maybe the Omega-AI will come up with some new calculations. Who knows, but if the world was ending, what did I have to lose? Anyway, are we done here? I will need Marco to meet me in my room to review a few things.

COMMANDER JANIS: Where do you think you're going?

THE SHEPHERD: To start packing. I'm retiring. And I'm certainly not going to stay in the Vatican for my retirement.

COMMANDER JANIS: You can't just leave!

THE SHEPHERD: Why not?

COMMANDER JANIS: I forbid it! I'm the Commander of the Entity!

THE SHEPHERD: And I'm the pope, The Shepherd, The Holy Father, the King of the Vatican. And who presides over the Entity?

AGENT BRUNO: The King of the Vatican!

THE SHEPHERD: The King of the Vatican, that's right, Bruno my man.

COMMANDER JANIS: I'm still going to send agents to track the creature down! He may be immortal, but he's not invisible!

THE SHEPHERD: Samyaza is one of the oldest and wisest beings on the planet. I don't think he'll have any trouble getting to his destination with the resources I've given him. You're welcome to try and stop him.

COMMANDER JANIS: Who do you think you are Shepherd? You said save the world and the church second. The world is going to be ashes anyway, and you've just killed the church with it!

THE SHEPHERD: I think I may have done the opposite, but we'll have to wait and let history decide.

(Subject exited the room. Interview concluded.)

Entity Commander Janis Borgman Personal Log, Manual Entry addition to Interview Record 2873, October 4, 2041:

I have reviewed all information on the prisoner escape, and it has been concluded that Liam S. Thompson, as the sitting Holy King of the Vatican at the time, has full authority to pardon himself of all actions. On retiring from his post as Bishop of Rome, Head of the Holy Catholic Church, that concludes the Entity's interests in The Shepherd.

As for the prisoner, our agents have sent drones into the caverns that we were led to by our informants in Ethiopia. If the sword is anything like Shepherd said, it is no longer found in the caves, however—there is more deep in that cavern to be investigated.

The pursuit of the creature has gone cold from there. Our drones and satellites have not found any sign of the Watcher Samyaza.

The Entity prisoner guards' last task is to clear the prisoner's cell of all items to be reviewed and cataloged.

The prisoner protocols are to be abolished from the Entity Order and will no longer be enforced. All Entity guards currently under the prisoner protocol will be released from those responsibilities and duties and given new tasks.

21

Dear Priest

S hepherd wasn't bluffing. He was already considering what Janis suggested about retiring and became one of the few popes in history to leave the Chair of Saint Peter voluntarily. A new conclave was called, and all the cardinals traveled to The Vatican again for the first time since Shepherd's election eighteen years ago. It was pointed out by Johns that since Shepherd was no longer the pope, he was never actually a cardinal and couldn't attend the conclave. Shepherd was initially to be excluded from the event by law but was unanimously given the honorary title of cardinal to skirt around the technicality, and he was invited back inside.

The cardinals all wanted to know why Shepherd had chosen to step down so abruptly from his seat. He didn't know what to say to them about Samyaza, and the apocalypse was already lingering. The cardinals needed to understand why Shepherd would resign in such a great time of unrest and need. Shepherd couldn't tell them his whole secret plot he'd just unraveled to potentially avert the apocalypse. Shepherd didn't think anyone would believe him anyway. So, he explained that he was stepping aside for a few reasons. One was because he was getting a little older and felt that he was a withered man who needed to step aside and let a new pope, with a spirit like his younger self when he first was elected, take on the role. He felt that it should be a new tradition that when a man is tired and weary and feels himself no longer fit, it was his duty to let another sharper leader take the reins. Shepherd hoped it would set a new precedent.

In his closing statement to the conclave, Shepherd said, "I think, if anything, I've learned with what I've experienced in my time as pope that the world needs younger leaders. We don't need old men set in their ways. We need young men still willing to get their hands dirty for what they believe in. Men who care about what is to come, rather than those pining over what was lost."

Shepherd went on to give reasons for wanting to do more for his home community and to see his family, which had grown much larger in his busy absence. Shepherd had many nieces and nephews now with children of their own on the way. Also, his older sister, Emily, was in poor health. She received the best in-home robotics assistance that Shepherd could find for her, but he wanted a human touch there. With her husband having passed last fall, she was fading quickly. Shepherd honestly did want to be with his sister more before her time came.

His last thoughts on the matter to the conclave were, "I've learned the world will keep spinning pretty much the same way it always has. People's hearts need to be changed, not the world. We need to see our neighbors, not the bigger picture. I've done everything I think I can from this position. Now, I will take back what time I have and save my world, but just a smaller piece of it. An old friend of mine, who spent a long time under—in the Vatican, taught me more than anyone else that doing something was always better than sitting and doing nothing. I believe the Creator's plan asks us to do what we think is right, and that as long as we are selfless and not selfish we're on the best possible path. I hope and pray this world doesn't end in the predicted apocalypse, but I truly believe at this point, if the predictions are true, it'll end all the same, with or without me in this position. Now, it's someone else's turn to take this seat."

After Shepherd's speech, the attention turned slightly from him, and the conclave began its process of deliberations and nominations. Initial votes were scattered. Some even had "Our Holy Shepherd" written on the cards, indicating they would not pick independently. After another vote, it was unanimous for *The Shepherd*. It became clear that the conclave wanted Shepherd to elect his replacement. Shepherd stood up from his seat and walked to the far end of the table where Johns was sitting. Johns was mainly retired but still part of the conclave.

"Jeez! Don't look at me, you fool. Oy'm older than you are! I'm gonna be in a 'over-chair like *The Shadow* within the next two years. That's if'n I make it that long!" Johns rattled off, pushing Shepherd away.

"Calm down, old friend. I wouldn't do that to you, but I have one last request," Shepherd said, comforting the old man. He leaned in and whispered something privately to Johns. After a brief embrace between the two, Shepherd stepped aside, and Johns asked everyone for their attention. Johns made his way to the far end of the table he'd been seated at and rounded it to where the papal staff was off to the side, taking notes.

Shepherd slipped out the side Swiss Guard entrance as Johns made an announcement.

Johns moved behind Marco's seat and rested his hands on Marco's shoulders. His silvery ponytail was draped over the back of his chair longer than ever. Johns cleared his throat and proclaimed, "My fellow cardinals, the man that Our 'oly Shepherd has agreed to choose since you have giv'n 'im yer votes, is the man seated before me!"

It had been two weeks since Shepherd last walked out of the Vatican. He flew back to New Zealand that very same day he slipped out of the conclave, leaving Johns to announce Marco as his replacement. He dawned his same Liam disguise from way back when he'd taken that day trip on the boat with Elias to get through crowds and airport security as unnoticed as possible. A few folks recognized him at security, but all being loving fans, they helped him keep his cover and kept things professional.

After arriving in New Zealand, he'd traveled to his childhood home and taken up temporary residence back in Dunedin. His sister's home was in the village, a short walk away. The Chain Hills house had been left in the family initially to Shepherd. Since he had joined the church and had no need for it, he'd given it to the family estate as a vacation home for anyone visiting to use and lend out. It was regularly up-kept by Emily's son and his family when they came to visit her from their place in the next county. Needless to say, Shepherd was more than welcome back in his own home, and it was his perfect base of operations for taking care of Em, visiting town, and having family and friends popping in and out, which was constant already. He was settling in and already contacting local community leaders and churches to find where he could be of service. Everyone he'd reached out to insisted he'd already done enough over the years with funding and projects and that he should enjoy retirement. Some people even said to enjoy the time he had before the impending apocalypse.

Shepherd still had hope for Samyaza. He hadn't heard or seen anything to indicate whether the Watcher succeeded, other than the sword missing from the caves, according to the reports he was getting from Marco. The two stayed in touch after Shepherd left the Vatican. Marco had a million questions after he got into the pope chest. All of which could be answered now that no more protocols were in place. There hadn't been any stories in the news yet to indicate whether Samyaza's Watchers were gone or if it was making any impact yet. One variation of the Omega-AI, version 332, the most current test module, gave some inconsistent results from previous versions. So far, nothing as far-reaching as an indication that all evil was gone from the Earth.

One afternoon, Shepherd was outside, enjoying breathing in the cool sea air while painting his home, when a car pulled up in front of the house. Shepherd stepped off his ladder, gently placed his wet bush on the top brim of the paint can, and walked around the house to see who it was. One man got out of the car, it was Bruno. He stepped out in plain clothes, which caught Shepherd off guard, having only ever seen him in the traditional black secret-agent-type suit Entity members wore at all times. Bruno wore a light button-up shirt, khaki pants, sunglasses, and loafers. He was hefting a large leather duffel bag at his side as he casually approached the house.

Bruno reached out his hand, but Shepherd brushed it away

and hugged the man. Bruno dropped the bag to the side and embraced him back.

"It's good to see you, Bruno!" Shepherd called out.

"Ciao, Shepherd!" Bruno whimpered back, grinning ear to ear.

"Please, it's just Liam now. Marco is the new *Shepherd*," Liam said sarcastically. Marco had chosen the name Pope Shepherd II in honor of Liam. Liam had insisted against it on a phone call right after he'd heard, but Marco wouldn't budge on the name.

Liam was also declared a saint by Pope Shepherd II for his accomplishments and, as Shepherd II put it, "for having one of the greatest impacts on the united souls of all mankind in the last thousand years."

According to Johns, Liam was also being considered for a Nobel Prize. Johns spilled the beans to him about an interview with the Nobel people just a few days before. As *The Shepherd*, Liam had created the world's largest non-profit empire. *The Flock* was run by one of history's largest and most diverse boards. With over 200 members, the board was like a miniature congress. The new world order had the checks and balances of the United Nations and international governments, The Flock Council, as the Flock board was being called, and the Vatican sovereignty over the church and land purchased in Africa. There was a new harmonious balance in the world.

Liam opened the door for Bruno, a serendipitous moment for them since usually it was the other way around, and showed him into the house. "Can I get you anything? Tea? And how's Rossi doing?" Liam asked cheerfully.

"Yes, thank you. Rossi is well. He's been learning the ropes from Janis on the Entity Commander position to prepare in case he needs replaced soon. I hope you don't mind me showing up unannounced. I had to keep my travel plans somewhat quiet. I have something for you, Liam." Bruno patted the bag he'd brought along at his side.

Liam was worried but intrigued. He joked as they walked into the house through the creaky front door. "What—did I leave some socks in a drawer or something, and you brought them all the way just for me?"

"Ha! Not so simple as that, no."

Liam switched on the electric kettle and grabbed his tin of tea fixings from a cabinet. Bruno walked over to a small family table in the adjoining kitchenette area where Liam's mother had long ago cooked and served for a family of six. While they waited for the water to heat up, Liam asked, "So Bruno, what do they have you doing around the Vatican now that there's no prisoner to guard these days?"

Bruno chuckled some. "Well, I didn't come to talk shop, but Janis has been so busy trying to track down Samyaza that the internal staff has mostly been holding down our desks lately, hence the ability to take some time off and come here today. I've been meaning to ask you, Liam, if you have heard from Samyaza?"

Liam grabbed the kettle as it started to steam. "I haven't heard or seen even a sign of Samyaza, no. I don't know how we'd tell if he fell on his sword. If he's out there somewhere, he's not bringing any attention to himself." Liam poured both cups and carried them to join Bruno at the table.

Bruno grabbed one of the warm cups from Liam's outstretched hand, "Grazie. Liam, what really made you decide to let Samyaza go? Was it the apocalypse predictions? They say those are faltering now, and there have been inconsistencies in the new data since you retired. You weren't allowed to share what you knew about Samyaza with anyone because of the protocols. You couldn't talk to your closest advisors. Not even Johns or Marco knew. Did they know anything?"

"No. I was true to my word. I stuck to the protocols. Well, till the last month mostly."

"So, how did you decide?"

"I decided—that the lesser of two evils—is still an evil. The right thing to do is the right thing to do regardless of the outcome. If the Creator had a plan for Samyaza to be punished, then I figured 3,000 years on ice should have been enough. The popes of the past and the Entity wrongfully imprisoned Samyaza for over 500 years. It was time to let the man go. He was made by the Creator and is a part of this world, too. Who are we to dictate whether he lives or dies and how he makes his way in the world? Samyaza has done no wrong since the Creator flooded our world, and whatever wrong he has done was washed away with the Great Deluge, as far as I'm concerned. Over thirty verses in the Bible instruct us not to judge others. That right is the Creator's alone."

"You lost me a little bit there, Liam. 3,000 years on ice? Great Deluge?"

"Oh, just some things Samyaza and I used to talk about."

Bruno set the leather bag he'd brought on the table's edge, opened it, and slipped out a package wrapped in cardboard paper and brown twine.

"What's this?" Liam asked, gesturing at the package.

"My last duty as Entity prisoner guard was to clean out Samyaza's cell."

Liam had forgotten, "Oh, that's right. Well, he was a tidy

chap. I don't suppose there was much too clean."

"There wasn't, you're right. But then, when we removed the furniture, I noticed something off about Samyaza's desk."

Liam remembered the old desk Samyaza had insisted on keeping along with his green chair whenever the remodel took place. "Yeah, the old walnut one. It was so torn up, but I couldn't get Samyaza to let me replace it. He said he loved writing at it and didn't care for an upgrade—something like that."

"Well, I was alone the second day downstairs for a few hours and moved the desk by myself. When I pulled it from the wall, a wood slat fell from behind, revealing a cubby hidden in a space behind the drawers. It must have been there all along for hundreds of years. No one ever noticed. They gave Samyaza some old desk with a secret compartment already built in." Bruno pushed the package closer to Liam across the table. "In the compartment was this package."

"Holy smokes! Why haven't you opened it yet? And why is it here? How did you get it out of the Vatican?" Liam was shocked at Bruno's gumption.

"I was in charge of overseeing the cataloging of the prisoner's cell. I kept my discovery out of the record and kept the package hidden. Once I could take a few days off, I planned a flight here and brought it straight to you from the airport. I scanned it with our security systems, and nothing appeared harmful inside, and nothing set off any sensors."

"You could get into a mountain of trouble, man! What if Janis found out?"

"Janis is too bitter towards you and too busy looking for Samyaza to worry about how many toothbrushes I cataloged when we cleaned out his cell. No one knows this package is here but you and me."

"But Bruno, what made you want to bring it straight to me? You don't know what it is, do you?"

No, but it's for you, Liam. This was tucked under the twine on top when I pulled it from the back of the desk."

Bruno showed Liam a plain letter envelope. It had written on the front in Samyaza's hand—*For The Shepherd.*

Bruno continued, "Samyaza must have left this for you after he knew you were going to help him escape. He left the letter to make sure if anyone found it, they'd know the package should go to you. The x-ray scan showed something dense, maybe books, but it hasn't been opened."

"Would you like to be here when I open it?"

"Hell yes! Thanks, I was afraid to ask," Bruno said, sitting up straighter over the table.

"Of course. You came all this way." Liam set the envelope aside first to see what was in the package. He untied the twine and tore away the paper wrapping. Inside were six different leather-bound journals. Massive ones that Liam recognized he'd delivered to Samyaza over the years. Each one a slightly different shade of leather—green, navy, rust, and each one a different level of wear. "These are some of his journals, I think. I gave him these blank. Samyaza requested paper and new journals occasionally. I never thought much of it. He did all his writing in plain sight on his desk under surveillance."

"Well, at some point, he found a way to drop these back behind the desk and then package them up unnoticed at the last minute. What do they say?" Bruno asked curiously.

Liam flipped one open. The text was all written in Watcher. Liam had a basic knowledge of it, enough to recognize it on sight but not read it fluently. Liam also recognized Samyaza's handwriting from having reviewed many of his journals over the years.

"Can you read that?" Bruno asked quizzically, looking at the strange language.

"No, but I can have it translated," Liam said. He pulled the letter back off the table and opened it. It was also in Samyaza's hand, but the language was regular English. Liam read it aloud for Bruno to hear with him.

Dear Priest,

I do not know if this letter will reach you or if Janis will bury it like he does everything else. I knew our goodbye after our last game together would be brief, but I owed you more than that for everything you have done for me. You have become my own priest in a way, and so here is my confession.

These journals are my transcribed copies of the six ages of the Watchers, almost precisely as I chronicled them in the time before the Great Deluge thousands of years ago. The original copies have been lost in the flood, and I have never shared these stories with anyone. Enoch's descendants have passed some of these stories through Noah and your Bible. These are my accounts. These are the accounts of the Watchers—an accurate history of the events of our time. I wanted to share them with you, Shepherd. I wanted you to see all that has come before to satisfy your curiosity finally.

We, the Watchers, were the reason the Creator sent the Great Deluge to flood the entire Earth. The Creator wanted to wash every sign of our existence from the land and sea. He wanted our children, the Bekori, nephilim, and all their beauty and wonder removed from existence. We had no choice. We were fathers put into an unbearable situation, twice by our Creator; once during the Bekori Wars when I used the Cherubim Sword to stop Azazel and Cain's armies. *The second was when the Creator asked us to lay down and die with the world we loved in the Great Deluge while he saved what parts he cherry-picked of nature and placed on Noah's Ark.*

It pained me not to share everything with you before I escaped, but I could not tell you about my oath. As you know, I am bound to my word. It cuts me deeply to do this to you, my friend, but I have deceived you. With these chronicles, you will learn of my true nature and of my true feelings towards mankind, the Archangels, and the Creator. I do wish to help mankind, but not in the way you have been convinced. I do not want to find the Sword of the Cherubim to fall on it and take myself and my Watchers back to our Creator. I wish to pull the sword from the ground and wield it for myself—growing my size and wings back to my original state as a fully embodied Watcher in the physical realm. Rather than end my life and the existence of my Watchers, I will take the sword's power for the first time since the Bekori Wars long ago. I will take the power of the Cherubim Sword to the phantom realm. There, I will finally use the sword to focus my Watchers' consciousnesses and rally them to my side, lifting them from the fog they have existed in almost twice as long now as when they were alive in this realm before. With my Watchers at my side and with the sword, I will draw focus to our powers together, and we will defeat the Archangels once and for all, ending their manipulative control over Earth's natural processes. I shall bring peace to nature as it once was in the garden and bring peace to humankind. We will destroy whatever spirits, demons, men, angels, Archangels, and Creator stand in our way and recreate a new world for Watchers and mankind alike.

Once the phantom realm is purged, I will return here. I will return with my Watchers, Priest. I will bring heaven on Earth back the way it always should have been, the way the Creator promised before my Watchers got confused and made a mess of everything.

I will fix all we have done wrong before. I will bring the Creator back to our side by saving humans and averting the apocalypse. I still wish to save you and your world, Priest, but I could not do so in the ways that you thought best. You do not know the true nature of the Creator and the apocalypse that he has planned for this world. I shall remove the Archangels from their seats and return within seven years to save you and all of mankind from the tribulations that the Creator has set in motion to befall you. Your friends have already put too much trust in this Omega-AI, as you called it. The Ether-Net is so very complex. Your scientists have flipped a coin several hundred times, and it just so happened to come up heads every single time, but that does not change that tails is just around the corner. They think they are pooling enough data when it is not even a drop in the ocean of what they are attempting to understand.

The Creator's plan is faulty. My plan is better. The Watchers must be able to fix what was broken once and for all. The Creator's plans continue to fail, and when they do, he destroys everything. I will remove him from the equation and make things new. I was almost successful before, but the Creator stopped me. The same Creator who says he loves you yet tortures you. The Creator who only lets you enjoy peace if you have experienced war. I will not stand for this to be how existence functions anymore!

I am so sorry I had to do this to you, Priest, that I had to deceive you. From the beginning, this was my plan. I was able to keep it secret from you while slowly moving you from the shadows in a direction that would eventually lead to my escape. I played the long con. I played a long game with you through each and every visit. Yes, you were a bishop in life, but on my board, you were a pawn. I was moving you slowly, space by space, hoping to go unnoticed until a pivotal point in the game when it would be advantageous. Leaving only one conclusion, checkmate. I knew my stories would entice you. If I explained to you how impossible everything was and where all the clues were to get you started tracking down the sword's resting place, someone of your adventurous spirit would eventually seek it out. After touching you that day in the cell, I knew that nothing would hold you back once I gave you the bits and pieces of information to devise your own plan.

So, we simply talked, and I gave you all the ammunition you needed to shoot and fire out into the world—and look what you brought back! Being trapped here, I could only inspire you and hope for the best.

I gave you just the right amount of information, in just the proper doses, to help you build a narrative of my life as one of penance and suffering, one deserving redemption, salvation, or a second chance. And you fell for every breadcrumb I left you. I grew fond of you and ashamed of how I used you, Priest, but the game had to continue. I have played this game before, but you see, I can only reset the board when there is a new pope. I led you to my journal, to the sword, and an escape plan.

You planned for my escape because you felt so guilty about my torture and my imprisonment, all of which were true. I did not have to do much other than sit back and let some of the facts do the work for me. I referred you to different journals and different parts where you would find the most awful and tormented days of my existence here. I leaned into your empathy, on your human emotions, to convince you that there was no real reason to keep me here. All the while, I hid my true intentions, not to die, but to fight, not to give up, but to take up arms. I swore to my Watcher brothers that we would remake this world again. I was bound to that oath when they were taken from me, and it has sustained me through everything I have endured.

The apocalypse may be coming, but it will never be what you or

274

I expect. I knew it would come someday. I knew that something, someday, would convince you that there would be no reason to keep me here. I trusted that you would one day find the sword, and a situation dire enough would arise, as it has, to convince you of the benefits of releasing me. I will do what I can for you, Priest. I am sorry for this deception, for what I have done to you, one who has treated me better than all others in this new world.

I will return to your realm once I have removed the physical universe's oppressors from the phantom realm and rally my Watchers to me. I will show the Creator, and we will make him see things our way this time. We will show the Creator there is no need to destroy the world again. This time, Watchers and Man can get it right. I will take back this world from his minions myself.

Mankind will suffer greatly before and after our return to the physical realm. Once we defeat the Archangels, the world will be in chaos until the dust settles from the natural order of the planet rearranging. Many humans will also deny the new order and cling to their social media technology and new gods they have replaced sanity with. They have not been listening to you. We will educate them.

Remember, we are all on the Creator's chess board, Priest, but you were also on mine.

Your friend,
Sam

22

Epilogue

From The Chronicles of the Watchers, Epic I, Descent

"We have spoken of this before!" shouted Samyaza as he paced before the ranks of his gathered host of Watchers, "There are too many unknowns!" Samyaza, the leader of the Watchers, was at an end. He let his head fall in consternation till his chin rested heavily on his chest. Samyaza heard more than enough over the last three centuries to know that the whispering, rumors, and now planning had to conclude one way or another. He would either have to take action or find ways to restrain his Watchers. The Watchers were miserable and relentless. They had become so enamored that they were to the point where nothing could sway them in any direction but forward on their chosen path. Samyaza lifted his gaze and asked the host before him, "Do you not see that once we descend, we may never be able to return? Are they worth the risk to you? To me? To all of us!"

"We would rather be destroyed than go on any longer without acting!" was Azazel's escalating rebuttal. "My Watchers and the other Chiefs' Watchers have observed them for so long, feel so connected and emotionally attached, that they want nothing else. We Watchers were not made to understand these feelings and desires fully, but we know that we cannot hold back and only watch any longer!"

Azazel was among nineteen of his fellow chieftains who had come before Samyaza, their leader, in such a pivotal moment. He was not a favorite amongst the Watchers, but in these last few councils, Azazel had become more and more vocal about the concerns of his Watchers, increasing his popularity. Samyaza felt the emotion in the words of his chief. Azazel was always the most combative in these arguments. There was never a time when Azazel seemed content, even for a second, with his task. Samyaza felt this in him, as it was Samyaza's gift being their leader, given to him by the Creator. He had the ability to sense the minds of those he was responsible for.

"I know the edge you feel to be walking," Samyaza acknowledged back. "I feel it myself and long for a relationship with them. But at what cost? The Creator sent us to this realm between worlds so we could report to him on man's progress. Not so that we would become so infatuated with their women that we would forsake our task and descend onto their plane!"

The realm of the Watchers was not the only place they had known. Samyaza, his chiefs, their lieutenants, and the whole 200 of those he was with had once been in the company of the Creator. The Creator made all, but what was his grand design or plan for the Watchers? Even Samyaza did not know. When he and all his Watchers were brought together, they were given simple instructions—watch, seek to understand mankind, and report.

"Can this not be one of the ways we better understand man?" Turel posed the question. "Is that not what we were made for?"

Samyaza again lowered his head. He knew this had been discussed each time the subject of crossing into man's realm was brought up. "Are we not Watchers? I am sure the Creator will see watching and interacting as two very different things," he discerned.

The council went silent. Samyaza could feel that he had made his point but also that they were not swayed. He looked hard at his Watcher brothers and breathed in all that they were feeling and thinking around him. He knew that there was nothing else to be said; their minds and hearts were already made up whether he gave his blessing or not. He knew the next step was inevitable, but he wouldn't approve without terms.

"What does our leader say?" pressed Azazel, again speaking for everyone toward Samyaza.

"I know your pleas and where your hearts are, and I see now that there is no other way. But if this is what must be, and if I am to make the decision, then you all must swear to me and bind yourselves to your leader in this action. We know not what the Creator will do; if he sees our actions as an offense, I will suffer, and I will not do so alone. We must all be willing to suffer any consequences together for such an undertaking. Do you swear and bind your fates to mine and each other in this endeavor?"

There was no hesitation from a single chief. In unison, without a moment of deliberation, they all cried out, "Yes!"

Samyaza felt no regret or second thoughts from those before him, and he knew the chiefs spoke for their Watchers. "It has been decided then," he said more softly to himself as he turned and looked down on the world beneath them. Samyaza stared quietly down at Earth for a moment, knowing that it would be their new home and that this was the last time he would see it from that place. "We will descend to the Earth, it will become our home, and we shall see if the women of mankind we have watched will have us as we hope." *And may the Creator show mercy*, was the final thought in Samyaza's mind.

No Watcher had ever crossed onto the same plane as man before; they had no permission to do so. The Creator made clear that their only purpose was to observe. The fact that the barrier between worlds was right in front of them the whole time made watching more agonizing year after year. Azazel was the first to cross over as they stepped up to the barrier. He spread his wings as he prepared for the leap. The giant Watcher's massive wings stretched ten feet on either side of him as he confidently walked to the ledge. Since no one had crossed before, there was no way of knowing what would happen. Azazel kept an intense expression as he pushed the invisible field before him. It bubbled out, and then, with one strong push, he was through and descending towards the Earth. After Azazel was through, the rest of the host of Watchers rushed right after, falling and twisting through the air like a hurricane of feathers and fury. Samyaza waited. He wanted to show his Watchers his caution and his protest of this act, conveying his disapproval by being last. They were all eager to descend; fear came over some of the Watcher's faces as they pushed through.

When the last of the other Watchers had moved off the Watchers' realm and descended into the realm of man, Samyaza stood at the edge—the Earth glowing with life stretching out far below. The Watchers all had the ability to reach the Earth's surface with their senses. The Watchers could listen and see all that man was engaged in, but the distance at the moment felt greater than ever. Samyaza stretched his wings, pushed through the barrier, and leaped. Down he fell. The air around him was calm and peaceful for a moment, and then he began to fall much faster than he expected. Looking down, he could see an expanse of Earth growing ever closer; there was no sign of the Watchers who leaped before him, only a strange smoke. Samyaza tensed as the thought that something had gone wrong washed over him.

A strange sensation began to shudder through Samyaza's wings, bringing his focus back to his current reality. Looking back, he realized his beautiful white feathered wings were starting to burn! *The smoke! The smoke was my Watchers burning!* He had never felt heat or the sensation of fire before since he was not only immortal but also impermeable. Such senses didn't exist for the Watchers in their realm. The fiery sting of the flames and heat ripping away at him made what was a short fall stretch with agony. The new experience of pain made him suddenly worry that he had made a mistake, that maybe he should call his Watchers to turn back. Samyaza had only felt emotions such as anger, fear, lust, and happiness. This new feeling in a physical form was utterly foreign to him. Even when he brushed shoulders with a fellow Watcher in their realm, there was no sensation from the contact. The horrible pain was what Samyaza worried would be the first of many hardships that the Watchers might face from their decision. Samyaza and the other Watchers knew there would be risks, but with no previous experiences of pain, the shock was horrendous.

The stinging in his shoulders caused Samyaza to cry out in uncontrollable agony. He was beginning to wonder as he fell what else was in store if only seconds into this journey there was such profound discomfort. His wings were almost charred to the bone! He experienced a new sensation of smell, burning sulfur, as his wings withered until nothing was left but a string of hot coals whipping in the wind hanging from his back. The feathers were blowing away like ash. When the last of the ash and smoke blew clear, nothing remained where the gift of flight once was. His back was a cauterized searing wound.

Samyaza realized he was through the thicker parts of the Earth's atmosphere and spread his arms, feeling the wind as best he could to slow his body without his wings. He looked out over the planet below him. Samyaza could now see the area where they would be falling. As he continued his descent, Samyaza realized that the fall did not affect his clothes, hair, and skin. *Why would just our wings be affected?* He wondered. This thought was quickly replaced with the horror of his possible mortality and the Earth below growing closer and closer. Samyaza's speed was increasing at an enormous rate. As he broke through the clouds, he could see pops of Earth flying into the air below him. Samyaza was terrified to realize this was his Watchers slamming into the planet's surface! They were hitting the ground at such a high speed that it was causing explosions of rock and dust hundreds of feet into the air. *Had they survived? Was this how quickly it would all end? What have we done?*

When first discussing how they would get to Earth if they tried, the Watchers assumed they would have the use of their wings. They had no reason to think all of them would immediately lose their wings and be unable to make a slow, controlled descent to the surface below. There was little time for Samyaza to think and nothing to be done. He closed his eyes and braced for the impact in darkness.

About the Author

J.S. Roebuck grew up in Northeast Ohio, where he won several young author competitions in grade school and continued writing as a hobby. He now writes novels in fantasy, supernatural, and sci-fi genres, as well as short stories, YA novels, and children's books. He lives in Colorado Springs with his family.

You can connect with me on:

🌐 https://jsroebuck.com

Also by J.S. Roebuck

more info at JSRoebuck.com

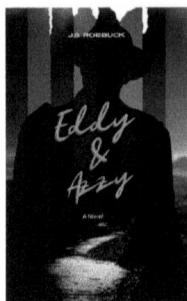

Eddy & Azzy
SUPERNATURAL THRILLER- *A 1950s
traveling salesman serial killer is possessed by
a demon, who takes him on a journey of chaos,
gluttony, love, healing, redemption, and risk.*
(Coming Fall 2024)

**Scan and find other coming
titles at JSRoebuck.com**

9 798990 905900